SACRAMENTO NOIR

EDITED BY
JOHN FREEMAN

BROOKLYN, NEW YORK

Published by Akashic Books
©2025 Akashic Books
Copyright to the individual stories is retained by the authors.

Series concept by Tim McLoughlin and Johnny Temple
Map of Sacramento by Sohrab Habibion

ISBN: 978-1-63614-201-2
Library of Congress Control Number: 2024940694

Akashic Books
Brooklyn, New York
Instagram, X, Facebook: AkashicBooks
info@akashicbooks.com
www.akashicbooks.com

For my teachers in Sacramento:
Jerry Enroth, Jim Jordan, Wayne Geri,
and Stan Zumbiel, honorary guru

ALSO IN THE AKASHIC NOIR SERIES

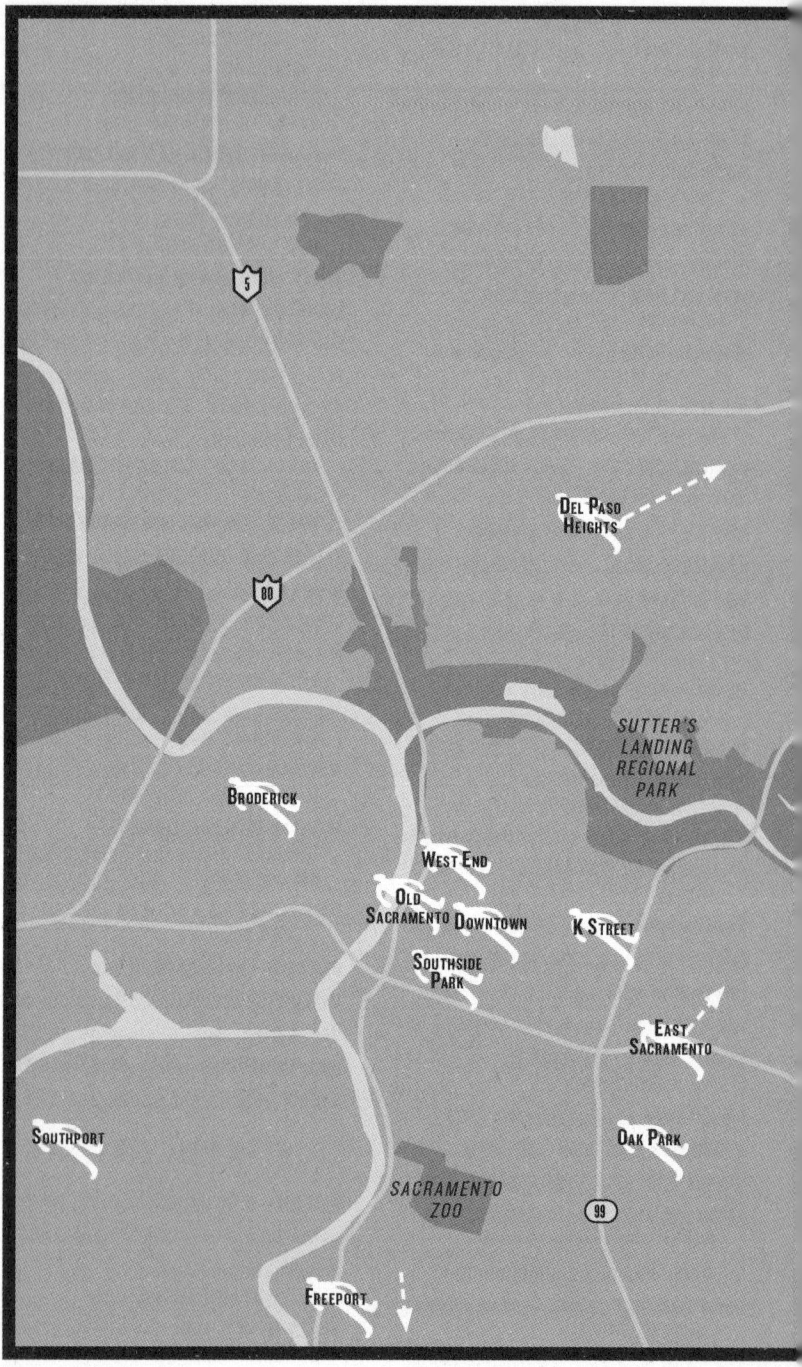

5
80
Del Paso Heights
Sutter's Landing Regional Park
Broderick
West End
Old Sacramento
Downtown
K Street
Southside Park
East Sacramento
Southport
Oak Park
Sacramento Zoo
99
Freeport

Citrus Heights
80
SACRAMENTO
50
Sierra Oaks
SACRAMENTO MATHER AIRPORT

TABLE OF CONTENTS

PART III: A TALE OF TWO CITIES

INTRODUCTION
Unburied Contradictions

Noir is a form I came to love when I began living in New York City, but it's a feeling I first felt in Sacramento. I grew up in the suburbs east of Sacramento in the 1980s and my father worked downtown. We'd take the bus into the city, so fragrant with its million trees, so empty of pedestrians in many places; it was a regular Saturday event, when my dad would go in to work on weekends, writing grants for the family service agency he ran. The stony silence around the capital. The dry soft air. The prevalence of older people, and old cars, like the ones you'd see in black-and-white movies. It all felt mysterious and large, and full of portent.

The capitol area was where adult things happened; my three great aunts lived around there. They resided in apartment buildings, and drove great big Oldsmobiles. Two of them had been single a long, long time. Their mother had been German and every time we piled into our own smaller car and drove west to visit them, especially Rose and Louise, I felt like I was simultaneously going back in time and farther out to sea—in a world where more complex things happened.

I wasn't ignorant of this world. I read the newspaper because I delivered it. Every morning around five a.m., my older brother and I would stumble into the garage and begin counting and folding copies of the *Sacramento Bee*. Some mornings both of us would scan the headlines—even as ten- and eleven-year-olds. Then we'd pedal out into the soupy early morning dark, our bikes weighed down by newsprint, our heads full of stories of the day: earthquakes, double-overtime losses in basketball, the occasional murder, and sometimes a secret pregnancy.

The paper route was more than a job, it was a kind of living map for both of us. We identified houses by who lived where, and by stories we gleaned in the monthly collection visits. There was no auto-pay back then, no tap and swipe. One literally had to go and extract payment every month from customers, some of whom would even dodge a ten-year-old. And so every month, between six and eight p.m., I'd ring people's doorbells and ask for $8.50.

Some things astonish me as an adult now with a niece the age I was delivering those papers. For starters, I can count on one hand the number of times in eight years I was invited into a house while someone retrieved their checkbook instead of paying with cash. Somehow I was never bitten by a dog, although a few of them all but learned English in their attempt to make it clear I was not welcome. It snowed just twice, and the look on people's faces who came out after it stopped made me a lifelong early riser. There were skunks everywhere.

Also, people revealed themselves. Sometimes with the door open into a house, I'd hear an argument—the long, grinding argument of an unhappy marriage. I saw people leaving furtively, like they didn't want to be seen. I smelled what was cooking, or sometimes just sour coffee. Whole worlds of stories piped out during the moments that front door was open, and then it would shut, and I'd go on to the next house.

This book is an attempt to prop a metaphorical door open a little while longer, a way to invite you into a variety of houses and apartments and spaces all over Sacramento, to imagine lives, not yours, or perhaps like yours, as told by some of the city's most talented living writers. What freedom is here in words: to travel, to visit, to linger, to hear stories from all across the city, and to some degree across time—both Naomi J. Williams and José Vadi set their stories in the 1940s/50s.

This is a book of noir, so the spaces we're beckoned into here are dark; they are sometimes not even moonlit. In Jen Soong's story, a woman is haunted by the ghost of the child of a next-door neighbor, or that's what she thinks he might be—she's too far gone on drugs she's been stealing from a pharmacy to know for sure. Meanwhile, in Jamil Jan Kochai's tale, an ex–police detective from Afghanistan stumbles on a body in the marshes beyond his apartment building; he's not even sure that's what it is until two men turn up to secretly bury the man.

The Sacramento River has a living presence in these stories. In José Vadi's historical noir, the river forms a mode of escape. In Maureen O'Leary's story, it is the last stop in a woman's return into the orbit of a chaotic and nefarious friend.

Dangerous dames are a hard theme for noir to carry into the twenty-first century without some rightful critiques. The stories here gesture toward that noir past, but reinvent it. Reyna Grande's story about two brothers—a priest and an artist, united by their fascination with a sex worker they've hired to pose for an artwork—carries an implicit critique of the way women are used to represent ideas men have created about them. In Maceo Montoya's tale, in which mural artists working in the early Chicano movement fall in love with a new female collective member, the narrator becomes so jealous that a schism develops within the group.

In Nora Rodriguez Camagna's story, a family living in South Sacramento confronts the risks of coming to this country while being stalked by an entirely different risk. In the story I contributed, a hit-and-run accident triggers a cascade of memories for an EMT worker who had nowhere to turn in a former life.

How a society treats those who are down and out, people who count as its outsiders, can reveal a lot about the way that society actually runs. In a piece titled "A Reflection of the Public," William T. Vollmann conjures a military veteran who has tumbled out of the housed life and is living in an encampment, where he finds unexpected tenderness in a lover, and in the politically charged conversation of friends. In Janet Rodriguez's tale revolving around an errant key her protagonist finds in a thrift-store purchase, the act of returning it leads her to an eviction, one she is powerless to stop.

Crime isn't always about single acts of violence. Sometimes it's a system devised to perpetuate other forms of violence and disenfranchisement. Two stories here situate themselves in such nexuses—within the law, and within academia. In Shelley Blanton-Stroud's story, a woman decides she's going to help her elderly grandmother around the house, and discovers an asset she might want to protect. In "A Textbook Example" by Luis Avalos, a young man studying confirmation bias finds himself in a situation almost predicted by his research: there's been a murder on campus, and the description of the perpetrator sounds a lot like *him*.

Here is Sacramento in all of its splendor and deep, not-at-all-buried contradictions. A frontier city that quickly used its wealth to gather power. A locale that is somehow not quite sure it is still urban. Darkly compelling, canopied, gusted by river smells, Sacramento emerges from these thirteen stories like a character itself. It's the kind of place that has sprawled widely enough, and covered enough different landscapes, that it is now many cities, some of which do not interact with each other. Some of which are only remembered in names of neighborhoods which people who once lived there still use with each other: Sakura City. The West End. Broderick. What a joy and vivid dream it is to see these stories here together, between these covers—for all to visit.

John Freeman
November 2024

PART I

FAMILY BUSINESS

TAKE AS NEEDED

BY SHELLEY BLANTON-STROUD

Sierra Oaks

It was only 101. They were projecting 107 for the Fourth. The TV meteorologist still called it state fair weather, even though they'd moved the fair from July to August years ago to try to catch a break on the heat. I couldn't blame them for the attempt, even if it didn't work. These days, August gave us heat *and* wildfire smoke. You think you've fixed something and it just gets worse.

And still I went. Last summer, before my senior year as a Sac State Hornet, I'd gone to the fair as part of the first-year orientation crew. I sat wilting at a picnic table between the deep-fried Twinkie stand and a laboring sow, picking at a corn dog, sipping rum and Diet Coke, worrying about how I was going to pay tuition. Then I joined a group headed to the Super Shot drop tower.

I was strapped in, feet dangling, next to Luis Martinez, orientation team leader and physics major, a nerdy guy who'd been acting like he had a crush on me. The ride began hauling us ninety feet up before it would plunge us back to earth. Luis must have noticed my pastier-than-usual face and so he explained that the magnetic brake system would stop the machine before we hit the ground. "The magnet's hidden behind the seats and copper's installed along the tower—it creates a magnetic field!" he shouted. "Even as you drop, you feel the metal resisting, saving you from a fatal crash below! It's perfectly safe!"

I didn't believe him, knowing that the thing you expect to save you never does, but I was already strapped in so I smiled at Luis because that was my only option. Well, surprisingly, the magnets did their job. We didn't die on the pavement. In gratitude for metallic resistance, I slept with Luis that night in his XL twin resident-assistant bed.

The way I felt *before* the sex with Luis, while I was still waiting for the Super Shot drop tower to plunge, was exactly how I felt right now, standing on the doorstep of my Grandma Barb's long-past-grand Tudor mansion on Crocker Road in Old Sierra Oaks, blue-blood dream-home central—it was state fair weather, I was all strapped in, out of options, slightly nauseous, and preparing to fake it.

My mom hadn't been crazy about this idea to involve Grandma in my problems, but she did want me off her couch since I wasn't contributing rent or anything else. I'd dropped out of Sac State to avoid a disciplinary hearing last year, right after the Super Shot drop tower and sleeping with Luis, and then meeting up unexpectedly with my deadbeat dad, who made it clear I wouldn't be seeing him ever again. He was dying of lung cancer, he told me. He was like a dog who wanted to die in the bushes alone. Either that or he just wanted an excuse to stop our pathetic little playact.

I'd tried to put my life back together since then, getting and then losing a Wienerschnitzel cashier job and then a State of California day-care center job after that. I wasn't sure exactly why I'd lost the last one, but didn't ask questions when the day-care center's supervisor gave me my final check in an envelope with my name printed in all-caps, underlined pretty aggressively. It seemed best not to ask.

Now my bank account was as dry as Mom's was before her

weekly checks arrived. She'd never explained exactly how the money worked for us, the sources it emerged from, but then neither of us explained much to each other. She did, however, share her version of why we were estranged from Grandma Barb and the rest of Dad's family, whose circumstances remained much better than ours.

Grandma Barb had been only twenty in 1946, pregnant with my dad, Bob, when she attended the Hippodrome Theater with her mother-in-law, my Great-Grandma Dot, Sacramento socialite. (Great-Grandma Dot's family had been around since the Donner Party and that gave her credibility in the finer local households.)

Apparently, Grandma Barb had talked my Great-Grandma Dot into seeing *Notorious* at the Hippodrome. They were in line to buy tickets when the marquee collapsed, fatally crushing Great-Grandma Dot and injuring Grandma Barb herself—her right leg and arm were never the same— and sending two other people to the hospital as well.

That was bad enough, Mom said, but then Dad's family decided not to forgive Grandma Barb because they claimed the old lady never would have gone to the theater to see that movie if Grandma Barb hadn't insisted out of her ambitious drive to achieve family bonding before baby Bob arrived. Gravity dealt her punishment.

So there she was, freak-accident victim, half her limbs ruined, pregnant, ostracized by her in-laws. Even her husband defected, staying later and later at the Sutter Club every evening after leaving Memorial Auditorium, where he conducted the symphony until dying at the podium in 1960. Grandma Barb spent her twenties alone in her bedroom in a massive crumbling Tudor with a housekeeping nanny and baby Bob, the root cause of all her trouble.

I'm sure that's what messed up my dad, driving him away when I was a baby, though no one really explained it. Some things don't need explaining, do they? I never even asked him about it when he dropped back into my life for an evening every few years. The way he did when he delivered his forever goodbye with the parting gift that caused me to drop out of school. That was him. Always absent when needed, only present when not.

Almost no one in town ever talked about the Hippodrome tragedy from Grandma Barb's point of view. They just always blabbed about her mother-in-law, dying under the marquee, the bloody letters that previously spelled *Mr. Hitchcock's "Notorious"* scattered around her like Scrabble tiles in a game gone wrong. The whole town, or at least the people who mattered, agreed it was Grandma Barb's fault. That didn't make sense, but that's the way things worked in Sacramento, an oligarchy of old families. Grandma Barb had married into it, she wasn't born into it, which made all the difference. So it's not surprising that Dad had always been off to Vegas or Phoenix or Anchorage, promising to see me soon. Not a big deal. You get what you get.

And it wasn't too surprising that Grandma Barb lived her life cut off from my mom and me, the only family members who'd never rejected her. Sometimes a person distrusts the people who treat her right.

Now here I was, on Grandma Barb's step, thinking maybe this could be a new chapter for both of us. I could stay with her awhile, help out, while looking for another job. Maybe we could actually get to know each other. I could use a grandma. Maybe she could use a granddaughter.

I knocked and knocked again.

Finally the door opened to a thirtysomething-year-old woman in those medical clothes that look like pajamas. "Yes?"

"I'm Abigail. Barbara's granddaughter?"

No response.

"I'm here to see her?"

"We didn't know you were coming," she said.

"I'm sorry, I don't know your name."

"I didn't tell you," she said.

Awkward. I waited. Her round brown eyes didn't blink. Just stared.

Then she stepped back and let me in.

It's weird to revisit a place you haven't seen since you were a kid. I'd always thought of Grandma Barb's as a fairy-tale house—turrets, a coiled two-story stairwell lit by stained glass, dark wood. Romantic, the kind of place I pictured living in one day. I'd write song lyrics up in the turret.

But now I saw other things too: a cracked entry-light fixture, a fan dangling from the living room ceiling by its cord, grimy velvet curtains of an unknown original color. I coughed a little from the dust. Worse, it was also very hot in the house. No AC.

"Is she upstairs?" I asked.

"Where else would she be?"

I waited for an invitation to go up, but when it didn't come, I headed upstairs anyway, this woman in scrubs a few steps behind me. The plaster walls were scarred, like from carrying big furniture up and down the stairs.

At the top of the first flight, she said, "End of the hall," nodding at the third door.

The rug had parallel ruts that looked like a wheelchair had etched tracks in the pattern. Could Grandma even get downstairs? She should be in her late nineties now.

I knocked lightly on her door.

"Who's there?"

I entered.

She sat in a floral wing-tip chair in the window alcove looking out on Crocker Road, with a standing fan blowing right on her face and a glass of ice water and box of tissue on the side table. Her left hand gripped the handle of a silver cane. Her right hand was lying limp on her lap.

She wore a dress, not the nightgown I expected: a garment out of the seventies, fall colors in an abstract pattern. She was so thin it seemed like somebody'd just draped a sheet over her. Her white hair was pulled back tight in a bun. She wore clip-on earrings, orange lipstick, and drawn-on dark eyebrows. Grandma Barb was making an effort, even when she was skeletal, even when she didn't expect any company. Or maybe this caregiver was making an effort on Grandma Barb's behalf.

"Who are you?"

"I'm Abigail. Your granddaughter. Bob's daughter."

She screwed up her face and stared at me. "Do you have some kind of identification?"

I pulled my phone out of my back pocket and retrieved my license from its sleeve, passing it to her.

"Glasses!"

The caregiver put a pair of readers on Grandma's nose.

"This doesn't make sense. You're too young to be his daughter."

"He had me at fifty-three. Mom was forty. I've come here before on Mother's Day and Christmas." Maybe it was only Mother's Day. Or maybe my dad's birthday.

She examined my ID more carefully. "You've gained weight since sixteen."

"I've been a little down."

"For what, seven years? You've been down for seven years?"

I nodded. It sounded bad when she put it that way.

She returned my license. "Why are you here in my house?"

"I thought maybe you could use some help."

"*I* could use some help?"

"I see you do have somebody here. But maybe I can do cleaning for you, organizing, or fixing?"

"Are you good at fixing and cleaning and organizing?"

"Admittedly, those haven't been my strengths so far. But I'm looking to change."

"So, a brand-new you. And in exchange?" she asked.

I hadn't expected her to be so direct. "I could stay in one of your spare rooms, out of your way, while I work on your projects? I'm between jobs and apartments right now . . ."

Grandma Barb snorted and rolled her eyes. "You don't say . . ." She coughed for a full minute, in a hacking style, before pulling herself back together. "Gina," she said, addressing the attendant, "find some sheets and towels to set her up. Back side, downstairs bedroom." No turret for me.

I'd only been there a couple hours, enough time to empty the contents of my duffel into a guest dresser, make up my bed, and head to the kitchen on a hunt for cleaning supplies, when there was a knock at the front door. Gina was upstairs with Grandma, giving her medicine or something, so I got the door.

"Helloooooo!"

A tall blond woman leaned down toward me, hand extended. I took the bait and immediately her left hand cupped our two right hands and she nodded earnestly. Her obvious

Botox treatment worked so well that it was hard to positively confirm if the look on her face was indeed earnestness or simply surprise at having caught an outsider.

"I'm Suzanne, from next door."

I pictured the freshly white-painted house behind the stone wall with tidy rosebushes and a lavender hedge.

"And you are . . ."

"I'm Abigail. Barbara's granddaughter, visiting to help out."

"Oh my God, that's wonderful! We *all* worry so much about your grandmother. How's she doing? All alone in this great big house. It's so much to manage." She craned her head to look around.

She sounded sympathetic, but not really. More like curious, with a veneer of sympathy, which was lacquered in contempt. Maybe not even curious. Maybe she was optimistically on task.

My hand still in hers, she pulled herself into the entry, then closed the door behind her. How'd she do that so efficiently?

Her lips glistened as her eyes canvased the space, taking in the wood, the leaded glass, the chandeliers.

"How can I help you?"

"It's the reverse, really. I want to offer some support while you're with your grandmother in this time of emergency."

She must have thought Grandma Barb was dying, what with the sudden appearance of my Honda in the driveway.

"It's all been too much for her to handle, I'm sure. I'd like to offer my gardeners to work in her front yard, get everything spiffed up a little."

For what? I wondered. "I'll ask my grandmother."

"Well, I don't think you need to bother—"

"Thanks again," I said, guiding her out the door.

Before she exited the steamy indoor heat into the searing outdoor heat, she handed me her card. "If you need anything at all." *Suzanne Locus, Broker, Coldwell Banker*, it read.

After the door closed, Gina said behind me, "You let her in."

"I didn't know."

"Now you've cracked it open."

"What?"

"Pandora's box."

The next morning I stood on the lawn, peering through the hedge at Suzanne's house, where a team of gardeners worked like Santa's elves around the already perfect property, feeding, shaping, polishing.

One guy in the crew looked familiar, that round face, the rectangular metal glasses, tidy collared shirt with a logo, *Just So Landscapes*, on his chest.

It was Luis! Physics major and orientation leader and pretty decent lay.

He gazed back at me through the hedge and his jaw dropped. He started walking toward the street. He was going to come around the hedge to me.

I felt sick. I looked down at my dirty, sweaty tee.

"Abigail?"

"Hey, Luis."

"What are you doing here?"

"This is my grandma's house."

"Nice." He took a look up and down the street. "So Suzanne wants us to work in your grandma's yard. Should we get started now?"

"You're on the gardening crew?"

"I own this company." He pulled on the fabric of his polo shirt at the logo.

"That's great." I thought of his being a physics major.

"Actually, it's my dad's company. He needed me."

I got that, sort of.

"I don't want to do this forever. I want to go to grad school."

It embarrassed me to hear him say that. He wasn't going to grad school.

"Should I bring the guys over now?"

I hadn't thought we would accept the gardening offer, but now it was confusing. I mean, this was Luis. Totally upstanding guy. And good-looking in a best-friend-of-the-hot-girl kind of way. "Sure," I said. "Whatever works best for you guys."

Fifteen minutes later, as I was cleaning kitchen cabinets, I heard the mowers and blowers and saw five or six guys through the window, doing everything at once, like they needed no instruction. They just started shaping the bushes into undulating waves, all these things you might have thought would require some executive artistic decision-making. I felt queasy about it, though the yard was immediately looking better. Even if they had only mowed the crabgrass, that would have been an amazing improvement. I was getting something done.

"She wants you," Gina announced from the kitchen door.

"What the hell is going on out there?"

"Suzanne next door sent over her gardeners to help out."

"Help *who* out? I don't want her gardeners!"

"I think she was just being nice."

"You're an idiot! Get rid of them! Now!"

And so I did.

I sat on the front step that evening when I was too tired to go on, having emptied all the kitchen drawers and cabinets and boxed the supposedly unneeded things, stacking it all in the basement. I didn't really know what was needed, what was not. But it didn't look like anything in the kitchen was ever used. Gina fed Grandma easy things, reheating frozen meals, making meat and cheese sandwiches. No real cooking. No need for all the old gear.

It had reached 106 today and it wasn't the usual dry heat. The air felt heavy. Sitting on the front step wasn't much relief. Sometimes the Delta breeze just wouldn't blow.

Luis walked up the driveway from the street.

"All finished for the day," he said. His face was so open. You hardly ever saw a face like that. That openness nearly broke my heart.

"Do you want a beer or something?" I'd made an Instacart order on Grandma's card earlier, adding chips and beans and salsa and beer to the white bread, bologna, and fake-cheese slices Gina bought.

Luis looked out over the weedy lawn, half-mowed. "Sure."

"Who's that?" Grandma Barb screamed from her window upstairs.

"It's me, Grandma."

"Who's that with you? You think I'm crazy? Think I can't hear you?"

"It's Luis. He's my friend." I thought it was better not to mention the gardening.

"Jesus Christ!" she yelled out the window.

I pulled a couple kitchen chairs, along with a little table, onto the lawn, and Luis and I ate delivery pizza out of the box, chasing it down with the cold beer. It was pretty out there, with our chairs turned to face the part of the lawn he'd mowed and, beyond that, the perfectly manicured neighboring houses. There was even a slight breeze now, like the inside of a convection oven.

"You just disappeared after that night," Luis said.

Something about the way he said it—his voice husky and soft, as if he really cared—made me want to answer.

"My dad met up with me the night after the state fair, right before the semester started. He gave me a gift, an old family thing, which I really wanted. My roommate found it, turned me in, and I dropped out."

"What did he give you?"

"A gun," I said, thinking of the old Ruger Standard wrapped in a towel in the top drawer of my downstairs bedroom dresser. "It belonged to his dad. My grandfather."

"That would definitely get you expelled."

"I wasn't expelled. I dropped out."

"Got it," he said. "Why didn't you just get rid of the gun?"

I looked at him with surprise. "My dad *gave* it to me. It's a family thing."

Luis nodded. He understood.

I noted that nothing terrible happened when I confessed to Luis about my near expulsion and my weapon.

The opposite, in fact.

I felt his magic lifting me above the crabgrass. I felt held. Supported. Things I didn't often feel.

When Luis and I woke in my downstairs bedroom the next morning, he hustled quietly out the French door, looking every bit as fresh and ready for the day as if he'd showered at home.

As I made coffee, Gina entered the kitchen. "Better hope she don't find out."

"Are you gonna tell her?" I asked.

"Why would I?"

I was beginning to appreciate Gina.

The next day was the Fourth of July. Luis texted to ask if I'd like to see some fireworks. I thought he meant we'd go to Old Sac and watch the big ones go off over the river, but that wasn't what he intended.

Around eight thirty p.m., his truck pulled up with a crew in back and they piled out, yelling hellos. Luis set a plywood board on the lawn and the guys started arranging the safe-and-sane pyrotechnics. Some of them looked less safe and sane, more homemade.

I was nervous. Grandma Barb wasn't going to like this. But I was also excited. This was going to be like a party, with someone I really liked, at my home, at least my temporary home, which, though decrepit, was still very cool. Very Insta-grammable, if I were some kind of social media maven. I felt competing instincts rumbling inside.

One guy pulled up in his own truck, which he backed onto the lawn to unload a barbecue, setting it just a little way apart from the fireworks, using the tailgate as a kitchen counter. He immediately started the charcoal. Luis laughed with the chef, occasionally turning to smile at me. I liked that smile.

I looked up at my grandma's window. Her white face appeared in the bottom third of the glass, Gina's a couple feet above her.

I went into the kitchen for more beer.

Gina came downstairs and stood next to me. "I gave her a Norco," she said.

"Does she usually take that before bed?"

"No."

"Is it okay?"

She shrugged her shoulders. "It's prescribed, *take as needed*. Must be okay."

That made sense. Take as needed.

"Do you want a beer?" Gina nodded and I opened one for her. "Grab a chair," I said. "There's sausage and corn on the grill."

"I'm your half sister," she said.

"Half *what*?"

"Bob is my dad too. He never married my mom. Our grandma took me in."

"Took you in . . ." My skin felt clammy. I wondered if my dad had ever visited Gina.

"I've been thinking you'd show up."

"Do you . . . want me to go?"

"Why would I?"

It's hard to know what someone else is after, even when you ask.

We went out and enjoyed the fireworks without Grandma Barb yelling or anything because she slept right through it, a miracle of modern science.

It was the most fun I'd had in forever. It was so natural. It seemed so right. Even with the neighbors conspicuously staring at us in the front yard through plantation shudders. This was our grandma's house, mine and Gina's. She invited us in. And these were our friends. *Get used to it*, I thought.

Everybody stayed over that night, even though they probably had AC at their own apartments. They were spread everywhere on couches and in unused bedrooms with bare mattresses. I think Gina even had one of them in her bed, upstairs next door to Grandma Barb, who got the best night of sleep of her life on the strength of her Norco.

I was feeling so open and happy that I told Luis about Gina being my half sister. About how we were the house's family. Luis kissed each of my eyelids, whispering, "I've loved you since school. Let's get married. I want to be your family too."

I felt a little alarmed at that, but also warm and relieved.

The next morning, looking out Grandma Barb's window as she snored in bed, I saw Gina speaking urgently to Luis on the street. I couldn't read her lips, but the way she waved her arms around, she seemed persuasive.

After Luis and I had cleaned up the lawn, he whispered in my ear, "I could help you fix up inside. Get things ready."

"Ready for what?"

"She's going to die, you know. She's ninety-seven. And then you and Gina will have some options."

"I don't know anything about that," I said. "I don't know what her will says."

"Why don't you look into it?"

"What, ask her lawyer?"

"Just look through the house. You're already cleaning and organizing."

My body jolted down and then up, like an elevator dropping briefly before catching hold again.

I was looking through her desk drawers, with a box on the floor next to me so I could reasonably claim to be cleaning things out, when Gina came in.

"How is she?" I asked.

"Pissed."

"I guess so." Gina did the hard work, serving Grandma personally. I was grateful that was her and not me.

"Are you looking for her private records?"

"Well, yes. I'm just wondering—"

"Look in the closet." Gina opened it up to reveal a filing cabinet. Then we worked together, going through each drawer, an unspoken sense of shared mission making us focus.

In the middle drawer, I found the lawyer files. Right at the front was her will. I read aloud to Gina Grandma Barb's intention to leave the house and all her financial accounts to her "*closest surviving issue, Robert Stratford, or, if he predeceases her, Robert's daughter Abigail Stratford. In the event that they both predecease her, the house and all financial accounts will be left to the Sacramento Philharmonic.*"

I looked up at Gina, sorry for what that meant. Gina slumped out of the room. Did Grandma not understand who Gina was? Did she understand who she was and still reject her? It was strange not to feel like the appendage for once. I was actually ahead of somebody else.

I took pictures of the will with my phone and then put the paper copy back in the filing cabinet.

I kept looking through the other drawers, not finding much of interest, until I came across a folder labeled *Caregivers*, where I saw a contract Grandma Barb had signed with a caregiver agency—Winged Angels. The contract named the caregiver: *Regina Martinez*. That was a very common name. But I thought about Gina's round face and thick, shiny hair, just like Luis's. Were they related? Were we really half sisters or had she made that up? Was Luis my half brother? What were they to me? What was *anyone* to me?

That night, I sat in a chair on the lawn, beer on the ground.

Gina came out from the house and sat on the second chair, fanning herself with a real estate brochure. She had an easy air about her tonight. Then Luis pulled up in his truck and joined us, sitting cross-legged before me. He drank from my beer, looking hot.

"So you're brother and sister?" I asked.

They looked at each other and at me.

"I really am your half sister," Gina said.

I turned to Luis.

"We had different fathers," he said hastily. "Don't worry about that. I'm not your brother."

Family was so hard to unknot. It always had been.

"Does Grandma Barb know about you, Gina?"

"She knows I show up and take care of her every day. Bathe her. Dress her. Change her diaper."

"Does she know you're related?"

She looked at Luis, checking, then back at me. "No."

Gina would be more valued by Grandma Barb as the one who took care of her, than she would be as an illegitimate grandchild.

Everything was muddled. Not just who these people were to me, but whether I even wanted them, or anyone like them—lovers, family. It seemed easier to be all alone than connected in such unreliable ways.

I glanced at Gina's face, pinching up like she might cry. I wanted to say what she wanted to hear. That we would work it out. That everything would be fine.

"I'm going to have to ask you to leave," I said instead.

"I work here," said Gina. "You didn't hire me."

"She has a contract," Luis added.

"A contract's just a promise. People break them all the time." This I knew.

"It's your grandma's to break. You have nothing to do with it."

I pulled my grandfather's Ruger out from under my chair, holding it up, shoulder level.

"Abigail," said Luis, his soft eyes wide.

I pointed the gun at Gina.

"Abigail, don't," said Luis.

"She won't," said Gina. I couldn't tell if she was trusting or dismissive.

I pointed the gun at the sky and pulled the trigger, making a sound like a crack of thunder that ripped everything open above me.

Gina hopped up, knocking down her chair. "Let's go, Luis!"

He deflated. Not like he was afraid. More like he was disappointed in me, a familiar reaction. He stood and followed his sister to his car, started it, and peeled off. The woman across the street peeked out her curtains.

The evening air seemed cooler now, like a door had opened.

"What's going on out there?" Grandma Barb screamed from her window. "Where's Gina? I need help!"

Grandma Barb was so anxious, the veins straining on her forehead, her hands picking at the blanket. I couldn't get her to calm, not with water nor a cookie, not with just sitting and stroking her arm and telling her stories about things I remembered from when I was little, like how my dad used to let me stand on his shoes as he danced me around when he visited sometimes—though I wasn't sure if that had actually happened or if I'd seen it in a movie.

"Where IS your father?" she shrieked. "I need him!"

"He's gone, Grandma. He told me the last time I saw him. It was last year. He was very sick and was going away. He said we'd never see him again."

"Oh no," she said, beginning to cry. "Not again."

I cried too. My dad never should have left.

But Grandma Barb's weeping went on too long. It seemed like it was making her worse, her voice harsh and scraping, coughing. I couldn't fix this. I felt overwhelmed.

The Norco sat on the end table next to her bed. I read the prescription: *Take as needed. Whose needs?* I thought. I took two into my hand and poured a little water from the bottle into a pretty glass.

"Try this, Grandma."

She looked at me hard for a minute, closed her eyes, and then opened them, nodding. She spread all five fingers in front of me. She wanted five. I froze. She waved her five-fingered hand in front of my face, her nostrils flaring. I picked three more pills from the bottle. She closed her eyes, nodded again, and opened her mouth, tongue extended. I put the pills on her tongue and raised the glass to her lips. She swallowed.

I arranged silky pillows carefully around her, pointing the fan away from her face but toward her body. I held her hand. And she drifted to sleep.

Everything was finally quiet.

I went down to the kitchen and retrieved another beer and leftover pizza and took them out to my front lawn and sat on my chair with my dinner and relaxed.

Things were settled.

The only thing spoiling the evening was a group of crows cawing and fighting on the unmowed portion of crabgrass over what looked like a little dead bird. Or maybe a rodent.

Then the old blue Camaro pulled up the driveway, my

dad behind the wheel. He got out slowly and walked across the lawn toward me, like a man who always knew his promises wouldn't matter in the end.

I tasted metal and set my beer beside my chair. Through the fabric of my shorts, I cupped the heavy weight of my inheritance in my right pocket, ready to use, as needed.

SAKURA CITY

BY NAOMI J. WILLIAMS

Downtown

Wednesday, November 3, 1954

Right before dawn, the temperature just above freezing, I was out in the alley as usual, lighting the day's first cigarette, stamping my feet against the chill, and waiting for Henry, who was, as usual, late.

For one suspended moment it was utterly silent, utterly dark. Then the ancient boiler of the Muramotos' bathhouse roared awake behind me, and a few minutes later the first white fingers of smoke escaped from their tall, thin chimney and traced their way across the purpling sky.

Henry rumbled up in his own cloud of exhaust and cigarette smoke, leaning out the window waving the front page of the *Sacramento Bee*.

"What's this?" I said. "You steal it from someone's front stoop?"

He laughed. "People should wake up earlier."

I took the paper from him and moved in front of the pickup to read by the headlight. The page was crowded with election results, but I found it—in small-enough type, but right up top: *SLUM PLAN LOSES*.

"Well, shit," I said, my breath visible in the air.

Henry shut off his engine. "Isn't it good news?"

"Sure," I said. "Supposedly."

"What's that supposed to mean?"

"Nothing," I said. I could feel the gathering, collective sigh of relief that would waft through the neighborhood as the news spread. Everyone I knew would want to celebrate—and chide me for not joining in. *Aw, George, always gloomy, try smiling for a change*, etcetera. I just knew there wouldn't be much to celebrate in the end. Turned out I was right, of course. But no one likes a killjoy.

Henry and I moved to the back of the truck, a battered Ford F1 my mother and I had bought when we hired him. It was supposed to be a temporary job until he found something better, but he'd been cheerfully and tardily making deliveries for us for four years now.

He spit out his cigarette and clambered up into the cargo bed. "You wanted this 'slum plan' to *win*?"

"Jesus, no," I said, unlatching the tailgate and hauling out a pallet of potted chrysanthemums. "It's just—you think the *hakujin* are gonna let us have this?"

He pushed a tub of delicate cut asters toward me. "The whites aren't our enemies anymore."

"You keep thinking that, Henry."

It was always like this. Six mornings a week, we wrestled hundreds of flowers off the truck and into my mother's shop. And arguing, always arguing. That had started when we were middle schoolers at Lincoln, continued at Sac High, then over my college breaks, and at Walerga and at Tule Lake. Henry had gone off to liberate Dachau while I ended up safely and inexpertly interpreting with the occupation forces in Tokyo. Somehow he'd still come out of the war an optimist.

"Hey," Henry said, jumping nimbly from the truck when we finished unloading, "Michiko working today?"

He was changing the subject. He knew Michiko only came in Mondays and Thursdays. He knew I was sweet on

Michiko. And I knew he was sweet on her too. Neither of us stood much of a chance.

Upstairs in the flat above the shop, we found my tiny prim mother setting out bowls of steaming rice and miso soup, slices of cold rolled omelet, and a plate of bacon, her concession to our Americanization. I set the paper down before her and pointed to the headline.

"*Slum Plan Loses*," she read aloud. She was a classically stoic *issei* woman from Fukuoka, but now her voice wavered. "We can stay," she said. "We not have to leave again."

"Hopefully," I said.

"What you mean, *hopefully?*"

"Nothing, *Kāsan*," I said. "Only—I hope you're right."

"*Tch.*" It was a sound she made when she was cross with me, which was often. "Henry-*kun*, what do you think?" she asked in Japanese.

"It's good, isn't it?" he said.

"What does he know?" I said. "You didn't even vote, did you?"

"What difference does it make?" Henry said, mouth full of omelet. "We won!"

My mother got up and cleared my food before I'd finished eating, another way she had of registering displeasure. "Work time," she announced, heading toward the stairs that led back down to the shop. At the landing she paused to change out of her house slippers. "Why you are so negative?" she called back.

Henry stood to follow her. "Yeah, George," he said, "why you are so negative?"

I sighed. "Just being realistic." But they were already mincing down the steep rickety stairs, where my mother would complete her Wednesday-morning floral arrangements for Henry to deliver.

I retrieved my breakfast and flattened the paper in front of me. Sure enough, the telling line:

Defeat of the redevelopment bond issue kills, for the time being, plans for beautification and modernization of the entire West End, shown by disease and crime statistics to be one of the worst slum areas in the nation.

For the time being.
One of the worst slum areas in the nation.

Prop B had failed. The city bond measure that was supposed to raise money to bulldoze the West End in the name of progress and "slum-eradication" hadn't garnered the required two-thirds "yes" votes.

But I'd seen the city's fancy posters with their color-coded maps—*Sacramento Redevelopment: Dedicated to a Finer Future!* I knew they'd paid a boatload of money to some tony LA firm to draw plans for what they'd build once they ran us out. No way they were going to give up so easily.

All day long the shopkeeper's bell on our door tinkled as customers came and went, bowing and exchanging congratulations.

"*Yokatta desu ne.*"

"*Sō desu ne, hontō ni anshin desu ne.*"

Thank goodness. Yes, what a relief, etcetera, etcetera.

I wanted to shout, *You people should know better! They're gonna find a way to screw us!* Instead I sullenly rang up their purchases—autumnal bouquets of yellow and orange mums, red and bronze button poms, sunflowers, bloodred roses.

"George," they'd address me, or "Jōji-*san*" if they were

speaking Japanese, "now you and your mother can really make something of this place, *ne?*"

"Maybe," I'd say, then feeling my mother's glare: "Sure. That would be swell."

Ironically, the only person with whom I could dispense with the compulsory pleasantries was a slick-haired *hakujin* who came in just before the noon rush. He claimed to be some kind of antiques or art dealer and had been sniffing around the neighborhood for months, looking for people anxious to unload their kimonos and scrolls and ceramics before eminent domain forced us to consolidate our belongings and start over—again.

The first time he'd come by, I'd laughed at him. "You're more than a decade late, man," I told him. "Shoulda come through in '42. We were practically giving away our family treasures to you lot."

"Oh, I was around," he'd said coolly. "I think a lot of heirlooms ended up stored by friendly neighbors and sympathetic churches till they let you out of those camps." He shook his head in mock dismay while glancing around the shop with his pale blue eyes. "Who knows what's languishing unused in your attics and cellars?" he said. "I'm just trying to help. Change is coming—and change is expensive."

"We don't need your help," I said.

His eyes had passed over me and my mother and landed on Michiko, who'd just come up from the cellar with an armload of pampas grass. "Speaking of family treasures," he purred.

"You need to go," I said.

"You have good taste, Georgie," he responded, wagging a finger at us in an insinuating way. He winked at my mother. "See you round, Kimmy."

My mother hated the overfamiliarity of Americans. She

especially hated it when people turned her name, Kimiko, into Kimmy. For my part, I was surprised the man knew our first names. Had he also somehow learned of the stash of pre-war Koishiwara pottery my mother had brought from Japan, the only "treasure" we'd managed to save from the plunders of forced evacuation?

After he left, I'd looked toward my mother and Michiko to share our collective ire, but they turned on me. "Why you antagonize man like that?" my mother had cried.

"Me?"

"*Okāsan* is right," Michiko said, pretty eyebrows drawn in disapproval. "He might have bought something while we pretended to be polite."

"But then he'd come back," I protested.

"Maybe," she said. "And spend more money trying to butter us up. Now he'll come back just to needle you."

"That man, he come back," my mother said grimly.

And now he *was* back, sporting a suit but no tie, chest hair poking out the top of his wide-collared shirt. "Hey, Kimmy, how goes it?" he called.

My mother was winding some wire around a cluster of heavy-headed gerbera daisies, her hands deft and strong. She nodded wordlessly in his direction. Sometimes playing "inscrutable Oriental" was the only power she had.

"Haven't you heard the news?" I said to him.

"Oh, I've heard." He languidly took a stainless-steel cigarette case from his pocket. "Thought you might be interested to know your neighbor Mr. Ito-*san* just sold me his collection of Kabuki masks."

"Ito-*san*?" my mother said, unable to hide her surprise. Mr. Ito owned the bakery across the street. He also taught traditional Japanese dance at the Buddhist church on O Street.

The man flipped open the case and drew out a cigarette. "Says he's thinking of retiring, moving to LA, be near his grandkids. I gave him an excellent price."

"We only have flowers for sale," I said.

The man fixed his frosty eyes on me. "Yesterday was a hiccup," he said. "I know it. You know it. Redevelopment: it's coming. All this—" He gestured around the shop with his unlit cigarette. "*Poof!* Change is coming, and change—"

"You're wasting your time."

He shrugged. "Maybe I just want some flowers for my girl. Where's that pretty Me-CHEE-koe?"

A current of rage shot through me, and he could see it. He lit the cigarette and tossed the match on the floor.

"Nine bucks for a dozen roses," I said.

"Sign says seven."

"Special nine-dollar deal just for you."

He laughed, then nodded to my mother. "Sayonara, Kimmy."

He didn't bother closing the door behind him. "*Aho,*" I growled after him. *Idiot.* Then kicked the door shut and punched the bell, which flew off and landed behind the counter with a jangly protest.

A daisy stem snapped in my mother's hands. "Why you act like that?" she said. "What if customer see?"

"No one else is here, *Kāsan.*"

"*I* am here," she said. She dropped the ruined bouquet on the counter. "Go get eucalyptus and red ribbon," she ordered. "And check on flower wire, we running out."

I was being sent to the cellar like a bad child. If I *had* been a child, it would certainly have felt like punishment. Our cellar resembled nothing so much as a secret underground bootlegger's hideout. It may have been that at one time. Its one naked, dangling bulb threw shadows all around, turning everything eerie—the wall of neatly arranged knives and shears and my late father's old handsaw, the tall urns filled with dried grasses and branches, the shelves stacked high with harmless florist's supplies.

When I reemerged, the damaged bell was on the counter and my mother was at the door in her Sunday shoes. "I go to beauty parlor," she said. "You finish daisy bouquet. And fix the bell."

"But it's Wednesday."

"So what."

"You always go on Friday."

"Today Wednesday and I go today, so I guess you wrong, Jōji," she said with aggressive cheer.

My mother wasn't getting her hair set. She wanted a break from her pessimistic, antisocial son and to rejoice with her friends about how, less than ten years after internment, we wouldn't be forced from our homes again. I couldn't blame her. Except I knew—man, I *knew*: we were not in the clear.

I also didn't relish handling the onslaught of sunny customers alone.

"*Kāsan*, we're pretty busy here," I said. "And I was counting on catching up on paperwork upstairs."

"Michiko-*onēchan* coming."

"Michiko?"

My mother regarded me with a knowing frown. I felt like she kept calling Michiko *onēchan*—"big sister"—to remind me that her once-almost-daughter-in-law, who was only two years older than I, was off-limits.

"You check wire?" my mother said.

"Shoot, I forgot—" But she had left, setting off down 4th Street with her formal, determined gait.

* * *

Michiko arrived a few hours later. A human bouquet. I'd always thought of her that way. Even at Tule Lake, with its swirling dust and tension, she'd radiated defiant grace. *Dusty rose*, I'd think every time I saw her. Even in grief, not hiding her pain, the dignified resilience of black calla lilies. And that November afternoon, when everyone else was celebrating, she entered the shop, and I thought, so help me, *Oriental poppy*. Under her gray half-coat, she had on an orange dress I really liked. It had three-quarter-length sleeves and was cinched at the waist with a shiny wide belt. She'd made the whole outfit herself. It looked amazing. *She* looked amazing. She smelled amazing. But I was still in a mood.

"What happened to the bell?" she said.

"Unfortunate accident," I mumbled.

She laughed. "What's wrong, Jōji-*kun*?"

I wished she'd stop calling me Jōji-*kun*. It was a kid's name, what my parents and older brother John called me. Michiko had started using it when she was engaged to John. She still did, years after John was killed in the Vosges Mountains and she should have married someone else, attached herself to some other family.

She shrugged now with bright nonchalance and plunked a purple *furoshiki*-wrapped package on the counter. "I brought you *o-bentō*," she said. "I made your favorites, so cheer up."

"You didn't have to."

"I know," she said, then laid her hand on my arm. "George." I turned to meet her lovely, steady gaze. "Let them have this day."

Without the bell, Mrs. Muramoto was already in the shop before Michiko and I noticed. She owned the Japanese-style *o-sentō* right behind our property and was one of Japantown's most importunate individuals. Our self-appointed *nakōdo*, she was forever trying to pair off her unmarried neighbors. But she was also, always, in some kind of legal or financial trouble and leaned on the *nisei* to help her decipher and reply to notices and threats from the city, the state, the IRS. The woman was exhausting.

"*Konnichiwa, Muramoto-san*," Michiko said now, drawing away from me.

The bathhouse proprietress eyed me warily and I stared right back at her. She'd been trying to introduce Michiko to more promising guys who'd managed to go back and finish college after the war. I enjoyed the fact that she saw me as a problem.

"George is about to take his lunch break," Michiko said. "How can I help you?"

"New flowers for *bandai*," she said, referring to the bathhouse entryway. I fled upstairs with my *bentō*. Entering the flat, I could hear her adding, in her faux-intimate way, "*Ne, Michiko-chan, chotto—*" then asking Michiko to help her read yet another complaint letter from the city. They were always on her about the height and emissions from her smokestack.

Upstairs, at the dining room table that doubled as our "office," I untied the *furoshiki* and found four *onigiri* rice balls: flaked salmon, *umeboshi* pickle, *tarako* roe, and *furikake* seasoning. I gratefully wolfed them down while churning through the unceasing round of tasks that kept our little shop alive: bookkeeping, always bookkeeping; making a note to check on that floral wire; calling about late deliveries; putting in orders for vases, carnations, ribbon, all from different merchants; signing checks to deposit; writing checks to mail.

Occasionally I heard sounds from below or from outside:

A boisterous laugh. Two dogs meeting in the alley. A muffled thud. A truck door slamming shut, probably Henry coming back. I winced, picturing him down in the shop, chatting with Michiko. Late-afternoon gusts rattled the street-facing windows. One pane, I noticed, had developed a second crack. I glanced up at the ceiling and hoped the slapdash job I'd done on the roof held when the winter rains returned. Once, looking up to rest my eyes after a column of figures failed to add up the same way twice, I found myself regarding the plain wooden box that contained my mother's Koishiwara ware. Guiltily I wondered how much we could get for them.

Darkness fell suddenly. With a shock I realized it was well past our closing time of six. I was due at my other job, at the Mo-Mo Club, at seven. Had *Kāsan* come back from the beauty parlor? It wasn't like her to be gone so long, or to return without shouting *"Tadaima!"* up the stairs. Or for Michiko to leave her shift without calling up a "Bye, Jōji-*kun!*"

And no one had asked for help with the cumbersome iron security gate for our storefront. Henry must have helped out, I thought, and unhappily imagined Michiko and Henry closing the gate together, laughing as they shut me in. But that grating metal sound: I would have heard it. I shook off my house slippers, jammed my feet into battered loafers, and padded downstairs into the shop.

No one was there. The shop was dark and closed up, but "not proper way," as *Kāsan* would have said. The inside lights were off, the front door locked, the sign that read *Closed* in both English and Japanese facing out. But no one had swept the floor or pulled the security gate shut. "What the hell?" I said aloud, then moved to check on the side door, the one that emptied into the alley. I turned the knob—left unlocked— and opened the door right into Henry. We both yelped.

"Christ, what's going on?" I cried.

"Nice to see you too, George," he said.

"Where is everybody?"

He shrugged. "I was gonna ask *you* that."

"I've been upstairs all afternoon."

I turned back into the shop and he followed, bouncing on his toes. "I'll help you close up," he said, snapping his fingers.

"No need," I said, but he grabbed a broom and started sweeping, bristling all over with weird energy.

I jingled open the till, which was close to bursting with cash. It had been a good day for us. No one had collected the money and brought it upstairs. "Seriously, man," I said, "you don't know where Michiko or my mother are?"

Henry seemed to be scattering rather than collecting the debris on the floor. "Pretty sure Michiko-*nēchan* went home," he said. "Maybe *Obachan* had a late delivery to make in person?" He'd called my mother "Auntie" since seventh grade.

"What delivery?" I said.

"I dunno. Who cares? Let's close up and go celebrate, get drunk, find some girls."

I laughed and grabbed the broom from him. "*Find some girls.* Do you even hear yourself?"

"Come on, George. Don't be like that."

"Look, I have, uh, class tonight."

"Oh, right. *Class.*" He'd stopped bouncing. "I still don't know why you need to be washing dishes for those *kokujin.*"

"Shut up, Henry," I said. The two Black men who owned the Mo-Mo Club had bought the place from a Japanese family during the evacuation. People in the neighborhood were still sore about it. Sore and prejudiced. Which was why I hadn't told my mother about the job. She thought I was taking accounting classes at the junior college.

I swept everything out to the street—a day's worth of fallen flower stalks and leaves, baby's breath, stripped rose thorns, the alley dust and street gravel tracked in by our customers, one dropped match, one aggravating best friend.

Henry helped me unhook and roll up the striped canvas awning that shaded the front of the shop. His anxious energy had evaporated. "What are you gonna do when your mother finds out you're not in school?" he said now. For once he wasn't challenging me; he seemed genuinely concerned.

"I dunno, man."

I unlatched the gate and we pulled it together across the storefront, me on the inside, Henry on the sidewalk.

"You should be celebrating with your own people tonight," he said.

"We didn't win, Henry," I replied through the grating. "Wait and see. No way they're letting us have this."

"*Tch*," he scoffed, imitating my mother. "Always the cynic."

He strode off toward the lights and merriment of 4th Street, decked out for the election celebration as if for New Year's. I clanged the gate shut and watched my friend disappear, and just for a second I was back at the sun-white afternoon in 1943 when John walked out of the Tule Lake Segregation Center in uniform. That had been a very different gate with an altogether different clang, and Henry looked nothing like my brother. Yet here I was on a cool autumn evening, three hundred miles and a decade away, cursing the bitch that was memory.

For the second time that day, I kicked the shop door closed. Thankfully the window in the door didn't break. We'd just paid thirty-five dollars for the lettering on the glass: *Sakura*

City, Florist, with our phone number and hours. It was quarter to seven. Mr. Hovey at Mo-Mo's had already reprimanded me once about lateness. Annoyance mounting over my mother's absence, I rushed through the rest of our closing routine: wiping down the counters, depositing the cash in the lockbox in my mother's bedroom, turning out the lights.

At the alley-side door I remembered I still hadn't checked on the floral wire. "Damn it," I muttered. That order should have gone in that afternoon; it *definitely* had to go in first thing the next morning. I spun around and made my way down the splintery stairs in the dark. At the bottom I crunched on broken pottery. *What the hell?* Was this the thud I'd heard earlier? Why hadn't anyone cleaned it up?

Then my foot bumped against something bigger, denser. A bag of soil? A *raccoon*? A jolt of unease flashed through me as I reached up and pulled the chain to the lightbulb. In the swaying light I found, crumpled on the dirt floor in front of our tidy storage shelves, surrounded by the shards of a heavy chartreuse vase, a dead *hakujin*. His face wore the expression of a man stunned by how things had turned out.

It was the antiques dealer, and someone had garroted him with floral wire.

It never occurred to me to call the police. We never called them to the West End if we could help it. But in any case, I could not stop thinking, *I'm gonna be late for work.*

I'm gonna be late, I thought, turning off the light and heading back up the stairs. *I'm gonna be late*, locking first the cellar door then the side door behind me. *I'm gonna be late*, running the four blocks to Mo-Mo's. The imperative to reach 600 Capitol Avenue on time, plunge my hands into the scalding water and come out with clean highballs and tumblers and shot glasses and snifters, overrode every other impulse.

I slid breathless into the jazz club's kitchen, unable even to begin to figure out what had happened, how the man had come to be in our cellar, where *Kāsan* and Michiko were. But standing at the sink trying to steady myself, scrubbing my rough florist hands clean, I suddenly remembered the way one end of the floral wire glistened sickeningly against the packed dirt floor of our cellar beside the *hakujin*'s ruined neck. It was an image I'd see over and over, that night and for many nights thereafter.

I don't remember who was playing at Mo-Mo's that night. It might've been someone I'd ordinarily have felt lucky to hear over the kitchen din or watch from the back during a break—Leroy Harold, the Rhythmettes, even Duke Ellington. I took an early smoke break, and Duane, a busboy I'd become friendly with, followed me out back and watched me try and fail to light a cigarette. "What's wrong with you?" he finally asked.

And I told him. I said I needed to dispose of a dead body.

Duane's handsome face snapped shut against me. "You're not trying to involve a Black man with some dead white man."

"It's not like that," I said helplessly and untruthfully. "I just thought you might know—"

"Stop."

"I'm in trouble," I said, my voice catching.

"We're not having this conversation, George."

He dropped his cigarette and went back inside, the noise of the club swelling then receding as the back door opened and shut, leaving me alone under the dark November sky, Duane's half-smoked Kool smoldering beside me. We were

both veterans, for Christ's sake, both hardworking, belea-
guered residents of the endangered West End, both peons at
the club. We'd shared jokes, cigarettes, complaints about the
bosses, longings for the unattainable gorgeous women in the
club. I'd thought that meant something.

Man, I didn't understand *shit*.

He didn't speak to me again that night. Or ever. In fact,
everyone at Mo-Mo's would give me wide berth after that,
even the Chinese janitor and the Portuguese short-order
cook. Mr. Hovey would wait till after New Year's to meet me
at the back door, hand me fifteen bucks, and tell me I was
done.

But that night, as Wednesday slid into Thursday, I trudged
home in cold, exhausted dread. I turned down my block expecting to see police cars pulled up out front, lights spinning,
a couple of Sacramento's "finest" ready to rough me up and
charge me with homicide.

But 4th Street was like an arty impressionistic photo—
streetlights diffuse in the mist, the neon *Sukiyaki Chop Suey!*
sign blinking blue then red, late-night revelers stumbling
past, the liquid asphalt of the street bearing all away. At the
side door in the alley, I was surprised to hear the rumble of
the Muramotos' bathhouse boiler and see white curling from
its smokestack. They usually closed at ten o'clock, and still
the city complained.

I padded quietly into the shop, unlocked the door to the
basement, and peered into the darkness below with nause-
ated apprehension. I knew what I needed to do: sweep up the
broken ceramic, shift the body aside, take everything down
from the shelves, move the shelving away from the wall, dig
a deep hole through the dirt floor, bury the *hakujin*, tamp it all

down, put everything back. It would take all night. If I could manage it at all.

I crept down the steps, breath held, then reached toward the lightbulb, pulling the chain, slowly, slowly, till it clicked on, filling the space with its barefaced glare.

There was no body.

The hardpan floor looked undisturbed. I lowered myself into a squat, careful not to touch the place where I'd seen the dead *hakujin*. But it was as clean as a dirt floor can be. Not one shard remained. Glancing up, I saw our Japanese broom hanging innocently from its wall hook alongside shovels and shears. The shelves regarded me sedately with their neat rows of baskets and vases (no evidence that one was missing) and the labeled boxes of floral foam and florist paper and—wire. Right. That box was empty.

Something still felt off, something besides the disappearance of a corpse I'd seen five hours earlier. But I felt a crawling, itchy need to be away from there, so turned off the light and felt my way back upstairs.

"What are you doing?" came my mother's voice in Japanese.

"Jesus Christ, *Kāsan*!" I said. She was seated very upright on a stool we kept behind the counter, her small figure silhouetted against the window. "What are *you* doing, sitting here in the dark?"

"Where have you been?"

"Where have *you* been?"

"*Tch.*" I couldn't see her expression, but I could sense fear under her annoyance.

"I went to class," I said.

"Till two o'clock in the morning?"

"Some of us went out afterward."

She switched into English: "You with *hakujin* girl?"

I snorted. "No, *Kāsan*, I wasn't with a *hakujin* girl. Or *any* girl."

A charged silence crackled between us. I finally gestured behind me toward the cellar door.

She shook her head slowly, decisively. "That story about Ito-*san*," she said. "Not true."

"It's not?"

"He didn't sell Kabuki mask. He not selling bakery or move to LA."

I pointed again toward the cellar door. "*Kāsan*, what—"

"No," she said. "No, Jōji. *No*."

And that's how the dead *hakujin* in the cellar joined Tule Lake, and John's death in France, and my father's slow suicide by bottle, on the list of subjects we could not broach.

The city lost no time finding a way around the failed referendum. The first building to meet the wrecking ball was a two-story Victorian on Capitol Avenue. Seventeen city blocks eventually leveled: how many lives did that comprise? One masochistic afternoon in 1959, I drove back to the old neighborhood to look at the blasted landscape. It reminded me a little of Tokyo in 1945.

Today the former West End is mostly government and corporate high-rises, overpriced apartment buildings with no character, parking garage after parking garage, sidewalks empty of people, and—this one really irks—some still-undeveloped parcels.

Meanwhile, my only clues about what might have happened that day came the next morning. When Henry hadn't shown up or called by seven o'clock, no doubt sleeping off the previous night's partying, I started calling around, trying to rustle up some last-minute flower deliveries, but my mother kept insisting I fix the damn shop-keeper's bell.

"We have to know when someone come in," she said while I climbed up a stepladder to wrestle the banged-up bell back into place.

"Sure, *Kāsan*," I said. She shook the stepladder with her hand. "Hey!" I cried.

"*Wakaru?*" she said sternly. *Do you understand?* "Someone come in, we *have* to know."

I pictured myself upstairs working on our accounts while Michiko went to the cellar for something, only to be surprised there by the antiques man whose entrance she hadn't heard—because of a bell I'd broken and failed to repair. For a moment I imagined her reaching up for a vase and bashing it over the man's head—but then? I looked down at *Kāsan* and imagined a length of floral wire in those strong, bony hands—

"Just *fix*," she said, giving the ladder another shake.

The phone started to ring, matching and drowning out some buzzing alarm in the back of my head, then Henry arrived, unshaven, heavy-lidded, his skin gray.

"Nice of you to show up," I said. "Looks like you found a vampire instead of a girl last night."

He glanced at my mother, then back at me. "Truck was stolen," he mumbled.

"*What?*" I said.

My mother pushed me away from him, then shooed Henry upstairs and followed after. She didn't come back for twenty minutes, and when she did, she ordered me to leave him alone.

"The truck," I began hesitantly, "should we . . . report—"

"No," she said emphatically, in English.

This time Mrs. Muramoto's entrance was announced by the restored bell. "*Ohayō-gozaimasu,*" I called out with exaggerated cheer. "You were open late last night, *ne*, Muramoto-*san*?"

From under her Lucille Ball–inspired poodle clip, she eyed me with more than her usual antipathy, then made a beeline for my mother. "*Wa-su-re-mo-no,*" she hissed. *You. Forgot. Something.*

Kāsan recoiled for a second before slipping an object into her apron pocket. I never saw it again, although I searched the apron that evening. But in that moment before she hid it away, I could have sworn I saw Mrs. Muramoto hand over a singed steel cigarette case.

"I need *big* arrangement today," Mrs. Muramoto declared. "All white." And until the city shut her down the following summer, we would supply Muramoto's *sentō* every week with ornate flower arrangements, free of charge.

Demolition work is impressive and compelling, even when it's your own neighborhood they're tearing down. I watched from the alley when the excavator peeled off the back wall of the *sentō*, revealing the boiler room, and it shocked me how small the boiler was. I'd imagined something massive, capable of producing that deep rumble and requiring that tall smokestack. Its narrow opening could hardly have admitted a child. The grisly thing I'd been imagining for months—it wasn't true after all, I thought.

It's a cliché of stories like mine: *I started to wonder if I'd dreamed up the whole thing.*

In real life, reasonably sane people don't confuse reality and dreams. Except I *did* start to wonder, after a while, when nothing happened. The man's disappearance never made the news. When the police finally showed up to ask about a missing *hakujin*, it was for a young white woman who'd last been seen at one of the nearby hotels. They never found her either.

Nothing happened—except that my mother and Michiko and Henry seemed drawn together by some secret urgency. At a certain level I understood: they were protecting my ignorance. But that didn't mean I didn't resent it. I accused *Kāsan* of preferring Henry to me, and experienced spasms of jealousy every time I saw him with Michiko. Yet Henry came around less and less often. He found another job, then another, then another, this time in Fresno. The rare times he returned to us—he was best man at my wedding and pallbearer at *Kāsan's* funeral—he'd drink too much and swing from forced hilarity to petulant silence. He never married, never had children, never settled in one place.

When he died at forty-nine, people said it was because of his wartime experience, that he'd been haunted by what he'd witnessed at Dachau. Maybe it was true. But graveside at East Lawn Cemetery, when Michiko and I threw our handfuls of dirt on top of our old friend, she said, face hidden under a black cloche hat: "You know that truck wasn't stolen, don't you?"

"What?" I'd been thinking of Walerga. At the temporary detention center east of the city where we'd waited for two months in 1943 while the feds finished building Tule Lake, Henry had stolen lumber and nails to build a treehouse for the kids.

Michiko turned her still-beautiful face up to me. "He drove it into a reservoir or lake," she said.

My mind pricked all over with questions, but the only one I could speak was: "Where?"

She shook her head. "I don't know."

I remembered: how jumpy he'd seemed that night, how anxious to draw me out of the shop, until he knew I was leaving for Mo-Mo's.

And one more thing came to me from that night, an element I could not identify till that moment. I know that a memory so old, so submerged, might not be relied upon, and yet I saw it: the wall of tools hanging in the cellar, the knives, the shovels, the short-handled broom, and missing from among them, my father's Japanese handsaw.

Body, handsaw, truck bed, furnace. Then a scuttling. The awful scene I'd once abandoned as impossible rose before me, grislier than I'd ever imagined, and I felt my middle-aged self slumping in my ill-fitting funeral suit.

Michiko put her arm through mine. "He loved me, you know."

I stiffened, and she jostled me. "He did it for you too, Jōji. And for *Okāsan*," she said. "And for Sakura City."

"It didn't save Sakura City."

"No, it didn't," she said. "But we made a life anyway."

We had, she and I. You might think I'd balk at marrying a woman I'd thought capable of killing someone and helping to dispose of the body and simply returning to work the next day, which she had, smiling as if nothing had happened. No—you want to keep a woman that fearless and beautiful in your life, if you can, if she'll have you. In 1957, when we were finally compelled to sell our place to the city—for a derisory settlement, of course—I asked her to marry me, move one mile south to a neighborhood with a large leafy park and no racial covenants, and start over with me and *Kāsan*. She said yes.

A SIGNIFICANT ACTION

BY MACEO MONTOYA

Southside Park

When the arts collective first started in the late 1960s, they called themselves the Rebel Chicano Art Front, but some people confused their acronym for the Royal Canadian Air Force, so in response they said that they were, in fact, the Royal Chicano Air Force, and not only that, they flew adobe airplanes. They even went around in WWII bomber pilot regalia. Scholars have written about them, and you can find their work in archives and museums, but at the time, all that mattered was art and revolution and the locura that would deliver us to that promised land. They had charm and talent in spades. They not only made artwork but wrote poetry and played guitars and sang. They also drank like fish. They were fun to be around, and when they showed up in their VW vans, which they called their airplanes, they made every party better. People wanted to be around them. This meant nonartists who just wanted to contribute to the cause, or partiers who wanted to join the revelry. This meant women too. There were lots of hangers-on, drunks who caused too many fights, artists and activists who were politically suspect, and eventually the RCAF learned to become suspicious of newcomers. They wanted members who were committed to el Movimiento, not just the latest party. Plus, just about every radical organization had been infiltrated by the FBI or the police. Everyone talked about the FBI's COINTELPRO as if it were the bogeyman. Which meant that when recruits like me showed up at their meetings eager to get involved, they kept us at a distance until we earned our way into the collective.

At the top were the founders, the Professors, and below them—though they would've denied such a hierarchal structure—were their most talented former students, expert printmakers and muralists. Below them were the "contributors," the fundraisers and organizers, the event planners, those who did all the work that wasn't art but made the art possible. They were all considered members of the collective, the "pilots." Then there were the bodyguards, the older vatos locos from the barrio, many with long rap sheets and stints in prison, whom the Professors kept around because they believed in second chances and because if things got heavy they wanted plenty of muscle on their side. Then you had the aspiring artists who weren't yet part of the collective but who were allowed to help print posters and paint—apprentices in training. They were people on the verge of getting "pinned," or receiving their wings as they called it. And then you had someone like me, who wasn't even an apprentice, who remained in a state of purgatory, just waiting for a chance to prove himself.

I was considered suspect, I knew that. I didn't look the part, for one. Most of the RCAF had long hair and impressive mustaches, and I was clean-shaven and kept my hair short with a neat part even though that had gone out of style ten years ago. I didn't dress the part, either. Tucking in my shirt earned me the nickname "The Accountant." I also liked to paint landscapes, mostly small rural scenes with horses and cows, and I sold these to help pay my way through Sac State. I was ready to paint revolutionary scenes if only they gave me the chance. Instead, they gave me another nickname, "Holy Toledo," as in a painter so white-bread I might as well be painting in Toledo, Ohio, but also a nod to *View from Toledo* by El Greco, which is the kind of wordplay the RCAF thrived on but could also be exasperating when it was at your expense. Anyway, I think I had so many nicknames because they never could remember my actual name. I was even once called "Afterthought," a nickname that never stuck, but it's probably the most accurate description of my role in the collective. I no longer wanted to be an afterthought. I was determined to demonstrate my value to the RCAF.

I was mostly just allowed to wash brushes. The muralists would climb down from the scaffolding, their brushes covered in paint, drying by the second, and I would rush over, bucket of water in hand. While they admired their handiwork on the wall, I would grab their brushes, dunk them into the water, and vigorously swirl them around. Then I'd carefully use my thumbnail to clean out the paint from the bottom of the bristles. Finally, when I was satisfied that all paint had been removed, I would take out my rag and carefully dry the brush, ensuring that not one hair was out of place. Then I'd hand the brushes back to the muralist, who by now would be engaged with some chavalito from the neighborhood or a viejita pushing a shopping cart, talking to them about the liberatory power of art, how it could transform society and uplift minds, and raza this and raza that, and then the muralist would take the brushes from me and climb back onto the scaffolding like a soldier returning to battle.

I rarely got a thanks, sometimes an *órale*, which felt less directed at me and more at the task at hand. But I was okay with that, it had been explained to me that we were community artists, an arts collective, and that we weren't like white artists who cared only about individual genius; no, we rejected individualism and did whatever the moment or the effort required, and this particular effort required some to paint murals bursting with color in Southside Park and others to wash brushes, put up scaffolding, order tacos, go on beer runs, or walk around the park like my friend Lety with a Folgers coffee can asking for spare change in order to purchase another gallon of paint. Of course, I aspired to be one of the artists placing the brush to the wall, and I dreamed of the day one of the Professors would stop by the mural, see my perfectly arranged paint canisters and brushes as good as new, and say, "You remind me of my navy days, kid, mis jump boots bien shainadas. Why don't you get up there and paint?" I had been waiting for this moment for well over a year.

I was the first to notice her lingering off to the side. She wore a knitted beret, a colorful poncho, bell-bottoms, and orange leather chanclas that we used to be ashamed to wear but now were all the rage. Her hair was long and black, and her dark eyes radiated intensity. After drinking from the fountain, wiping her lips with her sleeve, she held her hand over her eyes to block the sun as she stood admiring the mural's progress. She was beautiful, there was no doubt about that, but beautiful girls passed by all the time and stood admiring the murals in much the same way and sometimes they even called out flirtatiously to the muralists, distracting them from their revolutionary task, getting them to climb down from the scaffolding and chat for a while. I didn't mind these moments of distraction because sometimes one of the muralists would hand me his brush and palette and say, "Oye, fill in that sky and don't get crazy." I would climb up the scaffolding, my heart racing, my hands practically shaking with excitement, while the muralist flirted down below.

But the girl in the beret and colorful rebozo didn't call attention to herself. I was the only one who seemed aware of her presence. I watched her inching closer to the wall, one step at a time, her hand over her eyes until she was so close to the wall that the wall itself blocked the sun. She let her hand drop, revealing her full beauty, her lips still moist from her stop at the water fountain. I pretended to be busy, making sure the lids to the paint cans were secure, but I couldn't take my eyes off her. There was something I couldn't quite place about her. Something familiar.

It wasn't long before the muralists noticed her too. All of them did. Even Antonio and Eliseo, who were as disciplined as monks and likened painting murals to guerrilla warfare in a far-flung jungle, started painting distractedly, redoing areas that were already pretty much done. It was Bobby who swung down from the scaffolding first. He was the smooth talker, always quick to laugh and tease. He liked to call me "Piernitas," on account of my skinny legs and the fact that I often wore shorts because it was unbearably hot that spring, even in the shade. I couldn't hear their conversation, but she must've said something that impressed Bobby because his rakish smile disappeared, and soon he was pointing at the wall as if explaining the imagery. Then, to my surprise, because once Bobby was smitten with someone, he became the jealous type and cordoned off the object of his affection, he called over Ernesto, who was on the bottom level of the scaffolding painting hieroglyphs. They appeared to ask Ernesto a question, and Ernesto nodded his head as though thinking about it but was unsure how to respond. That was when they called over Antonio and Eliseo.

I was still too far away, and I usually approached only when beckoned, but I could hear batches of conversation about Aztec codices and female deities. I heard a reference to Orozco. Then Siqueiros. She made them laugh. Antonio and Eliseo, who could've been twins with their thick Zapata mustaches and their shoulder-length hair tucked under red bandannas, were soon engaged in the conversation. What could they possibly be talking about so raptly? I wondered. I couldn't bear the suspense. I walked closer to the group. Now I could hear them discussing the use of color in the wall paintings in Bonampak and how Aztec children were born knowing a color wheel of cosmic proportions. I don't know why but I felt the need to approach quietly, the grass masking the sound of my footsteps. I had practically joined the group and still no one registered my presence. But then her eyes, which had now lured over every muralist so that all painting had ceased, turned to me, prompting the muralists to look in my direction with the same exact expression on their face. Only Bobby voiced it: "What the hell do you want, Piernitas?"

"Any brushes need to be cleaned?" I asked.

They shook their heads and returned their attention to the girl. I was headed back to the paint table when Antonio called out to me, "Hey, Cuadro"—which meant canvas because I had once stretched a canvas for him, but it was also another way of calling me square—"get her a palette and fill it up with paint." Then he said to her, "What's your name, carnala?"

"Enamorada," she said, "but everyone calls me Ena."

Enamored. They were enamored all right. I opened the paint cans and scooped out huge globs of paint, dumping them onto the palette. They wanted to waste paint, then let them waste paint. I found her the worst brushes, those cleaned by my friend Lety who wasn't as meticulous as I was, and I watched while Antonio carefully guided the newcomer as she hesitantly climbed the scaffolding, she who had not been there twenty minutes already given the privilege of placing the brush to the wall. I wanted to fling the palette across the pavement, but I controlled myself. I respected the muralists. I believed in their devotion to the cause. They weren't frivolous bohemians, and sure, their heads were turned once too often by a pretty face and a flirtatious smile, but this was different. The muralists returned to the wall and resumed painting as if inspired, their brushes moving as if to make up for lost time, as if they were back in the jungles fighting for third world liberation. And I could hear Antonio, in his deep, mellow voice, explaining how he would walk her through the painting process. I climbed the first rung of the scaffolding and placed the palette and brushes on the platform where Antonio and Ena were sitting.

"Here you go," I said.

In the second before I hopped down from that first rung, Ena met my gaze and again I felt something familiar. By the time I made it back to the paint table, I was certain of two things: her name wasn't Enamorada, and even though at first I couldn't remember her actual name, our paths had crossed, however briefly, years ago.

I don't want to dwell on the memory. I see it all now from a distance, as though it happened to some other kid. When I was ten, my father got promoted to foreman at the Campbell Soup factory. We lived in Broderick, and my tía lived next door, and my tío lived across the street, and everywhere I turned there was a cousin to play with. But with my father's new salary, my mother convinced him that family was for floor workers and foremen lived in the suburbs, so they moved us to a brand-new three-bedroom house in Arden. The day we left, I choked back tears as my entire extended family lined up on the street to wave goodbye. I lost it completely when as soon as my dad started the car, my cousins resumed their game of football as if they'd forgotten me already. I cried the entire drive to our new home, and only stopped when my dad pulled over and said what he always said when I broke down in tears: "You want something to cry about, mocoso?"

We were the only Mexicans on our block, and I was only one of two Mexicans in my class. The other was a girl named Jenny. In the second week at my new school, we were paired together for a reading activity and almost immediately our classmates thought it would be funny to tease us about having a crush on each other—funny because we were both Mexican and that was the extent of their limited imaginations. I didn't mind, to be honest, because I was looking for friends and a brown face seemed to be my best shot. Plus, I thought she was cute. But Jenny turned bright red and screeched, "Ewww, he's dirty!"

All the white kids laughed until the teacher told them to pipe down. I buried my face in my arms and the teacher excused me to go to the restroom. That night—and this is the part I remember as though I were watching from a peephole in the ceiling—my mother found me in the bathtub, the water scalding hot, and I'm as red as a lobster rubbing my skin raw with a bristled brush.

My mother screamed, "What are you doing, mijo?"

"Am I not clean?" I cried. "Am I not clean?"

Then my father burst into the bathroom, and for the briefest second I saw a mixture of fear and even sadness in his eyes, which was quickly masked by anger. "Qué chingados is wrong with your son?" I heard him ask my mother on the other side of the door.

I don't remember what happened afterward, only that they found out about the kids teasing me at school. The next week I returned to live with my tía and cousins in Broderick. Not long after, my parents returned to the neighborhood as well, our time in the suburbs among gabachos just a blip in our lives. But from then on, I showered twice a day, trimmed my hair weekly, kept my fingernails filed and clean and my clothes perfectly pressed. Even the smallest stain caused me anxiety. My cousins accused me of trying to be white, but I just laughed because my cousins were Broderick boys through and through and didn't know what it was like out there. I never told them about the incident at the school in Arden. I never wanted to think about Jenny again. And I didn't, I really didn't, until she showed up at our mural in Southside Park telling everyone her name was Enamorada.

She could've had two names like my dad, Luis Francisco, and opted for one name over the other. So Enamorada could've been her real name too. And she could've left Jenny behind, the little girl who fit so well among the whites, and become politicized by el Movimiento as so many of us were, suddenly proud to be raza and to hail from Mexican revolutionaries and Aztec warriors, and shed her desire to assimilate. We all followed this path in one form or another. Antonio no longer let anyone call him Tony. Ernesto would fight you if you dared called him Ernie, even though that's what his mother still called him. So name changes weren't unheard of. This was a time of rediscovery, of reclaiming identities that had lain dormant. Jenny showing up out of the blue dressed like a radical Chicana wasn't inconceivable. But because of our shared past, I was suspicious. Maybe I didn't want her around because I didn't want to be reminded of that painful memory. But I also had another reason not to trust her presence: the only other detail that I recalled about Jenny was that her father was a cop, or in the parlance of our arts collective, a pig. The artists of the RCAF would find this troubling. They might not be as quick to welcome this newcomer onto the proverbial scaffolding. For the sake of the collective, I was determined to suss out Jenny's—or Enamorada's—intentions.

The goal of COINTELPRO wasn't just to monitor radical organizations, the FBI wanted to destroy them from the inside. Every organization had its differences, elements that believed in the slow arc of justice and others who wanted more radical change. Slow change was too stable, radical change demanded action, and those actions could be steered in nefarious directions. How many groups in those years blew themselves up in botched bomb-making workshops? But perhaps more dangerous than homemade explosives were oversized egos. Leadership squabbles led to splintering, and smaller groups were easier to monitor and control. If you're fighting each other all the time, then you lose the ability to fight the state. I mention this because if Ena wasn't COINTELPRO, then she was certainly following the manual.

Antonio and Eliseo had been inseparable since their first year at Sac State when they enrolled in the Professors' barrio art classes. They joked that the left-handed Antonio and right-handed Eliseo were an ambidextrous mural-painting machine. It didn't take long for Ena to jam its gears. I witnessed it happen. At first, they took turns instructing her how to paint, but they wasted too much time talking, leaning against the scaffolding railings, gesticulating with their hands, waxing philosophical. They almost stopped painting altogether. They grew jealous of one another and made fools of themselves as they vied to be Ena's mentor. They forgot about Bobby and Ernesto, who, though good painters, needed direction. They rarely called on me to wash brushes. Within weeks, progress on the Southside Park murals had slowed to a crawl.

I almost wished the handsome charmer Bobby had gotten to her first. He would've seduced her then lost interest, on to the next girl. But Antonio and Eliseo were such dedicated artists and activists that they weren't accustomed to these feelings. They kept telling themselves they were just teaching Ena how to be a revolutionary artist, and as long as they kept talking about muralism they could pretend that the ardor in their hearts was political, not carnal. She gave them equal attention, careful not to tip the scales in favor of either one. My friend Lety said she was "playing them like bongo drums," bouncing back and forth, a willing student, absorbing their lessons, adopting their language. She was even becoming a good painter. I spent more time washing her brushes than those of the muralists I was trying to impress. She barely acknowledged me. She just called me "Hey," as in, "Hey, can you clean these brushes? Can you refill my palette?" She hadn't changed. She still acted like the Jenny I knew back in the fourth grade. Haughty. Better than.

One afternoon she announced to the muralists that she had to leave for class. Antonio and Eliseo immediately deflated. She walked toward the paint table to grab her leather satchel and poncho, which she had left underneath for safekeeping.

"You taking art classes at State?" I asked.

She didn't even look my way as she gathered her things. "Yeah, Intermediate Drawing 2B, Beginning Painting 1A, Color Theory . . ." Her voice trailed off.

What a strange answer. I didn't ask for her course schedule. I thought on my toes. "Isn't Redfield an awesome instructor?"

"Oh yeah, he's great," she said as she walked off.

There was no one named Redfield in the art department. I had made him up. It's true, I was a nobody who didn't deserve her time. She could've just been blowing me off, but maybe, just maybe, I had caught her in a lie. I watched her cross T Street, a group of viejitos ogling her as she passed. She got into a maroon Datsun parked in front of the church. I noted her license plate and decided to start following her.

My suspicions were correct: she wasn't an art student. Two of her classes were in criminal justice, and somewhere between Southside Park and campus she always changed out of her colorful poncho, bell-bottoms, and chancla attire, and exchanged it for a plaid skirt, white blouse, and a ribbon in her hair. In my mind, she went from Ena back to Jenny. I wished the guys could see her. They would've called her Cuadra. After classes, she drove home to the same neighborhood in Arden where my parents moved for that brief miserable period. The homes no longer looked as if they'd dropped from the sky. The yards weren't so orderly. The trees had grown. I still didn't like being there.

These days, her father was always sitting on a folding chair in the garage with the door open, a cooler full of Coors at his side. He still looked like a cop, a mean one, with a closely faded flattop, his hair speckled gray, his biceps bulging out of his white T-shirt. And when his daughter arrived home one evening, she tried to slip past him, but he barked, "Jenny!" forcing her to stop and greet him with a peck on the cheek.

She entered the house through the garage, leaving her father staring at the street or perhaps at his spotless Oldsmobile in the driveway—but to me, he looked as though he were staring into an abyss. A neighbor—an old white woman with her hair in curlers who thought I was a Jehovah's Witness—told me that he was retired from the police force; forced retirement was what folks were saying, some incident involving embezzled funds and confiscated drugs, and she wasn't surprised because she'd never trusted him, never wanted him in the neighborhood, even if he was a police officer, and she probably would've told me how the neighborhood had gone to shit as soon as a Mexican moved in, but I extricated myself from the conversation. I had the information I needed. Ena was a criminal justice major recruited by the FBI to infiltrate the RCAF, which she did willingly because she needed to redeem the family name soiled by her father. I didn't know this for sure, of course, but these are just the kinds of things that enter your mind as you drive around town following someone. What happened next only heightened my suspicions.

Antonio and Eliseo were increasingly at each other's throats. I wasn't there and only overheard snippets of conversation, but apparently it got so bad that the Professors had to call a meeting to get to the bottom of their strife, and instead of confronting the problem directly—their shared obsession with Ena—they accused each other of reactionary and bourgeois leanings, of succumbing to individualism, and they endlessly rehashed political and artistic arguments that had nothing to do with what was tearing their friendship apart. The Professors insisted on a truce, an agreement to "let bigotes be bigotes," but Antonio and Eliseo left the meeting angrier at each other and more determined to prove their radical bona fides. This, I suspect, is when Ena started whispering in their ears.

It was my friend Lety who tipped me off that something big was brewing. Lety was also on the fringes of the RCAF, trying in vain to be accepted into the collective. In bitter moments, she thought it was because they were all sexist pigs and she wasn't pretty enough, but usually she chalked it up to her being half white, which might've been true. Her last name was Williams and I just took her word that her mother was Mexican because Lety looked like a run-of-the-mill white girl with green eyes and dirty-blond hair. She didn't speak a lick of Spanish either. But I suspected the main reason she remained on the outside looking in was because she hung out with me. I didn't have the heart to tell her because I didn't want to lose my only friend in the collective, or collective adjacent, whatever we were.

When I shared my suspicions about Ena, Lety offered to keep her ear to the ground. She was a good eavesdropper. I was amazed at the things she overheard—it was as if people didn't even notice her presence or simply didn't care that she was present—and it wasn't long before she informed me that something was being planned, and although she couldn't pinpoint what it was, Ena was at the center. One afternoon, Lety picked me up with her brothers Dale and Frank, and I joined her in the backseat of Dale's Mercury, where she filled me in on what she'd gathered. She had overheard Eliseo and Ena at a house party, she told me—her eyes growing wide as she described the scene—their faces just inches apart as if they were about to start necking, talking about a "significant action" that would "make the elite tremble." Later, she heard Antonio and Ena at the VFW hall also discussing in hushed tones a "significant action." She added that she kept hearing "the pincher Crocker."

"As in the museum?" I asked.

She shrugged. "They didn't say *the* Crocker Art Museum, if that's what you're asking. They just said *Crocker* always preceded by *pincher*."

"You mean *pinche*?" I asked.

"Oh yeah, maybe that's what it was."

I thought for a moment. The artists were always railing against the pinche Crocker. Museums were for gabachos, nothing more than warehouses for imperialists to house their plunder and for capitalists to wash their money. "Do you think this significant action actually involves the museum?"

Lety shook her head. "I don't know. I was sitting two stools over and there was a drunk guy between us who kept trying to talk to me. Then Oso came in and told us both to scram."

Oso was one of the RCAF bodyguards, an ex-con whose massive arms were covered in crude, fading tattoos. He seemed to relish scaring the sensitive artsy types in the collective, like the time he told me that I reminded him of one of the guards from his time in Folsom and that he was watching me, and he even lifted his shades to show he meant business.

"Did Oso recognize you?" I asked.

"No, I just think he wanted a drink," Lety said. "That man is so damn terrifying. I almost pissed myself."

I started worrying about COINTELPRO's strategy of pushing particularly strident activists to commit extreme acts, usually some form of violence or sabotage. I'd thought we were pretty safe in an arts collective consisting of muralists, poets, troubadours, and grant writers, but the repeated mention of the Crocker Art Museum had me imagining horrible scenarios. Would they deface paintings, or worse, blow up a wing? My suspicions only heightened when Lety reported back to me that Antonio and Eliseo, having finally accepted the détente, were making frequent trips to a hardware store. I pictured them in a basement apartment fiddling with wires and combustible materials, Ena at a chalkboard diagramming explosives. How could they not see that she was leading them to ruin, and by association, the rest of the arts collective? I needed to confront them, to at least give them the evidence I had already gathered—that her name was Jenny, and that she was not an art student as she claimed but was in fact law enforcement in training, and what's more, her father was a corrupt cop, and when she wasn't with them she dressed like a goodie-two-shoes white girl, and if that wasn't enough, she had once shamed a fellow Chicano when they were only ten years old, saddling him with a hygiene complex. I'd probably leave out the last part. In fact, I was feeling less certain of my case. I didn't have a smoking gun. Just suspicions. But couldn't I plant the seed, at least make them think twice about blowing up the Crocker?

Luckily, the Professors had ordered Eliseo and Antonio to resume work on the Southside Park murals, so I knew where to find them. Lety was on brush duty that day and I asked her to call and tell me if the coast was clear. Ena couldn't be around. I waited in my apartment, pacing back and forth, rehearsing what I was going to tell them. I would start off by professing my devotion to the RCAF and that I was voicing my suspicions only because I cared so much about the collective and its mission, and that I was happy to wash brushes if that's what the cause required, but that I also felt I was ready to start painting murals alongside them, and that once Ena's insidious behavior was recognized, we needed to recommit to muralism for the people without distractions, and I could be part of that recommitment. I even thought to bring along my portfolio of mural sketches to show them. Lety called at noon.

"Eliseo and Antonio are here," she said, street traffic nearly drowning her out. "They're working on one of the Aztec gods. The god of corn, I think. They're painting it together. It's nice to see."

"And what about Ena?"

"Not here."

"Okay, I'll be there as soon as I can."

I grabbed my keys and raced out of my apartment, and practically slammed into Ena, who was walking up the porch steps.

"What are you doing here?" I asked, startled.

She was dressed in her white-girl outfit. She looked around as though assessing the surroundings. "I followed you," she said, her voice calm and in control.

"What are you following me for?"

"To ask you that exact question."

I thought to deny it, but the expression on her face told me that was futile. "I don't believe you are who you say you are," I said.

"How do you figure?"

"Your name's Jenny, for one. Not Enamorada."

She looked at me disappointed, as if she hoped I would have something more substantial. "My full name is Juana Enamorada. I was named after my mom and grandma. The kids I grew up with couldn't pronounce Juana, so they called me Jenny. At home, everyone called me Ena because my mother is Juana."

"Your dad calls you Jenny."

She scoffed.

"You're not an art student," I said.

"So?"

"So, you've led everyone to believe you are. And I know for a fact that you're enrolled in two or three criminal justice classes."

"My dad says if he's paying for school and I'm living under his roof, then he'll be damned if I take any hippie classes. He makes me enroll in criminal justice courses because he thinks every other major is full of communists."

I had to think for a moment. This sounded 100 percent plausible, and I immediately felt bad about my suspicions. I started to blame myself. I was jealous that she had been invited up on the scaffolding to paint and I hadn't. I was scarred because all those years ago she had called me dirty, and I couldn't allow that she had changed, grown up, become her own person. "You don't remember me, do you?" I said, finally.

"Remember you from what?"

"In the fourth grade, I was new to your class . . . The kids were teasing us about being a couple because we were the only two Chicanos, and you . . . well . . . you . . ." I was having trouble saying the words.

"I said mean things."

"Yeah."

I looked up and her eyes were sympathetic, maybe even sad. She reached out and pulled me in for a hug. "Hermano," she said, "I was young and ashamed of who I was, and I'm sorry for causing you shame. It doesn't excuse what I did, but we didn't know ourselves then. El Movimiento changed everything for me. We'll never go back to that time again."

Her embrace felt good, her words even better. She pulled away and squeezed my shoulder. "Let's drop our suspicions about each other. It only causes harm to our larger goals. Aren't we stronger together?"

"Yes," I said, and for a moment I had a glimpse of what had driven Antonio and Eliseo so crazy.

Later that day I got a call from Antonio. The muralists never called me; I confirmed plans with them in person, either at the collective meetings or at the mural sites. He asked if I was free that evening and called me "compañero," which he used with a lot of people but never with me. I told him absolutely and offered to head over to Southside Park straightaway if he needed someone to wash brushes or maneuver the work lamps, which they used whenever they put in late nights.

"We'll come pick you up," he said.

"You mean at my place?"

"Yeah," he said.

"That's not necessary, I can head over to the park and save you time."

"We're not going to be painting," he said.

"We're not?"

"The Profes, they want to talk to you."

"To me?"

"Yeah."

"Oh, okay, wow, that's great." So the Professors had finally taken notice. Was I really going to earn my wings and be an official pilot of the RCAF? I wanted to believe it was true, but still I wondered what had sealed the deal.

Before I could tell Antonio my address, he said, "Al rato, vato," and hung up the phone. I felt a little bewildered, but excited.

I was waiting for them at the window. It was dark by the time they arrived, pulling up in one of the collective's VW vans. They honked the horn, and I grabbed my jacket and hurried outside. Eliseo was driving and Antonio was in the passenger seat, the window open, his arm resting on the door. They both wore dark shades. I slid the door open, the air thick with the smell of marijuana. I was surprised to find two men in the far backseat partially obscured by the darkness. It took me a second to recognize Oso's hardened face and another bodyguard whose name I didn't know. I hesitated before stepping into the van.

"How's everyone doing?" I asked as I slid the door closed.

Oso and the other bodyguard didn't answer. Neither did Eliseo as he made a U-turn, and Antonio just nodded his head. We drove in silence, and I began to feel nervous. If I was about to get my wings, this was not the welcome I'd expected from my compatriots.

"You said the Professors wanted to meet with me?" I asked Antonio.

He turned. I couldn't see his eyes behind his dark shades. "Yeah, sure, you'll get to meet them."

I leaned forward. "Did they happen to say what about?"

"Relax," he said, "we'll be there soon."

But I couldn't relax. I could feel Oso's eyes boring a hole in the back of my head. He was watching me all right. I focused out the window as the van sped through Midtown catching one green light after another. We were on Broadway, the old warehouses more derelict as we neared the river. We passed under the freeway overpass. The streets darkened. Eliseo pulled onto a gravel road, dust kicking up around us. I could see the lights of the city bouncing off the expanse of the river, and for a second I was almost relieved. Sometimes the guys liked to party down by the riverbank, a bonfire, carne asada, beer, and guitars, but it was cold and windy that night and all I could see ahead was darkness.

At some point the van stopped, and Eliseo and Antonio got out. "We'll be back," Antonio said as he shut the door.

I could hear Oso and the bodyguard breathing behind me.

"The Professors aren't here, are they?" I asked.

"No," Oso said.

"What are we doing then?"

They didn't answer.

Eliseo and Antonio returned to the van and got in. Antonio carried a box. Another car appeared, its headlights blinding us for a moment before they shut off. I recognized the Datsun. Antonio got out again, and this time he slid open the back door and got in beside me. The front door remained open, and I wasn't surprised when Ena hopped in the front seat as natural as a copilot. A cold gust of wind swirled and slammed the door after her.

The van was quiet for a moment, and I felt everyone's attention on me, as if I was the sole reason for this gathering. My heart began to pound.

"Ena tells us that you've been following her," Antonio said.

I was too shocked to respond.

Antonio continued: "She said you've been gathering information on her. Her classes. Where she lives. Makes us wonder if you're gathering information on *us* too."

I shook my head. "I didn't trust her," I spat out. "I was worried about the collective."

"She said that you and your little white-girl friend have been eavesdropping on our conversations."

"I thought she was COINTELPRO."

"Well, we're wondering the same thing about you."

"You guys know me." I was desperate. I imagined once they finished with the interrogation, Oso and the other bodyguard would drag me out of the van, beat me up, and leave me for dead by the riverbank. My voice rose, "I'm trying to get my wings. I want to be a pilot like you guys, that's all!"

I felt Oso's hands on my shoulders. "Calm down, vato," he said. "We're just talking to you."

"Why did you tell them, Ena?" I asked. She stared out the front window into the darkness. "I thought you said we needed to set aside our suspicions."

"I've seen you getting into the backseat of cars," she said without turning. "Talking to men who look like cops."

"What? That's not true at all!" I turned to Antonio. "She's lying, man. Ena, why are you doing this? Tell them the truth!"

Again, Oso's hands pulled my shoulders back. I could feel the strength of his fingers. He could've snapped my collarbone if he wanted. He spoke into my ear, so close that his mustache tickled my skin. He whispered so low that I could barely hear him, as though he didn't want the others to hear. "Listen, carnal, I know you're not a rat. No rat would dress like you, talk like you, paint like you—you dig, vato? We just need you to prove your loyalty, that's all."

Then his grip on my shoulders released and he patted me on the cheek.

We parked in front of the Crocker. Antonio slid the van door open and told me to get out, then gave me the box. My hands were trembling more from fear than the cold, but the cold didn't help. I cradled the box in my arms as though it would bring me warmth or comfort. Nothing good could come from this. This wouldn't further the cause. This wasn't art for the people. Whatever was in that box, it wasn't for liberation. Antonio instructed me to bring it up the front steps of the old Victorian mansion and open it there. I turned back to Ena and her eyes met mine through the window. She stared at me impassively.

"We'll wait for you here," Antonio said, but he wasn't as good a liar as Ena; I didn't believe him for one second. As soon as I got to the steps, the van would speed off, leaving me to my fate.

I walked forward, the ornate lampposts illuminating my path. When I climbed the first step, I expected alarms to go off, but even the wind had gone quiet. I labored up each step, my legs like lead. I felt as if those stairs went on forever. I reached the top and I placed the box down. They had told me that when I opened it, my mission would be clear. I started to undo the overlapping folds. I expected evidence of something mechanical, to hear the clicking of a timer, the culmination of all those trips to the hardware store. But when I opened the box, all I saw were a canister of red paint and a three-inch housepainter's brush. What was I supposed to do with this?

I turned back and the van was still there. They hadn't abandoned me. Antonio was leaning against the VW van, his arms crossed. He uncrossed them and made a gesture as if to tell me to paint. This was my mission? This was how I proved my loyalty? That's what they wanted. I had washed their brushes a thousand times. I'd peeled the paint off their palettes so that they looked as good as new. I had wiped the sides of the paint canisters so that the lids continued to fit tightly. I had refilled their water buckets. I'd gone on beer runs and taken taco orders. There hadn't been a task too small or beneath me. I was their errand boy and still they wanted me to prove myself.

I stared at the building's decorative trim and corbels, and

my eyes rested on the intricate molding on the hundred-year-old doors. I picked up the brush from the box and turned it over. These weren't the walls I wanted to paint. I dropped the brush back in the box and closed the lid and started walking down the long stairwell. I was going to refuse my mission. I would plead with them in terms that they understood, convince them that all I wanted to do was be like them, to paint so that chavalitos in the neighborhood could know their potential, so that exhausted workers could experience beauty in their daily lives and know that their toil was valued. But as I neared the van, I realized that Antonio and Eliseo were no longer paying attention to me. Oso and the other bodyguard were gone, and so was Ena.

"Look, guys, I don't want to do this," I said.

They didn't answer, they just stared down the street. I followed the direction of their gaze. In the distance, I could see the two bodyguards walking with Ena between them, their arms restraining hers. Then one of Oso's hands appeared to cover her mouth. She struggled to free herself, her feet lifting off the ground, kicking the bodyguards' ankles, but she was no match for their strength as they dragged her toward the riverfront.

"What are they going to do to her?" I asked.

Antonio took off his shades and looked at me as if recognizing me for the first time. As if I was no longer just the lackey who cleaned his brushes. I knew then that he despised my presence, and maybe always had.

"I wish *you* had been the narc," he said. Then he returned his gaze down the block. By now the bodyguards and Ena had disappeared. Were they going to hurt her? Would *she* be the one left for dead?

"I would've killed you myself," he said.

It took a moment to register his words. "Me?"

He was still peering down the street as if hoping Ena would emerge from the shadows, alone and safe. I set the box on the ground and pulled out the brush and canister of paint, then removed the top. It was cadmium red, my favorite color ever since I'd learned in art class that it was toxic, that it could make artists go crazy. It made sense to me that such a beautiful color was poisonous. I dipped the brush inside the paint, knowing that I was probably never going to be a member of the RCAF. Now I was going to make sure of it.

"Mira," I said, "I'm just an artist like you," and I took the brush and daubed Antonio's heart.

THE FORMER DETECTIVE

BY JAMIL JAN KOCHAI

Southport

N ow, in the parking lot, smelling blood, Zakariya should have muttered, *A'udhu billahi min ash Shaytanir Rajim,* and gone back to Massoud's apartment and apologized to his brother-in-law for not sitting through another one of his nighttime tirades, when Massoud would return from his shift at the Port of Sacramento to harangue Miriam about the cost of her thyroid medication. "I house you, I feed you, I clothe you," Massoud had said, "I pick you up from the border on my day off, I vouch for your husband to the Americans, and all I get in return is more problems, more bills, more more more more more mo—" Zakariya had walked out sometime between the sixth and seventh "more," and had been pacing in the parking lot, searching the lighted windows for life, until he smelled blood coming from the fields behind the complex.

With no papers, no money, no English, Zakariya wasn't in any position for trouble . . . and yet . . . and yet . . . the stench of blood wafting from the dark fields seemed so otherworldly in its intensity—the way it seeped into his body— Zakariya was reminded of his miracle in the jungle, his vision of the unborn child, and he thought that perhaps God, again, was testing him.

He hopped a fence to investigate. Wading through knee-high mud water, Zakariya lit his path with a phone light and picked through enormous reeds rippling in the dark. His eyes welled. His throat burned. His nose gushed snot. He roamed blind, led by the scent of blood, and when he emerged from the reeds, he found a trench dividing the field from another barren lot.

Inside this trench was a corpse.

Zakariya kneeled and examined the body with his phone light. Lacerations ran down the left side of its torso. Its chest had been cleft open, but the right side of its neck and face were riddled with puncture wounds. The boy had been jumped. Two attackers, at least. One of them stabbed with a short, circular object, probably a screwdriver, and the other slashed with a large blade, a butcher knife perhaps, but since there were no drag marks or blood trails, Zakariya assumed the boy had been lured into the field by friends. Or family. Who could say? The corpse's face had been cut up so bad, it took Zakariya a few moments to recognize him. A loud-mouthed teenager from the complex. An Afghan. Supposedly, the boy had taken quickly to America: dating girls and drinking beer and battling with his slovenly father, a veteran of the infamous 02 unit in Nangarhar. The boy had been lean and pretty, and seeing his svelte body sprawled out in the mud, punctured and torn, disturbed Zakariya in a way he hadn't anticipated. He was accustomed to bodies. Had learned to tuck them away in a desolate corner of his brain without lights or paved roads. He wondered about the parents, sleeping now probably, having eaten or prayed, unaware of the torment that waited for them in the morning, or in the afternoon, whenever someone else came upon the corpse and had the nerve to alert the police. A white woman, maybe. Or a dog.

* * *

Then—by the fence—Zakariya heard a rattling, a thud, two thuds, saw phone lights flickering, alighting into distant orbs, and he quickly placed a hand over his own light, until, fumbling with his phone, he shut it off and slipped back into the field, the mud, all the while staring toward the distant lights, the twin orbs, floating, bouncing, closer and closer, twenty meters, fifteen, ten, and as the lights approached, he slipped farther back beneath the reeds, crawling into mud and watching the trajectory of the orbs shift toward the trench, and he saw the backs of two shadows form as if their proximity to the corpse were providing them a material shape, and then the lights plunged into the trench, and he watched it aglow, a brilliant haze floating up out of the earth, and if he hadn't known better, if he had come upon the scene for the first time, as a child perhaps, a schoolboy, he would have assumed that he was witnessing a miracle, a resurrection, until, of course, he heard grunting and shoveling, and the lights dimmed, and he saw his chance to escape, and rose up, and the field seemed to belch with his rising, a terrible sucking sound that tormented Zakariya for a few impossible moments, but the work in the trench went on, and Zakariya lurched back through the field to the complex, most of its lighted windows having gone dark, but before reaching Massoud's apartment, he hopped the short fence for the community pool, and he slipped into the water with his clothes on, staring so intently in the direction from which he had come that he did not see the two men approaching the pool from the other side.

"Zakariya," one of them said, "is that you?"

Massoud had come through the side gate using a key he must have swiped ages ago.

Beside him, already shirtless and sweating, Massoud's acquaintance stood half-naked in the dark, exuding an incredible musk of charred lamb and cigarettes. He strolled over to a panel, flipped a switch, and dim blue lights floated up from the Jacuzzi. Despite his enormous beer belly and ravaged skin, Massoud's acquaintance moved with the arrogance of a man who had once been beautiful. He set a bundle of towels down next to the Jacuzzi and dropped himself into the water.

"What are you doing here?" Massoud asked Zakariya for the third or fourth time.

Zakariya didn't respond. He could barely hear Massoud. He was too busy peering at the man in the water. The father of the child in the field. Meters away, the man's son was probably being hacked to bits and buried, and his proximity to this violence—unseen, unreported—disturbed Zakariya in a way he found strangely exhilarating.

"Who's this?" the father finally asked Massoud.

Massoud had been interrogating Zakariya since he came in, but, strangely enough, hadn't lost his temper. "This is my brother-in-law," Massoud said. "The former detective Zakariya Kareem."

"You didn't tell me a cop was fucking your sister," the father said, and unraveled a six-pack of beers from his bundle of towels. "You should have introduced me."

"Major Fahim Faqir," Massoud said, gesturing back to his friend. "He's killed more Taliban than Dostum."

"You were with 02?" Zakariya asked.

"I ran 02," Fahim said.

"He didn't run 02," Massoud said.

"Fuck you I didn't."

"You took all your orders from the Americans."

"Orders? Americans? The Americans weren't kicking down doors. They weren't pulling triggers. Those girls couldn't shoot a bullet without filing a memo first. I was the one getting dirty. I ran the fucking show."

"Usually he's not this sensitive," Massoud said, standing awkwardly between the pool and the Jacuzzi, cradling his own bundle of towels, "but he gets animated about the war."

"*Usually*," Fahim said to Zakariya, "I'm a sweetheart. Come join me. I'll tell you a story." Fahim smiled, and his big bright teeth were tinted blue by the Jacuzzi lights. Slanted apartment buildings loomed on all sides, somehow larger than before. Zakariya followed Massoud into the small Jacuzzi where they each sat at an arm's length.

"Thirsty?" Fahim asked, and tossed Zakariya a beer.

But the can fell in the water, untouched.

"You're not one of those secret mullahs, are you?" Fahim said, and reached for the beer drifting back to him. He offered the can to Massoud, who took it, and held it, but didn't drink. "Wah, Police Sahib," Fahim said, "you've got my friend petrified. You're not going to report him, are you?"

"It's not my business," Zakariya responded. "He can do what he likes."

"But he *can't* do what he likes. Not really. Not now. His wife would beat him."

Zakariya forced a laugh.

"You'll think I'm joking," Fahim said, "because you don't see the beatings. Or hear them. But I know. He weeps to me. My poor Massoud. His wife is a tough one. She kicks him in bed. In his stomach and balls, and if he complains, she grabs him by the testicle, just the one, and ever so slightly . . . presses. Not even a pinch, really, just a bit of pressure. Just enough to make him whimper. Do you understand, Detective? How long have you been married?"

"Ten years," Zakariya said. "Almost eleven."

"No kids?"

"Not yet. But soon, Insha'Allah."

"Of course—Insha'Allah—of course. Ten years. Eleven years. I've seen stranger things. I have a cousin in Kabul whose wife was raped by Massoud's boys in the nineties. The Lion, you understand, during Afshar. Months later, when he finally gets his wife to a doctor, they tell him that she's damaged, that she'll never have a child. Still, my cousin sticks with her. Doesn't flee. They met in college, you understand, and he had stalked her for months, wrote love letters, asked for her hand, and they were married before Kabul fell. He stayed loyal. Even after her suicide attempts, he never left. They were together eleven years, both well into their thirties when they finally have their first kid. A son. Then a year later they have a second son. Two sons in two years. A miracle, you know, but the deliveries are rough on his wife. Emergency C-sections—the both of them. So, again, some doctor says you can't have any more children. You have to use protection. They don't. Of course. Who knows why. Maybe he can't afford the condoms. Maybe they think God will be upset. Whatever it is. She dies giving birth to her third son. The three boys grow up without a mother, and when they come of age, they all join the ANA. After a year or two, I manage to land them cozy positions in secure bases. But then . . . over the summer . . . one by one . . . each of the three boys, the miracles, they die in pointless shootouts with the mullahs. The country was already lost by then. I'd told them to flee. But they wanted honor. So they die. Afterward, I manage to get their father out of the country, another miracle, a last-second supply drop with space in the hangar, but now the miserable shit lives with five addicts in a studio apartment up north, killing himself with whatever he can smoke or snort or inject into his veins. It's a sad state. Sometimes, you know, I want to go up there and put him out of his misery. But it makes you wonder . . . you know . . . why? Why give them the kids . . . after so many years . . . a bona fide miracle . . . only to grind them up in the war? It makes you wonder . . . it does . . ."

"Do you have children?" Zakariya asked.

"I have a horde," Fahim answered, and lifted six fingers.

"Ask him how many wives he has," Massoud said.

Fahim put his hands down. "My first love has taken my apartment, four of my six kids, and half of my life savings. She lives there now." He gestured toward a building by the main street. "Wallah, Police Sahib, not even two weeks had passed, and she found some Pashtun lawyer, an American, to take her case for free. I was out every night, slaving away, and she was colluding with a lawyer the whole time. This was the love of my life. There were days I would have eaten my own hands for her. I would have torn my eyes out of their sockets."

"You don't have to tell him," Massoud said. "He's Majnun."

"Is he?" Fahim said.

"Almost got himself killed winning my sister from a Talib. A distant cousin," Massoud explained. "But Police Sahib here won out in the end."

"Our cop was a lover then," Fahim said.

"And he hasn't let up. Carried my sister for miles through the jungles. My wife half lost her mind with jealousy. Won't stop talking about it."

"What jungles?" Fahim asked.

"Colombian jungles," Massoud said.

"Was I asking you?" Fahim said.

Massoud took a long, loud slurp from his beer.

"It *was* Colombia," Zakariya said.

Fahim laughed, and Zakariya joined him. He couldn't help it. The warmth of the water and the chill of the night were making him sleepy and disoriented, as if the fumes from the Jacuzzi were intoxicating him. Massoud was now on his second beer.

Fahim had stopped drinking altogether. "Tell me about it," he said. "Tell me about the jungles."

They had never wanted to leave. Truly—Zakariya assured Fahim—they would have stayed on through an apocalypse in Kabul were it not for the child they had sought for so long. In the beginning, he and his wife had been so certain of the child's imminent birth, they had picked out names and even begun dreading the sleepless nights. But the childless months turned to years. They went into debt, borrowing thousands from different relatives to pay for fertility treatments and pills and injections. In time, Zakariya heard stories of miracles in America, and after the government fell to the Taliban, he petitioned for asylum, filling out humanitarian parole applications and calling on friends in the US, but when the legal routes fell through, he managed to wrangle visas to Brazil for him and his wife. They spent two weeks living above a soggy café in São Paulo, killing scorpions and brewing mochas until they contacted a trustworthy smuggler in Manaus. From there, they rode on ancient busses and horse-drawn carts all the way up to Colombia, where they marched through miles of flooded jungle, and it was there, climbing up a hill of mud—famished, feet bleeding, lungs burning, on the brink of death—that he saw a vision of a child, two or three years old, pudgy and beautiful, beckoning him. He followed the child and its pungent scent of blood. Later on, when Miriam collapsed from exhaustion, it was the vision of the child that gave Zakariya the strength to carry her on his back, to keep marching past trees, through rivers, up hills, beyond death.

"He won't save you," Fahim said.

Massoud was asleep. He had finished his six-pack and was resting his head on Fahim's shoulder.

"In the beginning," Fahim went on, "it will be good. You will hold him and think, *Oh, this is why God put me through this mess*, and you will watch him begin to walk and speak and fight, and even his farts will delight you. But, inevitably, you will expect too much. You will want him to carry on miraculously forever. But you will watch him grow *and* crumble. His limbs will morph and lengthen, but inside him, that thing from his infancy will choke and die, and you will begin to see in him everything you had once despised in yourself, and you might think that here, in this country, safe, never hungry, he will avoid those horrors we suffered, and it won't fester inside of him as it festers inside of us—but it's worse here, my friend, somehow much worse. There's a madness in this country. Life means nothing, or it means even less than it did back home. I can't explain how, but it will infect your children as it has infected you, and you will come to loathe your boy as much as you once loved him, and it will be even worse because he was once the vision that saved you."

Massoud stirred. A bad dream, maybe. His head slumped forward, almost falling into the pool, but Fahim held him up by his chest.

"What is his name, your son?" Zakariya asked.

"His name is my name," Fahim said, and smiled so brightly in the night. "What will you name yours?"

* * *

"Zakariya," Miriam whispered in the dark of the living room, "where were you?"

"We should leave," Zakariya said, lying on the floor. "We should leave right now."

"We can't leave."

"We shouldn't have left."

"What happened? Where were you?" Miriam asked.

"How is your hand?"

"It's okay. It was an accident."

"I should kill him. I should slit his throat in his sleep."

"It was an accident," Miriam said. She lay on the couch, peering down at Zakariya.

"If I killed your brother, would you run off with me?"

Miriam was quiet for a bit, her hands folded over her belly. "We wouldn't make it far."

"That's what you said in Colombia."

"That's what *you* said in Colombia. I had faith. Even in the jungle, I had faith." It was true. Miriam had always been an appallingly cheerful woman. Even in the jungle, on the brink of death, starving, she would tell jokes. Quips. Puns.

"Do you know that your cousin Mahmoud got a position in the ministry?" Zakariya said. "They gave him a house."

"What do I care about Mahmoud?"

"You never think of him?"

"Who do you think I am, Zakariya?"

"He messaged me on Facebook. Mahmoud."

"What did he write?"

"He told me to come back to Kabul. He said we need good policemen in the new world."

"You can't trust him."

"He sent me a photo of his daughter. Three years old. Looks exactly like him, the poor girl. But without the beard."

"Zakariya," Miriam whispered, "you shouldn't be messaging Mahmoud."

"He messaged me."

"You shouldn't have responded."

"But I needed to know."

"What?"

"I needed to know," Zakariya began, then stopped and tried again. "I needed to know how it is that God has shackled you to me? How it is that I have gone from depriving you of a child to depriving you of a home? How it is—"

Miriam reached down from the couch and pulled him up by his shirt, and pressing him against herself, she felt for his face in the dark and found his lashes, still wet, and she closed his eyes, and said: "Husband. My husband, do you remember our wedding night?" There had been a bed choked with flowers. "Do you remember how I pretended to be shy?"

"You were pretending?"

"Of course I was pretending. I was dying to get you out of that little suit."

"I didn't know."

"Of course you didn't know. I couldn't make you think I wanted you."

"But you did?"

"Did what?"

"Want me?"

"Silly man. What else can I say?"

"Say his name."

"Whose name?"

"Our boy. He should be nine now. Maybe ten."

"Zakariya. You'll drive yourself crazy like this."

"If you knew the night I had."

"I can only know what you tell me."

"I'll tell you."

"So tell me."

There are murmurs in the morning. Unanswered calls. An empty bed. A pointless search. The mother never stops looking. The father never begins. Zakariya sees the boy's face in the news. Just the same. Weeks pass. Months. Massoud's temperament changes. He helps Zakariya find a job at the Afghan grocery baking bread. Nine dollars an hour, ten hours a day, cash. With the help of an Afghan lawyer, Zakariya applies for asylum. Then citizenship. He Ubers. He Lyfts. He Door-Dashes. He saves up enough cash to rent an apartment on the third story of a corner unit overlooking the back lot: the field of reeds. Wildflowers grow in the spring and rainwater fills the trench. Then mud. Then concrete. The field is paved, and an Amazon warehouse is built in its place. Though he could make more money driving to and from Sacramento International Airport, Zakariya applies for a job at the warehouse, gradually moves up to delivery, and finally management. He runs the whole floor. He knows the layout of the warehouse better than his own apartment. There is a corner, between the restrooms and the emergency exit, where Zakariya likes to sit by himself and pray *salah*. Occasionally, he returns to the warehouse after hours, with his key card, to pray the evening *salah*, and when he bows down into *sujūd*, he rests his forehead against the bare cement, and he whispers supplications. His employers watch him on the surveillance cameras, but they don't stop him. It seems harmless. With time, he develops a prominent callous on his forehead that earns him the nickname "Sufi Sahib" from the other Afghan employees. He invites some of them to his home. Their families too. He keeps toys in the balcony closet for these guests, a habit which disturbs some of the parents, who warn their children to be wary of the childless "Sufi." Zakariya doesn't fault them. He imagines that he would be just as cautious with his own children. He imagines other things. Schooldays. Graduations. Weddings. But he tries to focus on sorrows. Escaped sorrows. Hospital visits and sleepless nights and gruesome injuries. Hateful arguments and tiny caskets and the dreams of Fahim's mother, whom he sometimes passes in the parking lot, or near the pool house. A stuttering, pale woman who refuses to leave the complex, though all of her children move far away. And he often thinks of her in the evening, near *maghrib*, when he sits beside his wife on their balcony overlooking the Amazon warehouse, and one day while sharing a beer mug of tea (alternating sips), his wife turns to him and says: "What an eyesore."

"They should tear it down," Zakariya replies.

"Build a park," she says. "A shopping center."

"What was there before? Do you remember?"

"Just fields," she says. "Reeds, I think."

"And a trench. There was a trench behind the fields."

"Really? I don't remember. What was it for?"

Zakariya takes a last sip of tea from their shared mug, leaving just enough for his wife, and responds: "I couldn't even begin to say."

THE SACRAMENT

BY REYNA GRANDE

East Sacramento

Jacob hated rainy nights. They reminded him of Paris. When it rained, his hands itched with the desire to hold a brush, to dip it in paint, to create something beautiful. But he couldn't. As he sped down Stockton Boulevard, he saw everything as clearly as if he'd been walking. The raindrops golden under the streetlamps. The blinking neon signs of the businesses twinkling in the wet puddles. The contrast between the foggy haze and the intense reflections. Rain transmitted mood. Only a rainy day provided the drama that could inspire an evocative painting. But this was not Paris. This was Sacramento, and life was different here.

Just as he was about to dial Tanya's number at the front gate of her apartment building, a woman appeared from the street. She was drenched, her long black hair stuck to her face. He could see her shivering as she took a key from her purse. In a hurry, she swung the security gate open. She did not look at him. She turned to shut the gate behind her at the same moment he reached for it. Their fingers touched.

Her hair wrapped around her round face like a veil as raindrops slid down her cheeks like tears. She had a saintly face, angelic. Her eyes were brown and wide, and just briefly, he had seen fear there, and hope, and longing, and need, and pain, and finally, hatred. She hated him, and he wanted to know why.

He stared at her, mesmerized at the way the raindrops soaked into her black hair, at how the lamp on the wall behind her streaked her hair with gold. He wanted to paint her. He imagined himself mixing Prussian blue, alizarin crimson, and burnt sienna to make the black color for her hair. But then another image of himself arose in his mind, the image of him holding a hammer and chisel, and he realized that he didn't want to paint her. He wanted to sculpt her. Carve her with his own hands. Know her in the most intimate way with his fingertips.

"I'm here to see Tanya. Do you know her?" he said, holding onto the gate. She didn't answer him. Instead, she turned and disappeared down the walkway.

That night, he fucked Tanya with the lights off. He knew she wondered at the change, but she did not ask. That is what he paid for, wasn't it? For her to do as he wanted. In the dark, as he twisted his fingers through Tanya's red hair while moving inside her, he thought of *her*, that woman-child with the rich black hair, with the eyes that bore into his soul, the eyes that asked, *Who are you? Who are you?*

It was his fourth teaching position in six years after having been asked to leave by other colleges. It didn't matter where he taught. They were always the same, the students. Drawing the same pathetic shapes. Their paintbrushes mimicking the works of others instead of creating something new. Something theirs and theirs alone.

Ever since that rainy night, he hadn't been able to get her out of his mind, the woman-child. He saw her hand, those long warm fingers reaching for something only she could see. Her hair, undulating down her back like a waterfall, or no, perhaps it would be twisted into a loose bun, wispy tendrils framing her face. No, that wasn't right either. He closed his eyes and thought of the wet night, of how the rain had pasted her hair around her face, framing it like a veil. No, but that was wrong too. Despite her angelic face, she was no angel. He'd seen that in her eyes. A toughness that comes from knowing only too well how the world works. She was a survivor, that woman-child. But she was also frail, tender . . .

"Professor Mills?"

Jacob turned to look at his students. They stood by their canvases, brushes in hand. None were painting. The clock told him class should have ended nine minutes ago.

"Can we clean up now?" one of the students said.

"Oh, yes, of course."

They moved quickly. Brushes were cleaned. Canvases and easels put away. Soon, the room was empty except for the lingering smell of paint thinner.

He had an hour before the next class. Usually, he would have gone to the Sandwich Spot around the corner, but today he wasn't hungry. At least, not for food. He searched for a sketchbook in his briefcase, but it had been so long since he'd drawn, he was no longer carrying one. He opened and closed his desk drawers until he found pieces of paper, memos from the office he'd forgotten to read, flyers for events he had not bothered to attend. He turned them over, and his pencil flew across the page in quick, steady movements. He sketched her eyes in one gesture. Her hand in another. Her lips. Her hair. Her chin. As hard as he tried, he could not draw her as he'd seen her that night. Her face eluded him.

He needed to see her again.

"I knew I'd find you here," said a voice from the doorway.

Jacob balled up his drawings and threw them in the trash, his heart pumping as if he were a child caught in the middle of some mischief. It always startled him to see his brother in black from head to toe save for the small white square at the collar. To Jacob, the collarino, rather than being a sign of good, looked like a scarlet letter. He still wasn't used to having a priest for a brother.

"Daniel," he said, standing up too quickly, his chair squeaking against the linoleum, "what brings you here?"

"I hope I wasn't interrupting something important," Daniel said.

Jacob blushed, glancing furtively at the trash can. "No, no. Just doodling."

"Doodling?" Daniel said, raising an eyebrow. "You don't doodle. You make masterpieces." He stood by the trash can as if he were going to bend down to retrieve the balled-up papers. He didn't. Jacob knew that the brother in him would have given in to his curiosity, but the priest in him would not. The church had taught him to respect the privacy of others. To keep other's secrets. *His* secrets.

"Join me for a cup of coffee?" Daniel asked. "I think some fresh air might do you good."

Jacob followed him out of the classroom and shut the door. As they walked under the magnolia tree in the courtyard, he glanced at the patterns the dappled light made on the walkway. He noticed the twisting branches of the tree beginning to lose its leaves, and thought of spring, of how beautiful the tree looked in full bloom, the vibrancy of its fragrant pink and white flowers in sharp contrast to the green of its surroundings.

As students passed by them, he noticed the females turning to get a second look at Daniel. Even with his priest's vestments, his little brother turned heads. Brown hair streaked with gold. His baby face made him seem younger than thirty-five.

He had eyes that enchanted, electric-blue eyes that begged to be painted, which Jacob had done often enough many years ago. His legs were muscular, his body, thin at the waist, flared up into a strong back and wide shoulders. Jacob knew his brother was not the gym-going type. Daniel was more at home at the altar, or in a garden, pruning rosebushes, turning compost heaps, or with a shovel in hand or behind a wheelbarrow. How, then, did he manage to look like Michelangelo's *David*?

"I have a commission for you," Daniel said as they neared the campus café.

Jacob stopped walking. "A commission? You know I don't take commissioned work anymore." For a second, he thought about Paris, about that past life. His art, the galleries, the parties, the champagne toasts, the applause. He'd been someone before, but that was long ago, and here in this country he was only a teacher of art. Not an artist.

"Before you say no, I want you to hear me out," Daniel said. "The church needs patrons. Times are tough right now. People aren't giving what they once used to give, especially not our parishioners, who can barely afford to feed their families. Repairs are needed, bills have to be paid—"

"What does this have to do with *me*?"

"We have been blessed with an angel. A woman, a wealthy patron, who has offered to give the church a large amount of money."

"And what can I possibly have to do with this woman?"

"She's quite fond of your work."

"How? Why?" Hardly anyone knew him in this country. Although born in Sacramento, he'd become an artist in Paris. He had been known in certain circles there, and those who still remembered his art would also remember that night when everything he was had been destroyed.

"She did not tell us much," Daniel continued, "except that she admires your work. She was in Paris once, at the time that you were there. She knows you haven't produced work in many years. She also knows you're my brother. She has offered to donate a million dollars to the church if you accept the commission."

"Which is . . . ?"

"A sculpture of Jesus and Mary Magdalene. Not for her *personal* use, but for the church. She wants it chiseled by your own hands, Jacob—what else can I say?"

"Why me?" Jacob asked as they sat at one of the tables outside the café. The coffee now forgotten, he waited for his brother's answer as students rushed to and from their classes. *Why now?* he wanted to ask. He had finally come to terms with the loss of his art, had finally fallen into the routine of living. His classes, his students, his empty house, the blank canvas he had set up in one of the spare bedrooms five years ago in a moment of desperation but not inspiration. No, inspiration had not come to him in years. So, the canvas remained a pristine white, still there in the empty bedroom, waiting.

"She likes your work, Jacob, why can't that be enough? Here is your chance to make a comeback. To make good. She will spare no expense. She will pay what you ask and on top of that help the church. I would not ask if things weren't so desperate. More than ever, the community depends on our charity. Their faith is being challenged. If my church cannot help them, how can we restore—"

"Your church is not my problem," Jacob said, standing up. "Their faith is not my problem." He turned to go. "I need to prepare for my next class."

"I'm not saying it's your problem," Daniel said, catching

up to him. "I am asking you, brother to brother, to do this. For me."

You aren't my problem, Jacob wanted to say. But as he looked into his brother's eyes, he knew it would not be true. He'd taken so much from Daniel. All his brother had left was his church. His God. His devotion.

"Jesus and Mary Magdalene, huh?" Jacob tried to recall his childhood Bible classes. It had been Daniel who was the model pupil, the altar boy, the priests' favorite. Mary Magdalene. He hardly knew anything about her. Didn't he hear somewhere that she might have been a prostitute? Or that she might have also been the beloved of Jesus? Vaguely, he recalled hearing a story about her washing the feet of Jesus. She was an interesting character. An enigma.

Suddenly, the rainy night came to him, and he saw her, the woman-child: the long dark hair, the round face, the expression in her wide brown eyes. Saintly, angelic—but there was something else in those eyes. Heaven and hell, that is what he'd seen in her eyes that night. *I want to immortalize her.*

"If I were to do this . . ." Jacob said, as they reached his classroom. "I'm not saying I will, but if I did, you know how I work, Daniel. You know my terms. I will not have my methods questioned. Would that be a problem for them, your church people?"

"Leave it to me," Daniel answered with a grin. "Just tell me when you want to start."

While not happy about it, Tanya came through for him by setting up a meeting with the woman. For that, he paid her triple the usual rate. Walking to the diner around the corner from Tanya's apartment building, he knew only three things about the woman-child: Her name was Margarita. She was from El Salvador. She never brought her johns to her apartment. Ever.

The diner was shabby, but it had a pleasant smell that reminded him of home-cooked meals. It had been awhile since he'd eaten one of those. He wasn't much of a cook, and he made do with frozen dinners and salad mixes. He chose a booth in the farthest corner, ordered a coffee and a glass of ice water, and waited.

Ten minutes later, she came in. Her eyes scanned the room briefly. Like an eager child, Jacob raised his hand and waved at her, smiling. Quickly, he realized his mistake and erased the smile from his face. She walked steadily to him, her hand going up to her hair to tousle it. She wore a tight yellow dress and black boots that reached past her knees. Her eyes rimmed with too much eyeliner, her lips a brushstroke of carmine. He thought about her in the rain, her face washed clean to reveal her true self. Somewhere underneath all that makeup, he would find her again.

He motioned to the seat across from him. "Please," he said.

She hesitated before sliding onto the seat.

"Would you like some coffee?" he asked, as he waved the waitress over. She shook her head no, but quickly changed her mind and nodded. She wore no jacket even though the evening was crisp. November was coming to an end, and even though during the day the weather would be pleasant, the temperature would quickly drop as soon as the sun went down.

She ordered her coffee black, no cream or sugar. That detail pleased him, somehow. Why mask its bitterness with sweeteners? He could tell that she was the kind of woman who would always want the truth, no matter how hard it was to take.

"Listen, I don't know how much Tanya has told you about me . . ." he began.

"What I need to know?" she asked. "You a man. I know what you want."

"No, no, that's not it." Jacob felt himself blush under her gaze. She had spoken the truth. Yes, he wanted her. Had they been somewhere private, he would have taken her by now. But he was here as an artist, not as a man. He quickly composed himself and continued. "I would like to hire you to pose for me. I have been commissioned to create a statue of Jesus and Mary Magdalene for a church, and I want you to be the model for Mary Magdalene."

She sipped her coffee as she seemed to weigh his words. "I no understand," she said. "I no model. There are girls, much girls who . . ." Her voice trailed off, and he could tell she was having trouble finding the right words in English. "And Mary Magdalene. I no . . ." Now it was *her* turn to blush.

He wondered what she was going to say. *Worthy? Pure?* Is this what she meant?

"Why you come ask this of me?" She angrily picked up her purse and began to slide from the seat. Her right hand rested on the table as she pushed herself out, and without hesitating he reached to grab it.

"Please," he said. "Another girl wouldn't do, don't you see? I will pay you what you ask. Two thousand. Three thousand. You name your price."

She sat back on the seat. Strangely enough, she had not pulled her hand away from his, and he took that to be a good sign. She gazed out the window. He wanted to know what she was thinking. He wanted to reassure her that he would not hurt her. Every second that went by, her face reflected different emotions. He saw her anger, but he didn't know what she was angry about. He saw her pain but didn't know what was hurting her. He saw the longing but knew not what she longed for. He saw the hope, and though not knowing its source, he knew it was a good sign. Something in her face changed. Her eyes lit up, and for a second he could see her, that pure, angelic face. The face of Mary Magdalene.

"Eight thousand," she said. "That is what I want."

"Done," he said. He took her hand and pulled her up.

"Wait. Now?"

"Now," he said.

She turned to look at a man sitting in the opposite corner of the diner. Jacob hadn't seen him come in, but he was rising to his feet now too. He reminded Jacob of some Latino movie star that always played tough guys in films. What was his name? Danny something or other. The man gave him the creeps.

"Is he going to be a problem?" Jacob asked as the girl got into the passenger seat. He saw the pimp walking to his own car, obviously planning to follow them.

She kept her eyes on her hands, which were shaking. "No problem," she said. "I deal with him, okay?"

In his excitement, Jacob had forgotten that he had not thought about where he would work, nor that he had not received his first payment yet. He hadn't officially accepted the commission, for fuck's sake! He would have to speak to Daniel first thing tomorrow. The bedrooms were too small for sculpting. He left the girl standing by the foyer as he perused the living room. The old Colonial Revival house in East Sacramento he and Daniel had inherited from their mother had tall ceilings, lots of windows that bathed the house in sunlight during the day. This was all that remained of the family money—everything else his mother had drunk away.

He pushed the sofa to the farthest wall of the living room. Some of the furniture was a bit too heavy, but adrenaline rushed through his body and within minutes he had managed to clear the room. He had sold most of his mother's belongings and had only kept what was necessary for daily living. If truth be told, the house was barely furnished. He'd hated his mother's ornate antique bureaus and tables, her taste for expensive but ugly decorations. And money, for these past years, had been tight, especially between teaching jobs.

The girl watched him but didn't speak. Her eyes wandered around the house. He imagined, judging from Tanya's tiny apartment, that the girl's own home would easily fit in his living room.

He placed two floor lamps in the center of the room and called her to him.

"Margarita," he said, her name like a caress. He shook his head and decided it would not be right to call her by her given name. It was crucial to get off to a good start. "From now on I will call you Magdalene."

"Call me what you want," she said. "But first, my money?"

"I don't have it," he said.

She let out a string of curses in Spanish as she darted to the front door.

He rushed after her. "Wait, wait," he pleaded. He took out his wallet. He had a hundred and twenty-three dollars. She rolled her eyes at the money and pushed past him, her hand on the doorknob. "Wait a goddamn minute!" he said, his heart pumping. Suddenly, he remembered his safe, upstairs in his bedroom. How much did he have up there? He would need Daniel to rush his advance, but tonight he had to do something, or he would lose her.

"Listen, I have some money upstairs, in my safe. Stay right here and I will go get it, you hear? Don't go anywhere."

It took him a few tries to get the combination right. He swung the door open and threw everything around until he found the envelope. *Shit*. There were only four hundred-dollar bills in there. He rushed back down the stairs, but he knew, even before his eyes registered the spot where he'd left her, that she was gone.

"We should get your first check in a couple of weeks," Daniel said as they walked the gardens outside the church.

It was a beautiful sunny day, but Jacob had not slept at all the night before and the brightness hurt his eyes. Today he could not see the colors in things, nor appreciate the textures, distinguish the contrasts between light and dark. "I need the money now," he said.

"Who is she?" Daniel asked. It was early in the day, and he was not dressed in his priest's vestments. He wore a plain white T-shirt and jeans. In his hand he carried pruning shears and the gardening gloves he'd removed when Jacob had shown up at the church.

He looks like an ordinary man, Jacob thought, and then corrected himself. *Ordinary* was not the right word. Daniel would never be ordinary. He'd inherited their mother's good looks. She'd been stunning once, before the drinking had taken a toll.

Jacob had not inherited her looks. Only her taste for alcohol.

"She's just some girl," Jacob said. "No one important."

"They are never just *some girl*," Daniel replied. "Not to

you, Jacob. Why won't you tell me? And why must you pay so much? Eight thousand is unheard of for a job like this, isn't it?"

"I warned you about my methods. And let's just say that your church wouldn't approve of her."

"Surely you're mistaken," Daniel said as they sat on the bench underneath the gazebo. "Who are we to judge God's creatures?"

"Just trust me on this, okay? And drop it."

Jacob took off his sunglasses. Now that they were in the shade of the gazebo, the light was not so blinding. Rosebushes surrounded them. Daniel had been tending to them all morning long. Jacob knew that come spring, the rose garden would be dazzling. Unlike Jacob, Daniel couldn't draw or paint to save his life, but he could will the earth to bring forth beauty. A beauty that Jacob could never replicate. Or surpass.

Beyond the rose garden with its brick grotto and a cheap resin statue of the Virgin Mary, and the tall black iron fence encircling it, lay the harsh streets of the community Daniel loved. Jacob knew that his brother had spent more time here as a teenager than in their fancy home in the so-called Fabulous Forties neighborhood. Only a few miles in distance, but a world away. When their mother died, Daniel had signed off on their home, saying it shamed him to look at it and wanted nothing to do with the house. His place was here, in this community that needed him.

Jacob thought about the girl. She and Tanya didn't live far from here. How ironic that his brother was trying to save people like Tanya, and Jacob was one of the people who played a hand in their corruption.

"You will be careful, won't you?" Daniel asked after a while.

Jacob lowered his eyes to the ground.

Daniel sighed. "I knew it was wrong to bring this commission to you, Jacob. God forgive me for what I have done. I thought that—"

"I'll be careful," Jacob said. The night came surging back to him then. The fire. The shrieks of the woman trapped inside the art gallery. He turned to look at his brother, who'd paused to stare at one of his rosebushes. Jacob wanted to talk to him about Paris, about watching the woman they had both loved go up in flames, along with his art, about how the guilt still ate at him. Just as he was about to open his mouth, he noticed that Daniel's bare hand was wrapped around a branch of the rosebush. He was clutching it tight, squeezing the thorns into his flesh. There was no pain registered on Daniel's face, only a small twitching of the jaw.

Jacob wanted to tell him to stop, but he didn't. After all these years, he still didn't understand the strange ways that Daniel would punish himself. As he walked away, thinking about the dreams that tormented him, he wondered if he, like Daniel, would ever find peace.

Margarita had known men like him. Men who took what they wanted from you. She didn't know much about this gringo whose house she was now walking to. What she knew was that she would allow herself to be used, not unlike previous times, to finally be set free.

As she made her way up Folsom Boulevard, she wasn't surprised she'd never been to this part of the city. Beautiful tree-lined streets. Luxurious houses surrounded by the greenest plants pruned and tucked into their proper places. She felt as if she had entered another world. Her clients were not of his class. She had gotten to know cheap motels that smelled of cigarette smoke and sweat, and she actually preferred that to taking them to her apartment, the place where she had saved a little piece of her soul.

She wondered what exactly he wanted from her. What a strange thing it was that he wanted her to pose for him, to be Mary Magdalene. There was once a time when she'd been a pious churchgoer, when among the scents of flowers and candles, she had prayed many a Hail Mary and Our Father. But that had stopped when the saints no longer listened. When she'd realized that they were nothing but stone or clay, and they would not, could not, help her.

The air smelled of rain, and the sky was dark gray, like dirty river water. She wondered if perhaps he would turn her away today. Although it was only noon, there would be no sunshine and he'd said he needed sunlight. Well, it wasn't her fault the weather was not to his liking.

She made her way down the driveway. The house, although magnificent in size, looked like a hag compared to the beautiful homes around it. Here, the plants grew wild. Trees in need of pruning hovered menacingly over the arbor. She felt a pang of pity for the house, for its evident neglect. For belonging to a man who did not love it enough to care.

He opened the door before she even knocked. "Magdalene," he said, then pulled her inside and guided her to the living room.

A few things had changed since she was last there. He'd put the dining table in the center of the living room and covered it with a sheet. Floor lamps were placed around the table and the lights shone on the center, on the spot she knew was meant for her.

She stood awkwardly beside him, staring at the table, at the blinding light. Had she made a mistake? She thought about what had brought her here and forced herself to stand taller, to look him in the eye and not be afraid. She had to do this right. She couldn't mess this up.

"The bathroom is over there," he said, pointing to a door to the side of the living room. "Everything needs to come off. I've left a robe in there for you."

She had known, a part of her had known, that it would be like this, but she'd hoped that she would be allowed to keep something on. Most of the time her clients were too impatient, or too short of time, to completely disrobe her. And she liked it that way. Liked to have her skirt hiked up around her hips, leaving at least a little bit of her covered.

"Magdalene," he said, putting a hand on her shoulder, "I will not hurt you. You can trust me."

She could trust no one, but she wanted to believe that no harm would come to her from him. She thought about her captors. The men her father had hired to bring them to this country and who had then forced her into this life, this hell. Maybe, just maybe, she could finish paying them her debt, and she could finally be free.

The robe he left for her in the bathroom was of the softest material she'd ever touched. She loved the way it caressed her bare skin, the way it enveloped her in warmth. As if she'd wrapped herself in a summer cloud. She walked to the living room clutching the belt of the robe. She wanted to keep it on and never take it off.

He extended his hand and helped her up onto the table. He was so tall that as she sat there, he still towered above her. "May I?" he said, grabbing hold of her shoulders.

She let go of her grip on the belt and undid the knot. She closed her eyes. He'd put the heater on high so that she wouldn't be cold, but still, she shivered when the robe came off.

He said, "Try to relax. It will be difficult, sometimes, to sit still for long periods. But you will get used to it." He stood a few feet away from her, his hands holding a sketchbook and pencil. He told her about Mary Magdalene, about the cruci-fixion. She knew the story. She had grown up knowing about Jesus, about how He had sacrificed himself for sinners like her. The man said, "Mary Magdalene was there, with him until the very end. Close your eyes. Imagine you are her, you are looking up at Jesus on the cross. Show me. Show me how it feels knowing that you are about to lose him."

She raised her eyes to the ceiling, but hard as she tried, she could not picture herself as anything but who she was. And Jesus? She had given up on Him long ago. She could not mourn His death now. She had mourned it enough, had brought Him enough flowers, lit enough candles, and kneeled for too many hours at His feet. And all for what?

"Not like that!" He tore the sheet from the sketchbook. She had not even noticed when he'd begun to draw her. He ran his fingers through his grayish hair. "Okay, forget Jesus. Think of someone *you* have lost. Someone you loved. A brother. A husband. A father."

Her body jolted and she glared at him. What did he know about who she'd loved? Who she'd lost? And what right did he have asking her to bare her soul to him?

He must have noticed her anger because he quickly added, "Okay, forget that. Just make it up, okay? Just pretend. Imagine anything you want, but give me what *I* want. Put your hand out like this, as if you're reaching for him. As if you can't bear to let him go."

He returned to his sketchbook. As his pencil began to move again, she watched the rain slapping the windowpanes, and the face of her father appeared in her mind's eye. She thought about that morning when they'd come to seek refuge in this country. They didn't get far. Not long after they'd passed the southern border of Mexico, they found themselves clinging with all their might to the roof of the train, made slippery by the rain. Then, suddenly, a branch hit her father square in the face, and he slipped. He'd left her to make the journey alone, to fall prey to bad men, to pay with her own body for a chance to make a life in this unforgiving country.

"Beautiful," a voice said.

Margarita turned to look behind her. For a moment, she'd forgotten where she was, who she was with. She reached to touch her cheek, to dry the tears that were rolling down, but Jacob stopped her.

"Leave them!" he said, his hand flying furiously over his sketchbook. One after another, sheets were torn off.

She wondered if his hand hurt, and if it did, would the pain even reach him where he was right now? Somewhere between reality and insanity.

"No, no, this is all wrong!" he yelled. His hand stopped moving at last, after what seemed like hours. She glanced at all the drawings he'd discarded on the floor. Her, over and over, from different angles. He bent to pick up the sketches, and as he looked at them, he started to tear them into pieces.

Margarita's breath caught in her throat as she saw her eyes, her lips, her hair, her arms, fluttering around the room, like a shattered mirror in which she could see fragments of herself. And then he started to cry.

She got off the table and wrapped the robe around herself, glancing at the bathroom where her clothes were folded in a neat pile. With a sigh, she returned her gaze to the poor wretch and went to him, cradled him in her arms as he sobbed. *Who is this man?* she wondered. *What happened to make him this way?*

At the end of the session she felt so tired, and she wished she could go home and sleep. He offered her something to eat, and she was ravenous, but she wanted to get out of there. Tuck her memories back into the deepest corner of her mind.

"You were wonderful," the man said as he walked her to the door. "Tomorrow, same time?"

She nodded, unable to speak. As she moved down the walkway, she realized she was glad that he'd torn up the drawings of her. She couldn't bear the thought of him looking at them, seeing her exposed in a way she had not intended to be. What her clients asked of her was to give them her body, but not her mind. They asked her to open her legs, but not her heart.

And this man, Jacob, he'd done that and more.

The following week, she made her way back to Jacob's house. The cup of coffee she'd bought at the donut shop around the corner from her place didn't do much to wake her up. She wondered if he'd notice how tired she was. He didn't say much when he opened the door. By now they had grown used to each other's silences.

Today, she would not be sitting. He'd removed the table and motioned for her to stand in the light.

"Look to the side," he said. "Imagine he is there, beside you. Your hands, almost touching." When she yawned, he raised an eyebrow at her but said nothing.

The second time she yawned, he stopped working. "I'm not drawing Sleeping Beauty," he said. "Where is Magdalene today?"

"I am sorry, the dogs no let me to sleep." Behind her crumbling apartment building was a dog kennel. Through the thin walls they could be heard at all hours of day and night, barking incessantly.

"The dogs?" he said, and then smiled. "Yes. They give me the creeps too." He put his sketchbook down and came over to her. "Come, let's get a cup of coffee. That should do the trick for both of us."

He handed her the robe. As she looked closer at his face, she noticed the dark circles under his eyes, the redness inside. She wondered what had kept him up at night but didn't ask. Better not to know much about him.

He poured her a cup of coffee from an antique carafe on the counter. Then he opened a cupboard and took out a bottle of whiskey and offered her some. She shook her head and watched as he poured a generous amount into his coffee. They sat at the breakfast bar side by side. His proximity un-nerved her. He was so close she could feel the heat of his body pressing against her.

"I have bad dreams that keep me up at night," he said. "Or I should say *a* bad dream. It's always the same one."

She watched the steam from her coffee curl up and disappear into the air. A part of her wanted to ask him to say more, but she stayed silent. She was pretty sure it was more than just a dream.

"There was a fire," he said at last. "A bad fire. Someone I loved very much died that night."

He told her then about his life in Paris, a world so foreign from her own. She had seen a poster once of the Eiffel Tower, and she had briefly wondered what it would be like to stand there at the very top with the whole world at her feet. He told her about a woman he'd once loved. And the fire that had destroyed his artwork and had killed her.

"I'm so sorry," she said.

"Me too. More than I can ever say."

She wished she could tell him about the demons that

haunted her, but she couldn't bring herself to do it. Thankfully, they were now done with their coffee, and they resumed their places. She felt the caffeine rushing through her body, and as she watched his hand fly over the sketchbook, she knew that the alcohol had done the trick for him.

This time, he wanted her to look as if she was in love. Had he wanted the sad face again, she would have easily obliged. The lack of sleep had unearthed the depression she tried to suppress. But today he didn't want her pain.

He said, "Think about Mary Magdalene. The way she must have looked at Jesus every day. A look of worship. Devotion. Unwavering love for the messiah. There are some theories that they might have even been lovers."

Margarita had had many lovers, but this wasn't what Jacob was talking about. In this, she knew, she wouldn't be able to help him. She had never been in love. She had lain with many men and had not once *made love* to anyone.

The only man she had ever loved was her father, and that had been a daughter's love, not the kind that Jacob was talking about. She had loved her father more than anyone in the world. And now he was lost to her.

"*Merde!*" Jacob yelled, bringing her back to the present. "How hard can it be to do as I ask?"

"I try, okay?" Margarita said, feeling the anger wash over her.

Just then, the doorbell rang and Jacob went to open it, leaving Margarita to swallow her words. *Don't mess this up*, she reprimanded herself. *Time is running out.* She debated whether to stay or run to the bathroom. She was exhausted. The session was not going the way Jacob wanted, so what was the point? Just as she was about to gather her robe, Jacob and another man came in.

"Don't move," Jacob said to her. He went back to his sketchbook while the man hovered in the dark entryway.

"I could come back later," the man said. "I don't want to interrupt."

Jacob waved his hand. "Almost done," he said.

Then the man stepped into the light of the living room, and Margarita gasped. Involuntarily, her hands went up to her bare breasts. *What in the world is a priest doing in this house?*

Her eyes locked with his, and she didn't know why, but instead of wanting to cover herself, as had been her initial reaction, suddenly she wanted him to *see* her. She didn't take her eyes away from his, and without knowing what she was doing, she dropped her hands back to her sides and stood up straighter, her breasts rising and falling with every breath. Her nipples became hard, tingling. And she stood before him as she had never done with another, feeling sensual, voluptuous, without any shame.

Then Jacob started to laugh. "Of course," he said. "How could it be otherwise?"

The priest coughed, then picked up the robe she'd left on the couch and approached her with it. He tried not to look at her as he handed her the garment, but right before she took it from him, his eyes betrayed him, and she'd seen his hunger. She covered herself immediately, her face flushed, her breath coming too hard. What had she been thinking? Baring herself like that to a *priest?*

"I'm sorry I disturbed you," the man said to Jacob. He wouldn't look at her anymore, even though it was now safe to do so. "I shouldn't have come." He headed to the door.

"Stay!" Jacob said. "For Christ's sake, just stay." Putting the sketchbook down, he turned to her. "You can go now, Margarita."

She didn't need to be told twice. She rushed to the bathroom to put on her clothes. But as soon as she zipped up her sweater, she knew that sooner or later she would have to come out and face him. She placed her ear against the bathroom door, and she could hear them talking. She couldn't make out the words but the priest had a deep rich voice, a voice that one could listen to in the intimacy of a chapel, with the intoxicating smell of flowers and candles. Or in the darkness of a bedroom, between sheets soaked with sweat.

Margarita, you sinner! she reprimanded herself. Then she giggled, and couldn't stop herself from blushing once more as she opened the door.

Both men stood up as soon as they saw her come out. She kept her eyes on Jacob. If she looked at the priest, she knew she would lose it.

"Come closer, Margarita," Jacob said, beckoning her. She did as she was told and found herself beside the priest. "This is my brother, Daniel. Daniel, meet Margarita."

This time, she had no choice but to look right at him. His eyes were bluer than she had first thought. His cheeks had splotches of red, as if it was too hot in the room. And maybe it *was* too hot. She could feel the sweat on the back of her neck. He took her hand in his and she immediately pulled away. Once more, she found herself unable to breathe.

Was she supposed to kiss his hand? she wondered, thinking about the priests back home. But those had been sweet old men with wrinkled hands. Not like him. Nothing like him, but still, he was a holy man, and she should not have looked at him the way she had.

Daniel made his way from the rectory to his room. He paused to look at the garden below him. It was late Sunday morning,

Mass had come and gone, and the afternoon stretched out before him. He looked at his garden again, his sacred place of devotion. He knew every plant, every rock, every contour of the land before him. For a week now, he had not gone to tend it. He longed to dig his fingers deep into the soil, to watch the miracle of life happen before his very eyes, to turn bare ground into something beautiful.

He went into his dark room and took out his rosary, pushing the thoughts of his garden out of his mind. He would not allow himself to go. He'd asked Brother Isaiah to tend to the garden in his stead. This was his punishment for his weakness, his sin. He kneeled on the floor and peered at the cross above his bed. He prayed an Our Father, but the words rolled off his tongue out of habit, and his mind was elsewhere, no longer on his garden. It would have been better to keep his thoughts on his roses—but no, his mind transported him to the living room of his childhood home. Again, he could see her standing bathed in the golden glow of the lamps around her, completely nude. He remembered handing her the robe, and how for a second, just a fraction of a second, his hand had not wanted to give it to her. He wanted to keep looking at her, at her skin the color of caramel, the delicate curve of her breasts, the way her black hair brushed against her hardened nipples. He'd wondered how they would taste.

Enough!

He rushed out of his room, down to the chapel where he knew he would find Father Matthew. But what would he say to his mentor? He entered the chapel, and instead of heading to the confessional, he sat on a pew. He recalled his ordination, how this very chapel had been full of friends and colleagues, but no family except for Jacob. His mother had refused to come, had refused to accept the path he had chosen.

But sitting here now, Daniel remembered the oath he'd made.

Father Matthew came out of the confessional and saw him sitting there on the pew. "Father Daniel," he said, "is something troubling you today?"

Daniel stood and took a deep breath. "No, Father. There is nothing to worry about." He had heard the calling of the Spirit and had pledged obedience and purity. He had no regrets. He had made an oath to serve the One and meant to keep it.

"Very well, my son." Father Matthew glanced at the entrance and Daniel followed his gaze.

"Excuse me, Father," Daniel said, "my brother has come to visit."

Outside, the day was pleasantly sunny, and he and Jacob made their way to the gazebo, their usual meeting place.

"I haven't thanked you for bringing me this project," Jacob said once they were sitting down. "You knew, Brother, *you* knew that I needed it."

"I knew you needed it; it is true. But was I wrong to bring this commission to you, Jacob? Should I have just let things be? All these years of watching you do nothing with your gift, I have felt a desire to help you find your way back to your art. But what if it was God's plan all along, to take it from you?"

"It wasn't God who took it from me."

Daniel heard the reproach in his brother's voice. *It was you, Daniel. It was you who took her from me, who took my muse, my inspiration.* He remembered that night in Paris when Jacob had set the art gallery on fire, not knowing that Juliette was asleep in her office upstairs. That was the night Jacob had learned that Juliette and Daniel were lovers.

"I have found it again," Jacob said. "When I look at Margarita, it comes back to me, the desire to create. When I see her, I know—I know that I still have it in me."

"So, are you done with her?"

"No. I know I'm close. But something is missing, and I haven't yet captured what I envision." Jacob removed some sketches from the leather briefcase he was carrying and held them up for Daniel to regard.

Ever since Daniel could remember, he had been the only person who Jacob fully trusted with his art. But today he didn't want that trust. He didn't want to see what was in those sketches. *With my whole heart I seek you; let me not wander from your commandments!* With trembling hands, Daniel took the sketches and began flipping through them. There was her hand, the delicate fingers so real they seemed to be reaching for him through the paper. The next sketch was of her eyes, and Daniel recalled the way she had looked at him that day, how his body had responded to the yearning in her eyes. On the third sketch, as he looked at her long neck, the lips that were slightly opened, beckoning, he felt his resolve crumbling and brusquely handed the sketches back to his brother.

"It's supposed to be Mary Magdalene, Jacob," Daniel said, taking deep breaths. "Not an erotic fantasy. That's not what you are getting paid for. Do your job. Be the professional I know you can be!"

"Erotic fantasy?" Jacob replied. He looked down at the sketches, then back at Daniel, and he began laughing. Daniel glanced at the sketches again and knew he'd made a mistake. There was nothing erotic here. They were exquisitely drawn. Jacob had captured the purity, the innocence in that woman's soul, and Daniel had been drowning in the turbulent waters of lust.

"Oh, Daniel," Jacob said, chuckling, "what you're seeing

here is only what you want to see. But that's fine. In fact, it's better than fine because, you see, I need *you* to pose for me."

"You're insane!" Daniel said, standing up.

"I still need Jesus. And you'll be perfect."

"I'll do no such thing." Daniel moved to go, loosening his collar, the brightness of the day now blinding him.

"Then I can't finish it. She won't look at anyone else the way she looked at you. I only need one day with you there, two at the most, and then I could do you separately. Come on, Daniel."

"Jacob, what you are asking, it's . . . it's blasphemy!"

"It's art, Daniel. It's something I thought I would never do again. And yet, you've given me that chance. Why would you take it away now?"

"Find someone else to be your Jesus," Daniel said, stepping away. "Because I won't do it."

Days later, after hearing the urgency in Jacob's voice over the phone, Daniel drove straight to Margarita's apartment. She was in bed, her face purple and swollen. Jacob told him she had paid off her debt with the eight thousand dollars, and in return, they'd beaten her until she was nearly unconscious.

"You should take her to the hospital," Daniel said.

"No, no hospital," Margarita said, clearly terrified.

"Here, drink this," Daniel said, holding a glass of water to her bloody lips.

"Why . . . how did you find me?" Margarita asked, looking back at Jacob.

"When you didn't show up at my house, I felt something was wrong. So I came. And found you passed out on the floor."

Daniel could tell she was trying to keep herself from crying.

"Listen, I called my brother here to stay with you," Jacob

said. "I must go out of town to choose the stone for the project."

"No, I no need—" Margarita began.

"You need help," Daniel interrupted softly. "Whoever did this to you might return. You won't survive another beating like this. Do you understand?"

Margarita nodded.

"Now rest, Margarita. I want you well when I get back." Jacob bent down and kissed her forehead, then nodded at Daniel before walking out the door.

"Father," she said, "I am okay. You go home, Father. Please?" She was acting like she didn't need his help, but when she lifted herself up, her body shook with pain, and she fell right back onto her bed.

"You must rest, Margarita," he said, his face inches from hers as he tucked her covers around her. If she leaned closer, their lips would touch.

"Father, you go now."

He shook his head. "You aren't well enough, child. What kind of priest would I be to leave you like this?"

Years later, he would remember this day as the day when it really all began. Because he could have walked away. He could have left her be. He could have found someone else to care for her, to help her find her way. Instead, Daniel had bundled her up and taken her to his most sacred place, the last place they should have been together.

As they walked side by side along the path, he could not help but look at her, admiring her beauty that couldn't be concealed by the gashes and large bruises that spread across her cheeks, a deep reddish purple like the pansies that lined the path. She walked slowly, trying not to wince with each step as they made their way to the gazebo.

"I like it here." She took a deep breath and looked around. "This place is paradise."

They sat on the bench under the gazebo, and he found himself becoming intoxicated with the smell of the earth and the scent of the woman sitting by his side.

He saw his garden reflected in her eyes, and at that moment he felt no regrets. This was the place he came to have his spirit renewed, reborn. And this young woman needed such a place. What little he knew of her was enough to see that her spirit was broken, her faith in God completely shattered. "You'll be safe here," he said to her. And later, after everything had happened, and despite what anyone said, Daniel knew that at least that day, he had meant what he'd said.

Despite her injuries, she insisted on helping him tend the garden. As they worked together, he taught her what he'd learned. He said, "Margarita, plants are like people: They are strong, persistent. They will overcome all kinds of obstacles and manage to sprout, to survive against all odds. They live even when everything seems hopeless."

She stopped for a moment to absorb her surroundings. He could see her trying to take it all in. He could see her words beginning to take root, but then a sadness spread across her face, and she returned to her task, digging her spade into the soil in quick, angry stabs.

"Is not enough to survive, Father," she finally said. "To survive and to live is not the same. What is the point, Father, to survive when all life ever do is hurt you?"

They kneeled over the raised beds as they cleared the weeds.

"We can't always understand why God does what He does, Margarita. Sometimes it feels as if He has deserted us, but that is not the case. All the troubles He puts in our

128 // Sacramento Noir

path are for our own growth." He pointed to the rosebushes growing around the gazebo. "I have to prune those down every winter. Now, pruning might seem a brutal thing to do to those plants. But in fact, pruning makes them stronger. This is what God does to us, Margarita. He takes his pruning hook and cuts into us, and it hurts so much we think we can't survive it. But we do, Margarita. We do. And we grow into a better and stronger self."

She looked at him in silence, her black hair falling down her shoulders, covering her like a veil, her eyes digging into him with a mixture of awe and fear and pain and defiance and lust. And then suddenly, there she was, his Mary Magdalene.

As his body ached with need for her, he knew that when Jacob came back, he would pose for his brother. He would be his Jesus. He would say, *Here I am, send me*, and let his brother's expert hands carve him.

PART II

COLLISIONS

GHOST BOY

BY JEN SOONG
Old Sacramento

Gina Lee hated Mondays, especially dank, wintry mornings. It was ten past nine. Outside her shoebox studio two blocks east of the Sacramento River, the wind was yowling and shadows waltzed across the kitchen like entangled lovers. A one-eyed crow was perched in a sycamore tree on 3rd Street, watching her. She was notorious for running late. Her tight-ass boss Yvonne at the Old Town Pharmacy threatened to axe her last time.

Screw Yvonne.

Without rising from bed, Gina popped three blue pills, then three red, downing them with apple juice. Tasted like piss. Empty orange vials littered the floor. She groaned and tramped across the room to case the fridge: beer, expired yogurt, and a moldy cheddar wedge.

When she banged the door shut, the light in the room began to glow phosphorescent green. Smoke spirals wafted in the empty nook above the fridge. A translucent boy with sunken eyes, missing front teeth, and a purple Kings cap clutched a bag of rainbow-colored gumballs.

Gina was irked because 1) she didn't believe in ghosts, and 2) she was definitely going to be late again.

"Gotta stop taking uppers," she muttered. "Freaking hallucinations."

"Hey," the ghost boy said, flinching as if insulted. "I'm

not a hollow nation. My name's Atlas. Used to live next door with my mom. Ring any bells?"

"Nope," she said. "Zero dings."

"You know it stinks in here, like a dead body," he said, pinching his nose.

"My housekeeper's on vacation," she said.

"You're funny." He offered her a blue gumball. "Want one?"

"Nah, I don't take candy from strange ghost boys named Atlas," she said, chuckling. She had heard the woman next door banshee-wailing through the walls the last three nights but never registered a son.

"Your loss, lady." He shrugged, tossed a gumball up, and caught it in his mouth. Then he faded away to a shimmer, his toothless smile disappearing last.

The first time had been a cakewalk. It was nearing midnight on a Friday (three months before Ghost Boy popped up in her kitchen). Gina's turn to close up the pharmacy. Pretend it's a dare, she told herself, and swiped the contents of three bottles into her purse in one motion. Her adrenaline spiked when she saw the pills nestled together like pearls on a silk lining, a small mound of white, pink, and baby blue.

Screw Yvonne. Screw the corporate mothership paying her minimum wage. She wasn't hurting anyone at work. Besides, she needed the dough. Wai Po's surgery wasn't going to pay for itself.

The thrill wore off as the weeks dragged on. Late on a Friday (three days before Ghost Boy showed up uninvited), she met her slimeball of an ex, Bo, at their usual spot, an alley off 4th Street near the Black Cat jazz club. A bearded man in camouflage panhandled on the corner, a dead bloody crow near his boots. A train by the river whistled a low warning.

Bo's black leather jacket matched his shiny motorcycle. Same sharp chin, weasel eyes, and greasy dark hair that smelled like fuel. What had she ever seen in him?

"I'm done," she said. "I want out."

He snorted and moved in closer. A mix of peppermint and gasoline choked the air.

"It's not just you and me," he said. "You're in Viper's ring. Viper will kill your Wai Po if you try to stop, and he'll kill *you* if you rat him out. You should be thanking me for protecting you."

"You sold me out? You scumbag!" she screamed. She'd heard rumors of Viper, a Chinese drug lord who once left a wake of bodies hanging from the I Street Bridge. Retribution for a deal gone bad.

Gina grabbed her crimson pocketknife from her denim jacket and slashed Bo's cheek with its serrated edge, drawing a thin line of blood. Then she shoveled a handful of pills into her mouth like M&Ms. "You can't sell what you don't have."

"Psycho!" he said with a snarl, retreating to his motorcycle. "You were always trouble."

Gina looked down at the small bloody knife in her palm. A sharp memory erupted from her chest.

When she was five, Ma brought her to a fortune teller in the back of Sam's Market in Old Town, one of the few Chinese grocers left over from the gold-mining days. An elderly woman with long droopy ears reeking of ginger put two bony fingers on Gina's forehead and declared, "This one, rotten egg." She knocked her head three times. "You can hide but trouble will stalk you."

"Nonsense," Ma said. "Wah, snake lady! Curse you!"

Shortly after their visit, Ma was high on meth when she dumped her at Wai Po's. She then ran away with a pilot named Ted who had a pencil mustache and promised her a life on the friendliest skies. All Ma left behind was a knockoff Swiss Army knife.

For weeks after her run-in with Bo, Gina holed up in her rancid studio, draining highballs from bed. She only saw Ghost Boy that one Monday so she chalked it up to a hallucination. An eerie one. Takeout cartons, pill bottles, and soiled clothes splayed on a peeling vinyl floor.

In front of a full-length mirror propped in the corner of the studio, she toyed with confessing. Her eyes glazed red. *I was conned,* she'd say, playing the wide-eyed damsel. But the reality of jail time sobered her up. Plus, local cops were morons. Viper would make her pay.

Instead, over the next week at work, she pilfered more pills—half for her, half for Grandma's fund. She swore she would never be a junkie after Ma split. But now she didn't give two figs. Nothing she did would add up to more than regret. The one person she loved—her grandmother, Wai Po, who told her she would never end up like Ma in a million years—couldn't remember who she was. Her decaying brain devoured by dementia. Good thing, because seeing Gina this way would break her heart.

We're all addicts anyway, sleepwalking through life, desperate for the next gamble, Gina told herself, the next high, the next heist. Some open their eyes sooner than others.

Gina stared at her reflection, studying the dumpling-shaped birthmark above her left eye, a blemish she had stopped trying to hide. Wai Po's nickname for her was *Bao,* which sounded like the word for treasure. Before things had soured, Bo used to trace the outline of it like a treasure map. They had once bonded over their stubborn streaks born from mothers who left and grandmothers who stayed.

Before she started losing her memory, Wai Po sold her tinctures to Chinese herbalists and had taught Gina as a child where to forage herbs for her recipes. They even grew jiaogulan, a climbing tea herb, on their small balcony. That was when Gina still believed in a future, before she needed to take pills to erase what she had become.

On the final Monday morning Gina overslept, she hustled to the hallway, leaking trash bag in hand. Black ooze left a trail from her door as she hotfooted to the dumpster. She tripped, and trash flew over a child's body. A purple cap flopped off his head. The boy's eyes were pried open, bulging like a dead swordfish. The stench of rotting sardines clogged the air. A one-eyed crow stood guard next to the boy. Gumballs scattered on the ground like marbles. Next to his twisted bony leg was a red pocketknife. Hers.

The dominoes crashed into place in her head. Ghost Boy had been murdered. The wailing neighbor was his bereft mother. A warning from Viper. Her fault. One she had ignored, too hyped up on pills, too zoned out to care. How had she blocked out this memory before? She was the target; the boy with the gumballs was just collateral damage.

Gina's chest erupted with sudden clarity. She *knew* what she had to do. She had to sell more and more pills until she could flee this wretched city, until time ticked on her side, until she stopped digging her own grave. A sharp pain jackknifed her directly in the forehead.

Ma's fortune teller was right. Trouble had ambushed her.

DOWNRIVER, NOVEMBER 1949

BY JOSÉ VADI

West End

The Dealer

A cold night approaching winter in the West End. Outside the Zanzibar, the Capitol building, the law incarnate, stares at me from one end, and on the other, destiny—the Tower Bridge. The Sacramento River swells beneath the bridge's silver steel belly, daring another casualty, the kind we read about every summer in the paper. I felt for the knot of money inside my jacket, my nerves churning like the river. Passing cars' headlights hit the club's front wall of glass blocks, revealing the silhouettes of those already grooving inside like ghosts at a haunted ball. My head felt as smoky as my second cigarette's contents, shrouding my face.

I've been here every night this year. The stream of car headlights illuminating army cadets from the eastside and lowlifes like me, lined up to get in, ready to fight our battles in the shadows, under the table. You're either gambling, selling, consuming, and, for your own safety, hopefully not all three, in this part of town, and I've been triple-dipping all week. I even added a fourth tonight to make it square—stealing.

I'd decided to make my way to Main Street by taking some side streets. So I started running a downstairs game at a speakeasy nearby. My life was a triad between the speakeasy, the Zanzibar, and my apartment in Southside Park, all walking distance from here. The speakeasy was a unit behind a tall

Victorian, with a work shed for a ground floor, and a walk-down basement. One entrance in and one out, with bouncers holding court at either end, blind to the extra hundred I was skimming every week.

I still had the audacity to cheat the speakeasy. The owner of the joint trusted me enough to be the dealer. He didn't know I was a bottom-dealing whiz, marking cards like alphabetizing my mother's shopping list. One night I met a rounder in town who caught on to my act, found me at the park, and made me an offer I couldn't refuse. I made sure enough good hands found his, with us both leaving the night satisfied, settling up in the dark of the park each night.

We had a good thing going, but something was telling me the best was behind us. And that I needed the band inside. I stomped my smoke, and exhaled my last puff before inhaling the club's energy upon entry.

The opening piano notes of Billy Strayhorn's "Lush Life" draws the attention of the crowd, bustling into the evening. An instrumental version tonight, but I hum the words to myself, *A lush life / in some small dive*. I can hear my pulse thumping like those ivory tones. The crowd responds, a realization of mind, body, and cocktails that propels hearts to do crazy things, especially for those drinking like they're old enough to remember Prohibition.

Life is a bore spent wishing excitement to come to shore, and the only shore that I'll encounter tonight could kill me. Fitting for a river rat like me, stealing a pathway to hell, or salvation, depending on how I get out of here tonight. The only way out was stealing something that floats and heading south, down the Sacramento River, and into the Delta, south of Freeport, where I got a woman with hips that make a brass band cry. A dirty way out is the only way I've stayed clean.

I'd spend my winnings here at Zanzibar before hiding the rest back at my place. The Zanzibar, to me, is both a finish line and a church, a place where a man can drift into the downturned collar of his coat, stare at the bar holding his drink, and swim into an evening abyss.

My life preserver was the house band, alumni of the Chitlin Circuit pluckers who brought acts big and small our way, playing new songs and standards between. I told time by the band's sets, their set breaks, how they dictated the rhythm of drinks poured, dates made, bets recouped. Their sounds soothed the worry I muted behind every dealt card, nervous I'd get made and might never see the Tower Bridge's tall steel face staring back at me again.

And that all ends tonight. It's the last night the Zanzibar will be open, one of the bartenders told everyone sitting at the bar. *Drink up because it's the last time you can!* Surprised a bar owned by Black folks even lasted this long, white and Mexican and Japanese patrons alike, but that's how hands change around here when it comes to houses, businesses. Everyone here knows this was a Japanese-owned joint before the war, before they were all herded into camps like most of this neighborhood, clear to the river.

Everyone thinks I'm white but my family is Mexican. I say I'm Italian to any Johnny Law in sight. Cards taught me enough gift of gab to manage the players in town, enough to navigate power to make a living in its shadows. And now I can't even find a good place to get a drink in town with decent music. This spot, the best in town, thanks to the ownership. Wurlitzer jukebox bars are all these straight-laced cops know of art, and they'll never know the beauty of those improvised tweaks of ol' classics I heard here night after night.

It feels like New Year's Eve and not a random Friday night in November. Singles become doubles with the bartender's pours heavy just the same. The voices and shouts from the crowd grow louder so the band responds boastfully, big-band numbers played between ballads that allow the crowd to have that smoke, get that drink, feel all three hundred and sixty dimensions of the lush warming their souls. That's the vice every suit in this town tries to keep away from you, but it's the kind of vice worth working, living for. Don't let anyone tell you it's a crime.

Neither is saying goodbye while the hand's good. I knew my time was up here a week earlier when, during a hot hand, an old rounder, a lifer like me, pulled up to my card game, knowing my knowing hands and what they could deliver his way. A couple of wins and delivered aces of spade later, someone called cheat and was promptly knocked out by my ol' friend, before he took his winnings and split. The bouncers must've been in on it too, since they were all shrugs by the time the knocked-out gent came to.

He was a cop, no doubt, an undercover wearing too good of a suit for this part of town. But I found out about all that after the fact, of course, having called it a night, and was back at my place before he woke up and knew which way was north. That old rounder was gray as a day's end but had a right hook that could've leveled San Francisco again, and explained why he always sat to my farthest left at the table. I knew that was my last memory of him, the last time I'd ever see him again. He'd meet another guy like me somewhere, I'm sure, just not me. Nobody here will.

I always knew the river was calling. It was only a matter of time until they figured us out.

I gave my girl a call awhile back, telling her that I'd be

finding my way south soon, finding a way back to card games dealing straight to my lady at our dinner table. No more bouncers, exchanges in the park, no more looking behind my back. Nobody knew where else to find me but a bar, and like an old flame it too ended, ash in another tray.

Sometimes the biggest hand you can play is knowing when it's time not just to leave the table, but to refuse to ever sit behind one again. And this night, the last night of my favorite bar in town, after my biggest come-up, it sounded right to call it quits. To finally follow through and see my girl. Creeping along the river's shore, I heard the Wurlitzer bars along the Sacramento River. Voices laughing and shouting, from suits and rats alike. A bunch of small boats were haphazardly tied along the docks. I found a welterweight option, but couldn't find an oar in sight, just empty bottles, and flasks, also cashed. The owners blacked out now, or soon to be, too drunk to remember the boat, let alone the oars. To hell with it, the river's current was in my direction, and I had no time to lose.

The streetlamps from what old-timers still call the M Street Bridge, and not the Tower Bridge, were hazy with the incoming tule fog, early this time of year. It hung in the still of the night like an exhaled smoke, the last note of a Sarah Vaughn song, the memory of a card shark who always seemed straight enough to trust with your hand. *Keep it steady*—I told myself, holding either side of the boat, searching for driftwood to fashion an oar, the moon lighting the water white as a domino's dare—*and try to count the waves*.

Brass Hips

Being old doesn't make you wise, least of all in the West End. Those men aged into better hustlers with the same goals of boys—women, money, maybe a car—with even sharper knuckles to claim them by. They didn't have to fight in the war because of the previous back-alley fights that made them incapable of running toward anything but a card game. Still, when I met him, he was running cards in such a way he could talk the white off cotton, at least, when he wasn't behind the table.

He'd saddle up at the bar where me and some other ladies would be sitting, sipping, enjoying the scene. The red across our lips welcomed conversation from strangers, and though he seemed to know everyone, everyone knew well enough to pay him little mind, it seemed. We spoke, though. Quiet platitudes about the night. Sometimes I caught a gleam of what might be joy spring briefly across his mug before I feared it was the reflection of a nearby match to a cigarette, glowing beauty all the same.

He'd come to the bar and wipe his brow when his shift had passed, drink Sahara desert–dry martinis (his words), and turn the night a lush shade of moon. I'd sit and imagine him dealing, refuting newbies or the overconfident with simple *All bets are in* or *Too slow, Jack, bets placed*, before settling the score, as he'd tell me at the bar.

Funny for a card dealer, when you think about it. The kind of bunch that thrive off pessimism and silence, connecting it with fatter wallets for them and another night of regret for their vics. But then again, hustler or patron, they all show up to a bar like the Zanzibar to hear folks with loose gums failing every night, knowing the risk of showing their tells. Was he only talking to me, I realized, at a bar full of regulars?

That was awhile back; I hadn't returned since autumn started. Laying low. Living off Uncle Sam's grid isn't out of the ordinary out here in the Delta. I miss the lipstick, the commotion, the presentation of oneself in a capital-c City.

Coming up for air in the local town is tricky, but stay low enough and you can find something steady. How long can anyone keep their head above high, legal water? Life's a long swim of short-time hustles, and we both knew it the night we met. The years after.

More and more weekends spent here instead of his spot near Southside Park, walking distance to his "night job," and it was those cheap, thin walls that convinced me no matter how long he talked about leaving, getting out, about how his paranoia reminded him of a veteran's (his words), about how the only time he felt alive, or that he could breathe at the very least, was outside capital lines—regardless, he'd live and die here all the same, unless I had something to say about it.

Over time I started staying here, standing my ground so to speak. He'd come down, hitching a ride, showing up at dawn in a loose suit, smelling of everyone's hands and the dames they spent their winnings on afterward at the Zanzibar. Some mornings, no matter how strong I made the coffee for myself and my bewildered guests, the smell of the bar on his collar would tell everyone just how well the band played.

My cousin hated him. He was my guy's age or just a bit older, and it's only me and my cousin here now. He's lives out back, in that bigger, somewhat insulated bunkhouse.

We both grew up here, our mothers sisters, and best friends, blood notwithstanding. They grew old through the Depression and banded to live and die here, together. Just beyond the bunkhouse, you'll find them, still together, resting. Tilling a bit. Keeping tidy. Some family moved to San Francisco, others Stockton, Bakersfield, others simply passed on. Me and Cousin remain. We started renting out the bedrooms upstairs, make guests a simple breakfast in the mornings and call it an inn. I cook and book, while Cousin fixes and, well, enforces.

Not a lot of bad intentions out here other than storms though. Especially compared to what most come here fleeing. There's one former city slicker Cousin mentioned was setting up shop nearby. Seemed to be connected to folks in the capital and is probably the only person I've seen who owns a new television. All ironed overalls and near buzz cut, he seemed the type who'd want a third world war just for practice. A lot of people told Cousin he's a Pinkerton. Cousin thinks he's after my guy, "the dealer" Cousin calls him. Time will tell.

We let anyone stay the night so long as they pay half up front, and each time a Japanese or Chinese family stayed here, one of them Pinkertons would come by the next day, asking if we're doing all right. Cousin would look at me those first couple of times I'd started back. I'd shake my head before finally just replying with a question—*Who called the cops?* He just put his hat back on, walked to his car, and stopped asking soon after that. Cousin said last he saw of the cop was when someone crashed into a gate nearby and we called the authorities. The guy was leaning against his car, just out of earshot, taking in the scene. By the time I'd come back from taking a call inside, he was gone, the smoke from his exhaust pipe stuck in the sky before it too disappeared.

In the morning the tule fog adds a second layer, like a second story, just above the actual earth for the spirits to trickle into town, or at least their memory. And it's then that I think about him most, even if he hasn't come home. I got a call that he'd be here by the end of the season, within a month's time. That was six weeks ago now. Farmers were preparing to wake the dead for spring. Sailors heading home for leave.

Would he hitch a ride this time and knock on the screen

door, the bar as thick as thieves on his back? Or another way, this time. The last time.

The Card-Playing Accomplice

I didn't know who I hated the most—myself, the cop, or the pipsqueak dealer I believed would let me get out of this clean—but there I was, channeling all the rage into a fist, hitting all the same. Hadn't struck a man since they announced the war was over and some kid tried to pickpocket me during the parade.

I was waiting at Southside Park, our normal meetup spot, for what felt like a century. Smoked every cigarette I had on me and even bummed a few from a drunk. A blue suit but dark enough in the shadows that when I asked for a smoke, I caught 'em by surprise. My nicest suit all shredded up now, the seams bursting where I redid them last week. I may be older but not dumb. Not weak.

Maybe it was the moon, the drink, the streets, whatever delirium concocted that cop to think tonight was the right night to pounce. Vice squad, probably, trying to get a lick in on a colored business before their time was done. Give 'em enough rope and stick 'em with debt. War bonds showed everyone that someone always pays.

And tonight, it was him. Gotta give it to an old-timer like me for hammering aces when need be. You can't play cards if you can't slug out a winning hand too. He should've known better. Rookie be damned (clean shoes, easy tell), he should've known better.

Except I had it mathed perfect. We both did. Where could he have gone? I left the park and headed to a different bar, using the pay phone every so often to dial his place. Nothing. Could he have been the rat? What's in it for him? Trying to make a buck before the Zanzibar clientele leave? I don't get it. There are enough saloons between here and the river to feed the back-alley games, why tonight?

He'd been talking about leaving. Delta this, Isleton that. Had he done it? Did he really have a dame? I mapped the here and there in the front of my brain, whether I could even get down the Delta this time of night. What's the use, what would I find? An old man with busted knuckles looking for a dirty card dealer at two thirty in the morning. I needed something tangible.

I settled up at the bar and walked back toward the park, toward his place. I found the building and, like most in the West End, half the lights were on, half off, everyone awake to some degree, minding their business. Guys like that dealer probably had several old hounds like me on his scent, trying to collect. I spotted his window toward the back and saw it open just enough. Shimmied between the windows and the gutter and voilà, I was inside his second-story situation.

And it was empty. Not cleaned up but cleaned out. He was gone and not coming back. I've been set up, I thought, how could he? I searched his bedroom, his drawers, nothing but dust and loose socks. And there on the bathroom floor a matchbook—*Freeport Inn and Breakfast, Isleton, CA.*

I found his phone book, tore out the page, and dialed the number from across the street. Busy signal, time and time again. Was he jamming it? Was I jammed up? I couldn't tell but was out of dimes and out of time.

Pulled the coin return enough times to get something in return, put the coin in, and one last time I called. A man answered. Said he was a state trooper, looking for a missing inn employee. Something about a girl and a man who lived out back who were missing.

I asked about my guy, and he responded that he'd seen the

guy, described him back to me, wanting me to confirm. He perked up when I did. I thumbed what was left of that match-book in my hand, the closest tangible thing I had to sizing up this guy over the phone; he sounded more like Johnny Law the more he talked. He responded, finally, and said he had a hunch that our guy was on his way, toward the Delta.

Brilliant guy, huh? Stealing my idea and reselling it to me all the same. A cop. Definitely. Maybe my partner in crime was still my partner after all.

I couldn't wait around this ol' part of town to find out. I ran back to my car, lit a smoke with the book's final match, and headed south toward its address.

The Morning Radio

The body of a driver was discovered in a damaged vehicle in ten feet of submerged water near the town of Locke, north of Isleton, in the Sacramento River's Delta, authorities said this morning. No name of the male victim was announced, but authorities said the car was registered to a retired police officer. Eyewitnesses re-counted hearing a large crash, a speeding sound from a suspected second vehicle, before local citizens attempted rescue. No leads at this time, yet authorities briefly noted the nearby recovery of a small boat reported stolen earlier that night in Sacramento, nearly forty miles north of the incident, but have made no connections between the two. Authorities did bring hounds to trace a small trail of blood along the river's shore, but there was no immediate de-scription of a suspect nor implication of foul play in the crash. Au-thorities do ensure a swift investigation and encourage witnesses to contact local authorities with any relevant information or reports of suspicious behavior.

THE KEY IN THE TIGNANELLO BAG

BY JANET RODRIGUEZ

Citrus Heights

Dorothy. *7228 Cabrillo Dr. West. CH 5-6345.* Robin imagined an older woman, partially blinded by cataracts, holding a blue ballpoint pen in her hand, laboring to write in cursive on the square sticky note she held in her hand. It touched her how perfectly the name *Dorothy* was executed—the woman must have been used to writing that name—inside the impossible boundary of the square. Robin had found the key in the Tignanello bag earlier that day, after she'd purchased it from a thrift store on the corner.

"Are you going to buy it or not?" the blond clerk asked her. "I need to get back to work." She looked fashionable and disappointed at the same time.

"I'm not sure," Robin said. "Can't I wear it around while I browse for a bit?"

The clerk shook her head. "Designer bags stay behind the counter with me."

"It's a little pricey," Robin said. "Do you have a cheaper one with a tassel like this?"

"Check out the tag." The clerk took the purse from Robin. "It's sewn into the pouch. It's a real Tignanello, not a knockoff. Just look at this stitching! And this tassel you like so much? It still has protective plastic around it."

Robin shrugged. "I'll give you twenty bucks for it."

The clerk sighed, then pointed to a chrome rack across the room. "There are cheaper bags there. Why don't you choose one of those?"

"None of those have tassels," Robin said. She reached into her wallet and took out a twenty and a ten. "My cat likes to play with tassels. I couldn't care less about labels."

She had paid the clerk, taken the purse, and left the store.

Back at home, Robin made a point of examining the stitching like the clerk suggested. It was then she found the secret flap with a zippered pocket underneath. Inside the pocket was a yellow sticky note with a brass key taped to its underside.

The key reminded Robin of her own key collection—the one she'd started when she was eight years old. She used to collect stray keys from her mother's junk drawers, Grandma's sewing boxes—even her father's bedside table. The keys were old, discarded, forgotten. She found them under a sea of pencils, markers, among spools of thread, beneath unopened chopsticks. Robin felt a connection with each key—she vowed to protect them—and kept them on a big silver ring. One day when she was fifteen, her mother found them, during a spring-cleaning venture. She had gone into Robin's room without permission and thrown them all away. Mom saw them as frivolous, like the "ridiculous clutter" of Robin's other collections: marbles, shells, hair barrettes, and feathers.

Robin had felt violated. She insisted she needed privacy, a basic human right.

Mom had disagreed. "Keep your room clean. Then I won't have to go in there."

The key was almost as big as Robin's thumb. It was thick brass, with a sturdy, round face and an official-looking *12* engraved on one side. The number seemed to elevate the purpose of the key. Robin took a picture of it with her phone and ran an image search. Several keys like it showed up: one for a sprinkler system at a middle school, one for a post office box in a private shipping office, and one for a portable cashbox. The closest match, however, was a bronze key for a safe-deposit locker at Wells Fargo.

Robin wondered if this key opened Dorothy's safe-deposit box, where her most precious treasures lived. Anything could be in there: her life savings, unopened letters from her sweetheart who never returned from the war, Krugerrands, diamonds in a black felt drawstring bag. Did Dorothy need this to open her safe-deposit box?

Right then Robin decided to return the key to Dorothy—if she was still alive, and if she was still living at 7228 Cabrillo Drive West. She decided that *CH* probably translated to *Citrus Heights*, the area where Robin was now living. She searched *7228 Cabrillo Dr. West*, using her phone's GPS. There it was: a house on the corner, almost obscured by trees and bushes. It wasn't far from her apartment.

It was four o'clock—she would have time to go before she had to feed Tiger, her sick cat. She still had to add chopped chamomile, calendula, and echinacea to his food, but she could hurry. Tiger was now on the apartment balcony, asleep with Peanut, a half-feral cat she had been feeding, bathing in the streams of radiant sunlight. Robin grabbed her car keys— the only ones that mattered—and left without saying goodbye.

Cabrillo Drive West had been designed in the 1950s, with long, curvilinear streets and clean sidewalks. Ranch-style homes, varying in color and size, stood back from well-manicured lawns, shaped boxwoods, and deciduous trees. Dorothy's house, however, was different.

Robin drove past 7228 twice, trying not to stare. She eventually parked directly across the street, in front of 7225: a cute pink house with white trim and a Japanese maple shading the sidewalk.

Robin turned off her engine and rolled down her window. Across the street, Dorothy's house was barely visible through overgrown vegetation that grew wild in her front yard. A small driveway in front of a dilapidated one-car garage had weeds springing up between crumbling paving stones. Dorothy's property seemed to be the eyesore of her neighborhood. Two willow trees stood sentry in the front, reaching sideways with bearded branches. Robin got out of her car on the passenger side and stood on the sidewalk, searching for any signs of life at Dorothy's place. The afternoon sun was intense, so Robin moved to the shade of the Japanese maple in front of 7225. She was startled by a loud voice.

"Are you here for the newscast?"

There was a woman on the lawn looking at her, waiting for an answer. Robin wondered if this was the owner of 7225, getting ready to ask her to leave. Instead, the woman smiled and joined her on the sidewalk, in the shade of the tree. Her silver hair, neatly styled, matched the gray floral dress she was wearing.

"I didn't mean to scare you," the woman said. "Are you Carol?"

Robin shook her head. "No, I'm not Carol."

"Oh, sorry," the woman said. "I'm Natalie. I live here." She pointed to the pink and white house behind her. "I saw you pull up and I came right out. I thought you were part of the film crew."

"Part of what?"

"The news team. The ones coming to film the cat lady's eviction today? You didn't know about this?"

"I was just . . ." Robin glanced around. "Is it okay if I park here?"

"Of course," Natalie said, waving her hand. "We call her the cat lady because she has hundreds of them living over there. She has no electricity, no running water." She lowered her voice to a whisper. "She's been going to the bathroom in her backyard. Can you believe that? I mean, that's toxic for our environment. Anyway, she's being evicted today. Finally."

Robin winced. "Wait, the woman who lives at 7228 is being evicted today?"

"Yes," Natalie said, sighing. "After she leaves, the animal control people are coming to round up all the cats, and next week the house will be demolished. Then the city will come in to clean up hazardous waste. We're all happy about this."

Robin watched Natalie closely as she talked. She was probably Robin's mother's age. She seemed to have the same need for order and cleanliness. Her makeup was perfect, even down to the shade of her lipstick. There were no stains on her clothes. Robin felt insignificant standing next to her.

"She changed when her husband died, years ago," Natalie was saying. "She let herself go, and those cats started multiplying like crazy. We tried to mind our own business, but with the cats and the smell, we had to get the city involved. Anyway, they condemned the house, but she still wouldn't leave."

"Do you know her name?" Robin asked. "Is it Dorothy?"

"Oh honey," Natalie said, slapping at the air, "I don't remember her name . . ." Her voice trailed off. Looking over Robin's shoulder, she straightened her dress. "Will you excuse me? That's the news crew, and they want to interview me." Without waiting for a response, the woman looked both ways and crossed the street.

Robin watched her head over to a shiny silver van that

was parking in front of Dorothy's house. The words *Excellence in Broadcasting* were written on the side. Doors opened and a crew emerged, including a young female reporter about Robin's age. She shook hands with Natalie, both women smiling like old friends. Soon, the crew was setting up lights, unloading rolls of cord, microphones, and a big camera. Someone snapped their fingers under a big microphone on a pole. The reporter checked her makeup in the side mirror of the van. A police car arrived several minutes later and pulled into the ruins of Dorothy's driveway.

Robin felt a strange urge to cross the street, rush through the overgrown vegetation, and warn Dorothy what was about to happen. Instead, she simply watched, open-mouthed, her feet rooted to the sidewalk. Soon the interview began and Robin wondered what to do. *Should I leave? Warn Dorothy? Go feed Tiger?*

Before she could decide, a black cat with white socks emerged from the vegetation on Dorothy's property and sat down on the sidewalk. He watched the taping with feline curiosity and superiority. Robin could almost see a question floating above his head: *Why are you filming my house?*

On the way home, Robin remembered her mother, who was supposed to come over for dinner that night. Robin expected to see her perched on her apartment stairs, holding a lasagna and looking pissed, but when she pulled into her carport, her mom wasn't there. Robin exhaled a sigh of relief, then gathered a wicker basket from her backseat and carried it into her apartment. Tiger and Peanut ran to greet her, expecting food and affection.

Before long, Robin was at her kitchen counter, chopping the herbs for Tiger's food into tiny, digestible pieces. There was a loud knock on the front door and she opened it wide to greet her mother, who stood on the landing with a home-made lasagna and a peach pie.

"Did you forget we were having dinner?"

"No," Robin said. "Can I take something?"

"Are you still in your pajamas?"

"No." Robin looked down at her clothes. "Come on in. I was just feeding Tiger and Peanut."

Her mother entered the apartment carefully, stepping over clothes and books in the hallway. "Look at this place," she said.

"I just got home, sorry . . ."

"Where will we sit?" Mom said, looking around. "This is a picture of your life, Robin!"

"Here, Mom." Robin lifted a basket of folded laundry from a round table in the living room. "Let's not start fighting. You just got here." Robin only noticed clutter when her mother was near. It did look awful.

"You're right," Mom said, setting the lasagna on the kitchen counter. "Let's wait till after dinner."

Robin smiled to herself and took the basket of laundry into her bedroom, a place she had considered livable before her mother arrived; now it looked disastrous. She left the basket on her unmade bed and closed the door. When she returned to the kitchen, Mom was putting the peach pie into the fridge and sighing.

"Mom . . ."

"What?"

"I have to finish chopping these herbs for Tiger's food. Why don't you sit down and relax on the couch? I'll turn on the news."

"I already read the paper today," Mom said, peering into the living room with disdain.

Both women tried to ignore Tiger's loud demands to be fed. He followed Robin, lifting himself up on his back paws and touching her legs as she turned on the TV. Robin forced herself to breathe. She didn't want to argue. She hoped the news would distract her mother from asking about her unfinished master's thesis, her clutter, the cats, her bank account. When she found the local news station with *excellence in broadcasting*, she smiled.

"I want to see if the cat lady made the news," Robin said. "Have you heard of her? I was there today."

This piqued her mother's curiosity. "What? Where were you?"

Robin gave her mother an abridged version of the story, starting with the purse and finding the key. Tiger whined impatiently as his food was being mixed. By the time his bowl was set on the ground, Mom was engrossed in national news: government budget hearings, climate change summits, the dismal prospect of another pandemic.

As she set the table, Robin recognized the introduction to the local story of Dorothy's eviction. "Here it is," she said, pointing at the TV. "This is it!"

A beautiful anchorwoman began the story, talking as she strolled in front of a large screen: Dorothy holding a cat. "A local septuagenarian was forcibly removed from her home today," the anchorwoman said, looking straight into the camera. "Dorothy Generay had been living on Cabrillo Drive West for forty-seven years before police came to remove her from her condemned home this afternoon."

Robin watched the TV, then her mother, who seemed transfixed. The reporter who had interviewed Natalie was now on-screen. "Here on Cabrillo Drive West, residents say this home behind me has long been a nuisance." She introduced Natalie as a neighbor who knew Dorothy well. Robin rolled her eyes.

"This woman has been a nightmare," Natalie said. "Her house has been condemned, because it's been deteriorating steadily, but she continues to live there with all those cats. She has no electricity or plumbing, which is why the smell is so terrible."

As the reporter asked Natalie questions, Robin realized that neither woman had called Dorothy by her name.

"The cats are multiplying exponentially," Natalie said. "They keep having new litters of kittens, but they have nowhere to go. At night they howl in the culvert, in our gardens. We wish her the best, but she needs to leave."

"Well," Robin's mother said, shaking her head, "she's a piece of work."

"I know, right?"

"Why are we even watching this?"

Robin moved closer to the TV. "Mom, please, I'm trying to listen."

"It's been a long road," Natalie was saying. "I'm just glad it's over."

The camera cut to two uniformed police officers escorting Dorothy to their car. She was a stooped, white-haired woman, and moved slowly.

"Generay will be taken to a local hospital, where doctors will assess her physical and mental health," the reporter said over the footage, "and try to locate family members who can help her move into a new and safer residence. The cats will be assessed by animal control and may soon be available for adoption." The screen cut to the property, where cats either darted about or relaxed in the sun.

The reporter's voice-over continued: "Generay even tried

to take a basket of newborn kittens with her to the hospital, but she was forced to leave them behind." The segment concluded with a shot of three gray-and-white fuzz balls, eyes still shut, mewing loudly from the basket.

"No!" Robin's mother shouted, standing up and covering her face. "Why did you make me watch this?"

"What?" Robin said, shutting off the TV. "I'm sorry, Mom—"

"What happened to those kittens?"

"Come with me." Robin took one of her mother's hands and led her to the bathroom. "I want to show you something that might make you feel better."

A night-light illuminated the windowless room with a pale-yellow glow. Once her eyes adjusted, Robin's mother saw the cardboard box. Robin stepped past her and kneeled next to it.

"I *had* to bring them home, Mom," she said, reaching into the container and bringing out a small kitten. "I couldn't leave them behind, could I?"

Robin's mother looked down where two other sleeping kittens were huddled. The yawning kitten in Robin's hand still had her eyes shut.

"I bought kitty formula to feed them," Robin said, stroking the top of the kitten's head. "It's close to their mother's milk."

"Oh, Robin," her mother whispered, "what have you done?"

After making some phone calls, Robin discovered Dorothy was being held at the county hospital. She canceled a morning appointment with her graduate advisor, promising to reschedule later. Her application for another extension to complete her thesis was due soon, but Robin knew it was more important to visit Dorothy and give her the note and key.

She walked through the automatic glass doors of the hospital entrance and stopped at the security/information desk. Two women with soft white hair and powder-blue smocks greeted her. Behind them, a uniformed officer, arms crossed, looked straight at Robin. His brass name tag read, JAMES. Robin wondered if it was his first name or last.

"I'm looking for a patient named Dorothy," Robin said.

The two ladies peered into the computer screen.

"Last name?" the first woman asked.

Robin bit her lip. "Generay."

"Spelling?"

"I'm not sure. She's the cat lady who was brought here yesterday."

Officer James stepped forward. "Are you family?"

"I'm not," Robin said. Three people walked through the double doors carrying flowers and got in line behind her.

Officer James waved Robin to the end of the counter. "What's the reason for your visit?" he asked.

Robin knew he was sizing her up, and she wished she had dressed in more professional attire. "I have something that belongs to her."

"What is it?" James asked. "Please tell me it's not a cat."

Robin smiled and shook her head, then reached into her bag and removed the key. She handed it to James, explaining how she found it in the Tignanello bag, drove to Dorothy's house, and watched her eviction. She didn't mention anything about taking the basket of kittens.

James examined the key, his face softening. "Is this for a safe-deposit box?"

"It looks like it opens a bank box, right?"

"Maybe. It's hard to say for sure."

"I have to give it to her, just in case."

James nodded, handing the key back to Robin. "Usually,

new psychiatric patients aren't allowed visitors," he said in a low voice. "Even family isn't allowed up there, not until the doctor says so. Got it?"

"Yes. So what should I do?"

"Come back when the hold is over," he said. "The best you can do is to be here, in the lobby, once she is released. That would be . . ." He walked over to his own computer and typed something on the keyboard. "Tomorrow at five forty-five p.m."

"Thank you," she said. "I'll be here."

"I will not," he said, smiling. "Hopefully, I'll be fishing. Good luck."

It was raining the next day at five o'clock, but Robin drove downtown anyway. When she arrived at the hospital, the parking lot was full, so she chose the closest metered space, one block away. After dashing to the entrance without an umbrella, she walked through the automatic doors, pretending to be calm.

The lobby was packed, with no seating available. An elderly man stood up and offered his chair to Robin.

"Thank you," she said, breathlessly, "but I'd rather stand." Nothing could have been further from the truth. Rain pounded against the glass doors and windowpanes of the hospital entrance. Self-conscious, embarrassed, and wet, Robin caught a glimpse of herself in a mirror. She was wearing the only dress she owned, and noticed a grease stain from an unknown substance on the bodice. She looked around for a warm place to stand, her flip-flops squeaking on the linoleum floor.

A loud *DING* resounded, and the main elevator doors opened. A tall nurse pushed a woman in a wheelchair out of the elevator and into the lobby.

Dorothy.

She looked tired and confused, but it was definitely her. A bright-green bag on her lap was labeled simply: *POSSESSIONS*.

"Here you are, Dot," the nurse said cheerfully. "Do you see your family?"

Dorothy stood up unsteadily. "Hmmm. Rain," she said, looking past Robin and out the windows.

"Dorothy?" Robin said.

The woman stared at her. As soon as they made eye contact, Robin wondered why she had said anything.

"Yes?" Dorothy responded, tightening her cardigan around her. "Who are you?"

"I'm Robin," she said, stepping forward. When she offered her hand, Dorothy frowned.

"I don't know you. Are you a reporter? Police?"

"No, I . . . I have something of yours." Robin opened her purse, unzipped the secret pocket, and took out the yellow sticky note.

"Oh no," Dorothy said, groaning. "You took Roberta's purse, didn't you?" She pointed at the Tignanello bag, its tassel dangling from the open zipper. "That's Roberta's purse. She loved that purse! Where did you get that?"

Several people in the waiting room looked up at Robin. A uniformed guard, smaller than James, started walking toward her.

"I b-bought it . . ." Robin answered, gripping the yellow note between two fingers. The Tignanello bag, slung over her shoulder, suddenly felt heavy.

"Liar!" Dorothy said, pointing at her. "You're a . . . LIAR! My sister would never sell *any* of her bags. They were her prized possessions. I bet you stole it, didn't you?"

"No," Robin said. "I didn't . . ."

"You were the most ungrateful child, Nicole! I'm ashamed of you!"

Robin held out the yellow square of paper with trembling hands.

"I'm not Nicole," she said. "I've never even met Roberta. I bought this purse at a thrift store, and found this note inside. It's addressed to you. Do you recognize this key?"

"You did it," Dorothy said, ignoring the key. "Always stealing everything your mother had! Stay back! Stay away from me!"

The nurse, who had been silent, took the old woman's arm. "Dot, please," she said. "Remember what the doctor said about your blood pressure?"

Dorothy pulled her arm away and held up two index fingers in the shape of a cross. "Stay away from me, you witch! You're the one who kept me locked up in this place!"

The security guard stepped forward. "All right, let's just calm down . . ."

"You son of a bitch!" Dorothy screamed. "Stay away from me! Get back!"

People in the lobby began to edge away from Dorothy.

The security guard held up his palm, signaling Robin. "Miss, step back." He pressed a button on his radio and spoke into it: "I need orderly assistance in the lobby. Fifty-one fifty detainee."

Dorothy covered her eyes and nose with her hands and her muffled sobs began filling the otherwise silent lobby. "All of you!" she cried. "You . . . you came to my house and took my cats away! You took them!"

"Dorothy, please sit down," the nurse said.

"All of you! Why can't you just leave me alone? You made me leave the kittens! I only wanted those three—"

"*I* took the kittens," Robin said, a little too loud. "They're safe. I took them home. I've been feeding them kitten formula."

The security guard and the nurse turned to Robin, then saw Dorothy soften. The old woman let her hands drop to her sides.

"You have the kittens?"

"Yes," Robin said.

"Good," Dorothy said, closing her eyes in relief.

The elevator doors opened, and another uniformed guard appeared, carrying a sealed hospital package. Robin knew it was some kind of straitjacket.

Dorothy sighed, then sat back down in the wheelchair.

The nurse kneeled down beside her and spoke tenderly: "Why don't we go back up to your room, Dot?"

"My room," Dorothy said, shaking her head, pointing a wrinkled finger at the nurse. "That's not my room and you know it."

"Take this key," Robin said, holding it out again. "It belongs to you."

Dorothy shook her head. "I'm not interested. Tell my sister I don't want any family blood money. She can't buy me off."

"Okay, let's go," the nurse said, pulling the wheelchair backward, toward the elevators.

Robin watched Dorothy retreat, and the elevator doors open. The nurse and guard stepped in, pulling Dorothy after them.

Robin stood still, holding the key and the yellow note.

The elevator doors closed, and the numbers above it lit up: 2, 3, 4.

Robin turned to the lobby guard, who shook his head. "Okay," he said, "that was fun."

"But . . ."

"I suggest you leave now," he said.

Robin considered his face. He wasn't angry, but he seemed pretty serious. As she moved across the lobby in her squeaking flip-flops, people watched her go, but when she stopped to look back, most of them turned away. Some scrolled on their phones.

She wanted to say something. Maybe she could tell them she wasn't trying to cause a scene, or that she really did buy the Tignanello bag with a key addressed to Dorothy. She could tell them keys were important things that no one should ever take away. Instead, she stayed silent and tucked the key away, back in the small pocket inside the Tignanello bag. She headed out the automatic doors.

It was still raining. Robin walked numbly through the downpour, knowing she had done what she came to do. Whatever happened to Dorothy now was out of her hands. She spotted her car a block away, looking shiny and clean from a distance, but suddenly remembered she'd left her windows slightly cracked. She ran to it, hoping the rain hadn't hurt the treasure inside.

She peered through the windows into the backseat. Her application for the extension for her master's thesis was soaked, ink smeared beyond recognition. Otherwise, the contents of the car seemed fine.

The box of kittens was still on the floor, the three furry balls huddled together, until one sensed her presence. He lifted his face, eyes still shut, and started to mew loudly. His siblings joined his song, so pure and innocent. Inspired by their desperate need for her, Robin opened the door and cooed over them.

"Don't worry, babies," she whispered, "Mommy's here!"

INTERSECTIONS

BY JOHN FREEMAN

K Street

"The first thing you need to realize is everyone wants to talk about UFOs."

We're sitting in the van, parked around the corner from Café Shah, and Danny is giving me advice again. It's been a slow night. Thankfully, most of them have been slow lately.

"Your instinct is, talk about family, right, your close connections? *Wrong*. Don't ever say the word *cousin*. Arabs with malfeasance on their mind always have cousins."

"Danny, we all have cousins, *you* have cousins, it's not a crime."

"That's what those guys in San Diego said. The twenty-first hijacker crew? *Coming to visit their cousins.*"

Most of my cousins are dead, but I haven't told Danny this yet, it's too much to introduce in a small van on a quiet street at two thirty in the morning. The police radio fuzzes and stops, like someone is turning the channel on an old-fashioned radio. Then someone says the word—*banana*. Which makes both parties laugh.

The police dispatcher at this hour is named Cindy and speaks to the officers like they are her favorite horses. It's my third month at the ambulance company and still the codes are confusing. I understand what they are saying—basically. When Cindy talks, the tone though is unmistakable.

I've heard that tone once, a long time ago, before I had what Danny some days calls my haunted face.

"Jesus H., Vincent Price, did you dance with a shovel last night in the dark?" This is how Danny talks, like he's a very old man assembling a cartoon. It's what he said the first time I came to work after a sleepless night. *Dance with a shovel in the dark?* It was a joke but also a warning. Americans don't like you to wear your sadness, it makes them uncomfortable.

Danny's not American, though, he likes to say, he's Italian, and most of the time I consider myself lucky I didn't get stuck in this van with a Jason or Brad, but Danny Marino of East Portal Park. He's specific that way. Some days when it's slow, Danny simply rewinds time and replays the journey from East Portal to San Francisco to Trapani where his great uncles and aunts used to fish *tuna big as this van right out of the ocean.*

"You and me, we're sea brothers, Ramy, I bet there's a tuna that swam from Sicily to Palestine and back, did like a round-trip, *pow pow,* evading your great uncle and mine!"

Most days I say a prayer and thank God for the chance to come here and work in Sacramento, a very, very long way from Bethlehem, where there is no sea, at least not that near, but again, I haven't told Danny that. There are so many things I can't really say yet, but I think one day I will.

In the meantime, I just sit in the right front seat, mostly silent, Danny's audience and partner, waiting for calls. Most of them are people in their homes who need a ride to the hospital. "We drive a bus, Ramy, that's all it is." I like these days. Picking people up all night, walking or wheeling them slowly to the van. Dropping them off into the mouth of the hospital like they're coming home.

Many aren't enormously sick. They are other things.

Lonely, or poor, or very heavy—I never understand quite how Americans get so big. But okay, we cope in our own ways. Some are all of the above. Some are suffering with that other thing next to loneliness—not quite disturbed, but no longer right. Where they can't go back to reality. I worry I have permanently entered that state. And so I ride this van.

"You need to get a dog, Ramy," Danny says, putting the ambulance into drive. Then he starts flicking through his phone with one hand, driving with the other, showing me his favorite dogs. Small ones, big ones, dogs that look like they should wear top hats or ride in limousines and others who look like bouncers or assassins. "Look at this guy," he says, and I look at a brownish-tan dog with a flat face the size of a small pony. "These are called bullies, but they're just sweethearts, total mushballs if you treat them right."

We haven't got a call but Danny grows restless, so most nights we move around, stopping at convenience stores where Danny has crushes on the workers, which he shows by buying gum silently. "Girls don't like it if you talk too much," he explains, and I feel sad he can't be his usual self. We pull into the gas station on Folsom Boulevard, where the ambulance looks more at home—shiny and too bright. *Hand me that Binaca.* Danny is old school when it comes to breath.

It's when he's inside flirting by not flirting that the call comes in. I can tell it's not going to be a good one by the dispatcher's attempt to neutralize her tone, even though she uses our nickname. "Med Brothers, Med Brothers, we've got a hit-and-run on K Street, what's your location?" It's not far, so I get on the radio to explain how close and click on the lights so Danny knows we need to go. A moment later he's in the van and we're off, moving slowly down Folsom. Ambulances don't go that fast.

By the time we get there, Sacramento PD have already made a perimeter around the scene. "Ah shit, that guy's dead," Danny says, as we park the bus. I don't ask how he knows because I recognize the posture too, when someone looks too comfortable lying on the roadside. A group of what must be witnesses stands in a clutch on the curb, their faces contorted. An officer speaks to them in gentle tones, they're white people.

"Ramy, go talk to the officer, I'm going to check this poor guy out."

So much energy is spent in this life protecting the protected from what they ought to know. I approach the group, trying to mentally de-haunt my face. A woman and two men are relaying information to the officer. His pen is moving but when I am next to him, I realize he's just scribbling. Then he says, "He left his calling card," and he's holding up a license plate. "Hold on, folks, let me talk to Ramy here."

That's when I realize I've met this officer before. Another accident, not a bad one. A fender bender turned argument. Maybe it was the irritation of those near fights. People yelling and threatening each other. Right away I saw he was not someone who ever stopped being an officer, the way some do when they recognize you're an EMT—then talk to you sideways like fellow undertakers of the world. This one never gave up that power. And he repeated my name so much I began to hate it. He's doing it now.

"Ramy, a bit of savagery here, as you can see. Blew the light or whatever and this guy is definitely DOA. You must recognize it, Ramy, right? See his neck? Anyway, these folks saw it and gave me a statement, but the guy was going so fast, knocked his license plate right off the car. We'll find him, Ramy, we always do."

The soldiers in Bethlehem used to talk to me that way. *Ramy, Ram-E!* The ones who shouted it were the ones I was most wary of. I was often not the first on scene there too. Someone had held someone too long in a certain position and then the ambulance company would be called and since Holy Family Hospital was close, we'd be there in seconds and they would delay our departure until whoever it was they'd been talking to wasn't ever going to talk again.

I had planned to be a doctor. Like my father before and his father before. They had such gentle hands. If I was cold or hot, or tired, or hungry, my father's first instinct was to put his hand on me, on my neck or forehead, like his fingertips were the most sensitive temperature gauge on the planet. Back in those days, we'd play outside and get hot and feverish. *You're overheated, son, you got yourself overheated*, he'd say, maybe the most spoken words of my childhood.

I walk over to Danny now and he's got his gloves on and is touching the victim's neck. It's a white guy in his late twenties, our age. Except his skull has been slightly crushed in and his neck is very clearly broken. "I think impact did this, maybe bounced off the windshield or something," Danny is saying, touching the body softly.

Shards of glass cover the intersection, as if life were a miracle held together by a bit of blown sand. Maybe that's it. I know this isn't Danny's first DOA, he's had a couple of suicides, a bad car accident; one gunshot victim died in the back of his bus. All stories he's told me on slow days. The placement of this body now—the way it's right on the medium strip—makes it all so public. It's like a crèche.

Once it's clear the man is dead, a different set of wheels begins to turn. And Danny and my job takes a backseat to evidence gathering, and interviewing, and I can tell the small crowd which has assembled has noted we aren't driving away in a hurry, and they must know too, which has laid a hush on top of all sounds like something or someone must not be disturbed.

An hour later, we drive to the hospital with the body in back. It's very late and the streets are empty, except for drunks getting into taxis, and the odd delivery truck dropping off milk or today's *Bee*. I used to love this hour, sitting by my window in Beit Jala, smoking cigarettes and listening to the night, the real city coughing and turning over in its sleep.

It's because of this hour that I started to work at the hospital. When the Israelis came for our downstairs neighbors, and we could hear them beating Abu Shwami like it was work, like they were annoyed how hard his hard head made them work, my father put his clothes on like he was going to race downstairs. *Do you think they care you're a doctor?* my mother hissed. *That is a gift to them, George.* "Good, we get a professor and a doctor in one night!" And the look on my father's face as he sat down and stayed still until the beating stopped.

Son, you need to get a job, he told me the next morning. *You need to get a job at night, because that's when they're going to come for you. Me, they will not be able to hold me so long, the hospital will call. But son, you they will keep for years. For years, do you hear me, son?* I still remember my father sitting on my bed saying this, his breath sour and sweet and his slacks pressed; he was going to the clinic that day. I wasn't going to be like him just yet.

Most people would have killed for my job. But my father called a colleague, who called a colleague, and within a week I was pushing carts of dirty nappies and laundry and other human liquids around the hospital at night. We were a maternity hospital mostly, and so a lot of what happened there was good news. It's where people came to watch life begin. The hospital had been there since the 1920s, and many of the doctors there were the grandchildren and great-grandchildren of many of its first doctors.

Very few babies are born between three and six a.m. A bit more after midnight. So unless I was taking items to or from the nursery, where occasionally a woman's scream of labor might brittle the walls, it was quiet. Peaceful, even. Gliding by with my cart in my new sneakers and white pants, I felt like an angel of reprieve. *Do you like it, son, do you like the hospital?* my father asked the first morning I came home. *Yes, Baba, I do*, I said, *thank you*. And he just rubbed my head and went to work.

How I wish this is where our story ends, and I wasn't here now, riding in this too-quiet van to a different hospital, where it's not peaceful at night. But do we ever really control our stories? I used to think not, that some things are truly chance, or accident. God or some other hand just reaching down to pluck the strings of a day to make a different music, a new song. I don't know if this is the case anymore, not since I came to Sacramento, not since I left.

Because wasn't it my fault I was in the hospital last spring? Sitting in the lounge among some sleeping grandparents, farting and snoring through their first night as grandparents, when I saw Layla. My father had told me to leave, yes, and I had chosen to do it, to not stay home. I'd chosen not to ask him, *Are you sure they won't take you?* No, I agreed and went to the hospital and took the job and then she walked into the lounge at three a.m. like it wasn't night at all.

There is so much beauty in being at one with your purpose. Layla walked like someone who never questioned why she was there, not in that building. Not with a patient. Never with a child. Later, never with me. Even though what we did destroyed everything I've ever known. That night I couldn't imagine such a thing, I wouldn't have been able to, watching this woman walk with liquid calm across a night floor like an angel. And smiling.

Before long we're at Sutter Memorial, the great sliding doors opening and closing thanks to the smokers outside who don't understand they're standing by the door censor. Danny has been humming the whole way there, and now finally he says something. "Final trip for this dude, let's take him in easy," and for the first time since I arrived in Sacramento I have to pause to catch my breath. The tenderness with which he reaches into the back of the bus and slides the man's body out on its tray, lifting the legs so they don't bang anything or bounce, so the body doesn't jolt—a dead man doesn't need this care, but I guess that's why he's doing it.

And then we're on our feet, beside the stretcher, wheeling him into the hospital, the body covered, and that always makes people nervous, because they know. I've known when I've seen it. Everyone can see what we're doing, especially the nurses and doctors moving around as we push into the building, brightly lit, everyone almost cheerful with industry, even though it's not at all a joyful time of night in Sacramento, as I have found. It's when drunks and suicides and nighttime heart attacks come in. And men like this one, though not that often.

Immediately they're on us. A clutch of nurses and a doctor —asking questions. Now I feel protective and eggshell-fragile as we sign the body over, like it's a large package, like *he* is a large package, and I wonder how often my father could stand doing this—with parents too. The part of life that was meant to be the biggest, happiest, freest, most magical, and instead on some occasions, there he was with the worst news in the entire world, and a delivery no one can ever imagine.

"All right, buddy," Danny says, as we walk back into the soft, dry night, "let's go get ourselves a Slurpee. I have to not think about that."

It began with the tea. That's how Layla and I began talking. I was standing in the small kitchen at the back of the hospital, where only the nurses and orderlies went, and she walked in with her liquid walk trailing a scent of lavender. I'm not sure what came over me, I was normally shy. Most of what I said back then, I said with my eyes, sometimes without even meaning to. But here I said, *Would you like a tea?* And just like that, it became okay to talk.

I knew she was married. The ring on her hand said that. Her posture. The clothes she changed into after work, which I saw one day. Beautiful dresses and long silken pants. Tops that hugged her chest. And, of course, her husband picking her up in front of the hospital in their green Mercedes. I remember thinking then that if I was married to someone like Layla, I would pick her up too. I would make sure she never had to deal with something so tedious as soldiers harassing her on the street. Or getting her own tea.

Watching from the third floor of the hospital, dressed in my orderly outfit, I felt for the first time how impossibly small my part in her life might be. I might have been something one forgets when it's out of view. But maybe not? Not knowing was at once torturous and a pleasure unlike any I had known. Some mornings when I came home smiling, my mother would give me juice and tell me how beautiful it was to see me smile, and it felt glorious for once to have bounced light into the room, rather than to have come home bringing her worry.

I might have continued in this state of bliss had we not actually begun a conversation. We'd started on a break, at first by accident, something simple, *Can you pass the tea bags?* And then every time I went to the kitchen, there she was—so often it couldn't have been an accident, maybe it was luck? And we'd smile and say jokes and she would compliment me on my outfit, which was funny, because it was the same every day, white on white on white. And the fact that she was nearly old enough to be my mother made this all safe, since of course we were merely colleagues.

There was also all that life always pouring out of the hospital. It required so much attention and care and joy, and Layla was one of the focal points of directing this attention. Less so because her shift was at night, but still, at any point in time she might have to leave, and go back to a baby who wasn't sleeping, or was struggling to nurse, or a mother who woke up and wept, which they often did. Until that job, I never understood what a thing my mother had taken on by having me. I also understood for the first time why I had no siblings, unlike so many of my friends.

Maybe that was it—the precariousness of all that joy. Or the fact that it was quiet. Like church, or a secret place. Maybe that was why one night, as I was standing by a window, Layla approached me from behind and wrapped her arms around me. She was so close I could feel her breasts against my back and her breath on my neck. It was sudden and then utterly familiar and before I could think, I turned around and kissed her, and she kissed me back.

* * *

I still don't know why she trusted me. Maybe because I was quiet, and seemed older, and was often alone. Maybe she sensed something in my manner. But from that shift on, rare was the night where we didn't collapse into each other in a closet or empty room, or walk quietly to a park where she'd tempt me with her hand or once her mouth, until I zipped up and we went hustling back to work breathless. I had only dated women my age until then, and to have a woman tell me what she wanted—and for it to be me—turned me into a flame.

There have been times since I came to Sacramento that I've shuddered at the risks we took. That she took. If we'd been found by a doctor, I'd always assumed she'd lose her job instantly and, well, my job was so new, and she was so beautiful, so incredibly soft, so sweet smelling, so quick to laugh, as if what we were doing was humorous—not a joke, but a prank, almost, on the mad, staid world—that all of this would have been worth it. And it was, until the soldiers came to the hospital.

They weren't dressed as soldiers, which my mother and father had always warned me of. Had we not been in the hospital closet, I would have known right away they weren't Palestinian. They were dressed like doctors on a TV set, not our hospital, where the doctors all look a certain way, as if they shopped at Harrods, their coats pressed and starched white, and their hair combed. These doctors who were not doctors entered in a group and moved right through the hospital. They threw open the door of the closet we were in and there was a gun pointed in my face.

It's not him, a doctor who wasn't a doctor said in English.

Another man dragged me out of the closet anyway and threw me against the wall. *Stay there*, he said in poor Arabic.

My first instinct was to cry. Layla was buttoning up her shirt, her hands shaking. A female soldier came into the room and yanked her out by her arm. *Come here,* she said in Arabic, *come here,* like she was scolding an animal. And she sat Layla down in the waiting area.

Then we heard the shooting.

I'd heard gunshots many times before. There are pops and bangs, there are things which sound like buzz saws. There are booms. Then there are sounds which seem to suck all the other sound out of the air. That's what the shooting in the hospital sounded like.

The soldier came back to me and grabbed me by my hair and began dragging me out of the ward. One of the real doctors, a man my father's age, stepped in front of him and the soldier chopped him down with his rifle—one swipe and Dr. Khoury was on the ground, bleeding from his head.

Anyone else need to check in? the soldier shouted in Arabic. *All right!*

And then we were in the elevator; I could smell his sweat, the acrid sweat of rage or fear. When we got to the ground floor, he kicked me up to a standing position. *Come on, let's go, come on, you dog. Get in the truck.*

Another soldier zip-tied my hands, while a third opened the back of their armored vehicle and they threw me in like a piece of trash.

There were no windows so I couldn't feel where we were going, just the diesel engine surging and drifting, surging. Then we were stopping and the door had been opened and my heart dropped.

We were at my family's apartment building.

Come on, Ramy, let's go, one of the soldiers said, now in American English. They pounded on the ground-floor door.

Let me call them, I said.

Shut up, Ramy, the American said. Then they started buzzing the apartment.

My father is a heavy sleeper.

You better hope he wakes up, Ramy.

Finally his voice came over the door buzzer. Lights were beginning to turn on across the street in the upstairs flats.

We walked up, their boots heavy behind me. My soft hospital shoes silent. At the top landing, my mother and father stood in the doorway with a look of terror on their faces.

What is this? What happened? my father said. He was wearing his galabia, and my mother her nightdress.

You need to invite us in, Mr. Aoun, we have to talk to you about Ramy, one of them said, and that's when I saw he was holding my IDs. I hadn't even noticed them rip them off me.

A moment later we were gathered in the front room, my mother half sitting, half standing, my father looking with bewilderment at the soldiers, who seemed to take up more space than they actually occupied, clustered inside the apartment now, examining our things, our photos, our books, their doctor disguises undone so that their bulletproof vests were visible.

Your son here, yeah? Your son is fucking one of the nurses at the hospital. And before you congratulate him on his zub working so well, this one's married, okay?

My father looked at me with utter disbelief, and utter sorrow, like he had somehow brought this world upon us all.

Mr. Aoun, I need you to hear this. It was the American talking. *From now on, Ramy is going to work in the ambulance corps, okay? You're going to get him a job in the ambulance corps, and he's going to check in with us. Right? He's going to check in with us once a week and he's going to tell us some things.*

You can't possibly ask this, he's a boy.

176 // SACRAMENTO NOIR

No, no, I think Layla Haddad's husband might disagree. And if for some reason Mr. Haddad has a special relationship with his wife, if we don't hear from Ramy, we're first going to call the hospital. And then come over here and shoot him in the fucking head. All right?

My mother was weeping silently. One of the soldiers peered out the window at the still-dark street, yawning. Meanwhile, the one leading the interrogation grew impatient and shoved my father.

Do you understand, Mr. Aoun? I need you to agree. Because if I have to come back here again and talk to you fucking pieces of rat shit, I'm not going to come nicely. Do you understand?

Yes, yes, I understand, my father said, his head dropping.

And that was the beginning of the last period of my life in Bethlehem.

Danny is sucking contemplatively on his straw now, and I want to say something to him. I have an urge to fill the silence of the ambulance with something real, something I've been carrying, but the radio crackles instead and it's Cindy again from dispatch with a fatigue in her voice. It's nearly daybreak.

"Hey, Med Brothers, where you boys at? The precinct wants to know if you're heavy sleepers. We've got detectives starting on this accident in the morning—they're going into it as a homicide."

Danny picks up the radio and holds his mouth open in quiet agony for a second. "Sorry, Cindy, brain freeze there. Postmurder Slurpee. You should try it. Impossible not to go back to the best part of childhood with cherry. But yeah, we're here. Any chance we can talk to these guys before we get off?"

A few hours later, two detectives pull into the parking lot at the gas station where Danny and I are dozing in our seats. Both of them are white, and one has her hair in a ponytail. They walk over to the bus and tap on Danny's window.

"You guys have a moment to talk to us?"

Over gas-station coffee, we walk them through what we saw. They're good detectives, scalpeling off anything that is irrelevant or conjecture. The one with the ponytail has eyes so stern I can't look at her, and so I just watch her hands, which appear soft and unchapped, but there's a deep scar running from her pinkie to her wrist, like her finger might once have been nearly sheared off.

"Car accident," she says, catching me looking. "Would have lost the finger if it wasn't for one of you people." For a second I think she means Palestinians. "I apparently picked it right up off the roadway like it was something that had fallen off my car, walked it over to the EMTs, and said, *Can you fix this?* and fainted."

"Stop telling your war stories, Helen, we've got *this* one to figure out," the other detective says, a man who looks like he belongs on *Law & Order*. It was on in Bethlehem all the time. "What's your name again?" he asks me then.

Spelling my name had always been the hard part. I don't know why Americans had trouble. Four letters. R-A-M-Y. I tried to come up with a pneumonic, but everything I could think of only made it harder. Back in Bethlehem, the American soldier didn't care. He just changed it at will. *Roni. Loni. Money.* Then he'd get it right like this whole thing was a huge effort. *Ramy*, he'd say, slowly, like it was a gift to me. *What's* your *name?* I asked him once when we were sitting in a windowless van not far from the hospital. *Joshua*, he'd said, and the look of pride on his face made me hate him.

We had met weekly, as planned. I was reassigned to the hospital's ambulance service, which was small, since most of what they did was deliver babies, but the fact that some women needed picking up allowed me access to many homes. I tried not to take notes, and I hoped my eyes wouldn't help, but whenever we returned to work and dropped off a grateful mother-to-be and sometimes a husband or grandmother, I found I could remember everything. I marveled at and despised how desperately my memory wanted to make sure we stayed safe.

At first my shifts had continued as planned, but gradually our ambulance would get called out to what I realized were interrogations. We'd arrive and find a man on the ground bleeding or sometimes barely breathing and the soldiers would ask us to make sure he was alive, and on one or two occasions he wasn't, and then it became our problem to deal with, mostly—the wrecked apartment, the body, the fact that we had to tell someone what happened. On one of those trips, Salim, who worked with me sometimes, asked what happened. *I don't know*, Joshua had said. *We found him that way.*

I never saw Layla again, except for once, from the corner of my eye, getting into the green Mercedes. We'd never exchanged phone numbers, since I would always be seeing her at the hospital, or so I thought. She walked briskly to the car, got in, closed the door, and they sped away.

Without her, the days there stretched open to become a sea of nothingness. Of people I didn't know, who had important, happy, sometimes terrible things going on in their lives, lives which touched mine for the briefest of moments when I ferried them to and from a hospital, taking notes on anything that *jumped out*, as Joshua would say.

The way he'd excavate my memory when we got together felt like what I imagined being fucked felt like. Each question followed by another thrust. *What was in the room? What color were the walls? Did they have books? How old are the children? Did you see a computer? What was the view out the window? Did they talk in Arabic or Hebrew? How many months have they lived there? What kind of dog was it?*

I tried to imagine where this ocean of information was going. To what use it could possibly be directed. No matter how much I provided, though, they wanted more, clearer, cleaner. More names. More ages. More dimensions. It was like every single living thing and space was being mapped in 3D. As if they'd crawled into my body and were directing my eyes with *their* eyes.

"So tell me what you saw again," the detective is saying, the one with the brush-cut hair and the *Law & Order* face.

It's light now, a smear of pink emerging on the horizon. Danny's smoking a cigarette, his one and only of the night, a ritual, over at the back of the van. The smell reminds me of my father.

Once again, I walk the detective through the scene upon our arrival. The body, the glass, the crowd, and this time I remember the officer doodling in his sketch pad.

The detective shakes his head. "What a fuckup."

The one called Helen sucks her teeth.

"I'm sorry you had to see that," he says, sounding genuinely pained. Like somehow this is all a mess that officer had created.

"Okay, if you don't mind, could we all drive over there before you clock off for the night?"

For months Joshua sucked me dry. What began as once-a-week meetings turned into twice a week. Some days I'd leave the hospital and he'd be standing out there dressed as an American tourist with his Bible and fanny pack and he'd motion to me with his eyes, and I'd follow him. I sometimes thought they'd care if I was caught, but at a certain point I came to the conclusion that Joshua wasn't very important, and that I was some kind of extracurricular activity—like he was practicing for something more important.

On days I'd talked to Joshua, I'd come home and go straight to my room and take off my clothes and run a hot shower. Then I'd come back downstairs wearing as much cologne as possible and neither my mother or father would say anything about what I'd done at work that day, or why I was a little late. I had a cell phone but Joshua had told me, *Don't even think about texting anyone anything, we can read all your messages.*

One day I came home for work and my father was waiting for me outside the apartment, smoking a cigarette. It was nearly summer, and still light, but it was unusual for him to be standing there on his own and I grew worried. *What . . . what's happened?*

He just grabbed my arm and steered me toward his car. *Come with me, son,* he responded gently. *Don't say anything.*

And then we were driving through the city, stopping, moving, the radio tuned to the news. My father smoking with his hand out the car. It was warm but not hot yet, and I loved this feeling normally, being in my father's car with him. Going somewhere, anywhere. We couldn't travel very far usually, but still, it was something, the feeling of air on our faces. My father's elegant profile. I always hoped I'd look like him when I grew older. *Like Omar Sharif!* my mother's mother used to say, when I was little. I still don't know who that is.

After a while, we stopped at a house and my father said, *Stay here.* Five minutes later he returned to the car and got me. *Come with me*, he said, and I followed him to a different car. *Get in.* When I didn't move, he motioned with his head and repeated it with emphasis: *Get. In.* It was a newish Toyota with Israeli plates.

Whose car is this, Baba? I asked as we drove off.

Son, be quiet, he said, and we entered the freeway that sped through the settlements on the way to Jerusalem.

Eventually my father handed me a piece of paper with writing on it: *My dear George, I have received your letter in which you've done everything necessary to enable Ramy to stay with us in Sacramento.*

I read on for a moment. *What is this? What does this mean?* I asked him.

My son, he said, breathing heavily, *you are my heart. I cannot live without you, but I also cannot live with this gun pointed at you every day. You have to leave. You must leave, you are leaving.*

And I left.

At the accident scene at nearly eight in the morning, there are still shards of glass blown this way and that, like someone had made a half-hearted effort at sweeping up everything. I remember how my father used to sweep the sidewalk in front of our house, where on some days drunken tourists would drop bottles of beer or Coke and just leave them there. He always looked so peaceful from above. It's been six months since he dropped me off at the airport in Jordan, and heaved once in my arms before shoving me into the terminal.

Danny looks as exhausted as I feel. "Ramy, what do you think an actual UFO would do if it set down to land here?" he asks as the detectives walk around, taking more notes. "Look at this, wouldn't this be perfect, this intersection?"

I glance at the four stoplights, clicking from red to yellow to green, and the wide boulevards, and I have to admit he has some sort of point, if what a UFO would need is a space where nothing is as it seems. There are palms at the intersection; I hadn't noticed that before.

We stay for an hour, the detectives still taking notes, and I can't tell then—but they've seen something that will help them solve what they have decided is a crime. Interviews and clues over the next year will lead them to a construction site where a man is supposed to work, but never comes. One witness and then another will come forward. And finally, when it seems like nothing will happen at all, and all the glass has been swept up, a man will take a plea to involuntary manslaughter and go away to prison for a year.

All this is months away, hard to imagine. Just as six thousand miles away in Bethlehem, it's hard to imagine that one day my father will sit down to breakfast and have a fatal heart attack, and die before we see each other again.

PART III

A TALE OF TWO CITIES

ONE THING ABOUT BLUE

BY MAUREEN O'LEARY

Oak Park

One thing about Blue, she always had a scheme. The summer after high school I drove a van she got from her cousin who we just called Cousin. Blue got Cousin to take out seats and cut a hole in the floor so I could drive over the metal circle thing at gas stations. I drove and Cousin unscrewed the bolts to siphon diesel. We got the job done six times and Blue knew a guy who drove his own long-haul truck to sell gas to, so there was money to be made. That's something Blue liked to say.

I was afraid of Cousin because he was big and grumpy, but he didn't talk much. I wasn't supposed to drive but Blue said I was smarter than people thought and taught me how, so I became our driver. Nobody suspected me bumping over the metal thing in the middle of the night except for the sleepy-looking man who worked at the 7-Eleven on Broadway in Tahoe Park. He called the police.

Me and Cousin served the time. Blue made the money. I went to County for eighteen months and that's where I got caught in the middle of a bad fight one time and ended up with a ruined face.

Mr. Cox who was my teacher visited right before I got out. I looked messed up compared to before and his eyes wobbled when he first saw me. He had on a nice shirt and I bet his shoes were shined. Mr. Cox always dressed like he was headed somewhere better than room 32, which was where the special-ed kids learned. I felt sorry for him sitting there with a phone to his ear and his red face and his ironed shirt. He liked showing PowerPoints of his vacations. There was a picture of him and his wife at the Grand Canyon and he told us that every year somebody got too close to the edge and fell off because the canyon could hypnotize you if you weren't careful. He also said he got to go to fun places because he worked hard. He said, I work hard and so should you.

He held the phone thing away like he was afraid his lips might touch the plastic. He asked me how I was.

My shirt was not ironed. My shirt was orange and white stripes and I would never enjoy a Creamsicle again in the summertime, I will tell you. The color orange made my teeth hurt forever after two years of that's all I got to wear.

I said I was going home to my mom in Oak Park and he said he gave my name for a job cleaning classrooms at the charter high school there.

You can't be haunted by the past, Georgia, he said, and wouldn't look me too long in the face. He said the most important thing was hard work.

Cutting the circle hole in the bottom of the van was hard work. Sparks flew everywhere. Driving so the hole in the van matched the circle in the ground was hard work. But he didn't need to know all that.

Mr. Cox told me to remember I had a disordered brain. Whenever I thought I found a shortcut, I had to remember it was going to be a disordered shortcut. Period.

Mr. Cox was a nice man. Not a creeper. Nice dresser. Worked hard. Always visited his former students when they were about to get out of jail.

* * *

My first night at the charter-school job, I didn't recognize Blue. I went in to the office and there was a lady standing at the copier, the machine's light going back and forth.

She collected the papers and smiled like she knew something about me. Her hair was blond and in a twist. She also smelled like a whole other person than last time I saw her at Cousin's house in West Sac. Back then her perfume was diesel and french fry grease and her hair was black. Back then she wore Dickies and men's undershirts and a ball cap from Mobil gas. This lady looked like the waitress in the steak restaurant my mom took me to after I got out to celebrate. But this was still Blue. Same face. I would know her no matter what.

I said, I didn't know you worked here, and she smiled without showing any teeth and didn't say anything about my face. She didn't like her teeth because of the gap in the middle, though when we were kids I made her laugh so she couldn't help showing the gap. I loved her teeth.

What I mean to say is I can only tell what happened the best I can, but do not think I will say a word against Blue.

I was supposed to empty trash and dry-mop the floors in the classrooms, yet Blue said no. She told Mr. Cox that there was an opening for a janitor so he would not ask questions, but there was more to the job. *There was money to be made.*

My neck got hot because I hated fighting with Blue. I wasn't mad about my time inside. I made the choice to drive the van. She didn't force me. I never wanted her to suffer same as me. But I didn't want to do her schemes anymore either. I didn't want to get in trouble ever again.

Then she proved herself by showing me the empty rooms with no desks, no garbage cans to dump out, nothing but shiny floors. In the office we ordered clothes for me off Amazon using the school's account. Pencil skirts and high-heel shoes. Button shirts like a steakhouse waitress. Blue gave me an envelope of cash and told me I should deposit the money in a bank. She said I needed to be smart and put my pay in a checking account I could look at online.

Then we went to her apartment in Midtown and she cut off my split ends and dyed my hair blond same as her. After she rinsed out the bleach, she held my head and made me look at us in the mirror side by side, her jaw square and whole, the side of my face looking like I fell into a wall. When I tried to look down, she held me tighter and forced me to look.

You are beautiful, she said. You are smart.

Her long nails scraped the back of my head lightly when she used the blow dryer and her touch made me shiver and want to cry.

She said we had to change our names at the job. She was Bea Andersen. I was Jo Little. We used to call each other Bee and Geo, short for Blue and Georgia, when we were kids, so there would be no slipping.

We're different people now, she said. So we must change our names at work.

Blue dropped me at home at midnight and my mom was waiting with the light on in her room. She worked at Costco and went to meetings four times a week so she got tired a lot. She called for me, lying on her side all tucked in.

She said I smelled funny. She asked who did that to my hair and I said Blue.

She sat up in bed. Please, Georgia, anybody but Blue. And she was crying. I patted her cheeks with my fingertips and I was sorry to make her cry. But Blue was a canyon I fell into just by standing near the edge. Explaining this would not be a comfort, so I said, I love you, Mom. I said, I promise I will stay free.

* * *

I went in a few more nights to dust-mop the already clean floors. I emptied the garbage in the office. The school was big and the classrooms were empty except one hallway had a few rooms with desks in rows, white boards, and signs on the walls saying *Work Hard* and *No Excuses*. The garbage cans never had trash. The boards never had writing.

On Friday, Blue gave me a bottle of Dior perfume and the clothes. She said she had an idea for us. Like she said, there was money. I would get paid way more but I could not tell anybody what we were doing. My ears got hot. I thought about my mom crying in bed. I wanted to go home.

The look on your face, Blue said. Girl. She put her arms around me and I was a baby bird made of light bones and skinny feathers. She was meaty. She smelled like particles and money. Her face was wet pressing against mine and the salt from her tears burned my skin.

Georgia, I owe you, Blue said. I will never hurt you again. Trust me.

I trust you, I said. But I didn't.

I went to work at five o'clock the next day. I was Blue's assistant and she didn't want me to talk to anybody at the meeting. Me being her assistant made her seem like a boss and that was the important thing.

The lobby was big as a parking garage and there were three tables set up in a U around a screen. Blue was making the projector work with a clicker. You look good, she said. She sniffed me. Good perfume, she said. Not too much. Enough. You smell rich.

Her top was silky. Her nails were shiny as vanilla ice cream. She said to pretend to take notes. There was a man coming to the meeting. That is, there were many men coming to the meeting, but only one was important.

How would I know which one was important?

Blue said I would know.

The men were coming in. A wash of them in suits, ties, dress-up shoes that made noise on the concrete. This is the superintendent, Blue said. Mr. Lewis.

Mr. Lewis's eyes were above me watching the door. This was not the important man. The important man was entering with a lady with short blond hair and a purple dress. Her heels clicked on the floor like Blue's. Mr. Lewis greeted the important man who was tall and thin and wore a tie. He was dad age. Grandpa age. He moved like a dancer on television. He wasn't dancing but he moved graceful. When the tall graceful man entered, the other men talked faster, their voices a hum of bees. I became dizzy.

Blue moved me to a seat by the short-hair lady. The important man shook hands with everybody. When he came to Blue, he leaned down to talk in her ear. I wondered what he said. His hand was on her back. She brought him to me.

I'm Jim Bell, he said. I shook his hand firm like my mom taught me. You must be Jo. Ms. Andersen speaks so highly of you.

That's nice, I said.

The meeting started. Mr. Lewis was talking. The blond-hair lady whispered to me, Jim has a Purple Heart from Vietnam. He doesn't like to talk about the war but I think people here should know. Jim is a hero.

Blue showed a video of kids in black polo shirts and tan pants walking into the school. In the lobby there were pictures of kids in black shirts sitting in front of computers and holding basketballs. I never saw these kids. These kids who made no mess, left no garbage, whose teachers never wrote on the whiteboards.

Mr. Lewis was saying the charter high school had the best graduation record for minority kids in the city. The kids in the video walked in slow motion across the lobby. I never saw their footprints when I swept at night.

We send more minority students to four-year colleges than any other school in Northern California. This was Blue now talking. The movie was over and there was a graph with a jagged line full of spikes and valleys. Mountains. Canyons.

The woman whispered next to my face, her breath minty fresh. She said, Jim is the kindest man I have ever known.

Blue said to come in the next day at four p.m. She said to sit at her desk and she would be back soon. I opened her laptop and researched Purple Heart. A medal for bravery. When Jim Bell told the meeting that he planned a substantial donation, the short-hair lady whispered to me, I told you so.

I researched Jim Bell. There was a Jim Bell who was a soccer player in England. The important Jim Bell was in charge of Bell Partners Developing.

A man came in looking mean, and when Mr. Lewis stepped out of his office the man asked where were the students and Mr. Lewis said to remember we were a year-round schedule and this was our fall break. They closed the door and there was stern talking. My head tingled like when people were fighting in jail. Something bad was happening and I was going to get stuck in the middle. I was going to get hit.

I was about to run out when Mr. Lewis banged the door open. He rushed me yelling questions.

What did you do with that permit? You said you filed the permit.

The man behind him shook his head like he couldn't believe someone was as dumb as me. They were mad at me. My face bones hurt. I looked down at my hands.

Goddamnit, Ms. Andersen depended on you. *I* depended on you. This is unacceptable. There are legal repercussions to your mistake, Jo. We can only hope nothing comes of this. We can only pray to God that the city council decides to give us another chance. Do you know what you've done? Do you know?

I clutched my skirt to keep from shaking. I squeezed my eyes closed. The mad man left and nobody said goodbye. Mr. Lewis kept yelling at me. I saw purple hearts bursting.

Suddenly Mr. Lewis stopped yelling and I heard him step into the hall. I heard him go into his office again and close the door.

Blue came in carrying her purse and jacket. I'm fired now, I said. Maybe they will arrest me.

Blue said no and to get my stuff. We were going somewhere fun.

Normally I loved riding around in the front seat when Blue was driving. In high school she took me everywhere and we sang along to the radio. We drove over the Yolo Causeway sometimes because Blue liked to look at the owls that hid in the trees by a dirt road there. On the way back into Sacramento toward the tall buildings coming up out of the flat land, she liked to say that we were headed to the Emerald City, and whenever I was with Blue I could believe that we were.

In the car was where she explained things to me, such as who at school was nice and who was only pretending. Teachers to trust and teachers to avoid. But that night in the passenger seat of Blue's car, the sun was setting and the sky was on pink fire and my stomach hurt from getting in trouble. My head hurt too and I said I felt like I was dying.

Oh baby bird, she said, I wish you didn't feel that way.

She took me to Dutch Brothers for a blue drink, which made me feel better. Don't spill, she said. After we drive, we are going to dinner with Jim.

We took a turn through the Delta by the river that was a broken mirror for the sky that held storm clouds purple as hearts.

This is haunted country, Blue said.

I shivered in the way only she could make me.

She explained things when we got back to town. We're not supposed to have those kinds of meetings on public property, she said. Not without a permission slip.

I didn't know, I said. I tried to remember a permission slip. My mom signed a permission slip for camp at Sly Park when I was in seventh grade. That was all I could think of.

There wasn't one, Blue said. If we filed with the district, we would have had to say what the meeting was for and we can't do that.

I didn't know what she was talking about. The ice cubes rattled in my cup over a bump in the road. They sounded like cracked glass.

We pulled into a parking lot and went into a restaurant. White tablecloths. Candles. Blue said to the lady we were guests of Jim and she brought us to a table where Jim was. He shook my hand and kissed my cheek. I felt that kiss in my body, and even though he was as old as a grandpa, I wondered if he could like me.

Mr. Lewis sends his regrets, Blue said. You just have us tonight.

He told us he was delighted and that we should get what we wanted, and I looked at Blue, who laughed with her teeth out and said we would have steak and shrimp but first we needed red wine.

This is a good night, Jim said. The work you are doing with the charter is really something. You are changing the world. Gives me faith.

Blue touched his arm, her fingernails white beetles on his sleeve. She asked him if he knew how she met me. She said, I met Jo at the Sacramento Children's Home. We were there together. Roommates. She laughed again.

I wiped my mouth. Ran my tongue over my teeth in case there was lettuce there from the salad. In our front room my mom kept a photo of me sleeping on a hospital bed, my bald head covered in a beanie and wires, tubes everywhere. To remind her to never drink again, she said. The red wine burned in my stomach, which was already having a rough day. Jim looked at me. I wondered, Why tell this to the important man? My mom got sent to jail after my brain was injured in her DUI. I didn't like people knowing about me like that. I can hide better if people don't know. I was wondering if maybe Jim could like me, but how could he like me now?

Blue touched my hand under the table where Jim couldn't see. I studied hard and got into Berkeley, she said. I worked to pay my way through and I just want to pay that forward, you know? Give kids like me a chance.

My grandson just graduated from Berkeley, Jim said. I don't suppose you would know him. It's a big school. Franklin Bell?

Blue tapped her finger on her chin. She was thinking. Wait, she said. Alpha Delta Phi?

Jim smiled like he was the happiest man in the world.

Oh, he was way too cool for me, but I knew of him. Everyone knew of him. Great guy, Blue said. Really great guy.

He would be lucky to know you, Jim said. I don't know what happened with your parents, but if you were my daughter, I would be very proud.

When Jim excused himself to the bathroom, I said to Blue, I didn't know you went to Berkeley.

Oh Georgia, she said.

When he came back to the table, Jim wasn't looking at me or caring anything about me. He was falling off the cliff of Blue. The air was filling his jacket. He was dropping through the sky.

When the bill came, Blue grabbed the leather folder thing. This is on me, she said. Your gift to the charter means the entire world to those kids. She blinked back tears, building diamonds on her mascara. I remembered Blue in a ball cap and undershirt in Cousin's backyard off Jefferson Boulevard. We covered our ears as he cut a hole in the van big enough to siphon gas through. She taught me when there was money to be made.

She set her purse on the table and took out a pink wallet. My wallet. I looked down and there was my orange purse we bought on Amazon, open.

Jim tried to insist. Blue didn't care. She signed my name on the bill. The money was everything in the account and more. I did not speak. I felt wind against my face. Jim's blue eyes crinkled at the edges when he smiled at me. We were both lost. And yet me, the one with the injured brain, I was the only one who knew it.

When I got home, my mom called me from her bedroom but I stopped for a minute to look at the pictures on the shelf.

The school photos of when I was little with no front teeth and then up to junior high. In seventh grade I had a big smile because I didn't know what was going to happen.

There's one picture of me and Mom in our backyard and we are happy. That was right after she got out of jail and before I got arrested. There were no pictures of me since being in County but I knew what I looked like. I was broken to pieces in a jail-yard fight and glued back together by a jail infirmary doctor. I had a crescent-moon scar under my eye, and my right cheekbone was sunk so far in my face was crooked.

Sometimes I looked at the girl in the seventh-grade picture who wasn't in the car wreck yet. She didn't have an injured brain yet. She never took a disordered shortcut. What happened to you, girl in seventh grade? She was off at Berkeley, working her way through.

Mom was looking at a show on her iPad with earbuds. She took one out for me so I could watch too. Her body smelled like cinnamon. I rested my head in the soft part of her shoulder and watched that show she was into about bikers with a tough mom who is in charge of everybody.

I worry about you, my mom said into my hair. I remembered that my bank account was empty and my stomach hurt. My mom would be so pissed if she knew. I didn't know why Blue wanted me to pay, but I couldn't be mad. She didn't force me.

Blue didn't tell Jim Bell everything. She didn't tell about how after Sacramento Children's we landed in the same group home on 59th Street with windows that had locks but no bars. She didn't tell about the nights we ran through the park, playing on the swings and singing our favorite songs to the moon.

I'm proud of you getting a job, but Blue is rotten, Mom said. I don't trust her.

I was so tired. My head was full of static. There were gunshots in my right ear from the show and gunshots in my left ear from down the street.

Blue is mine, I said. You can't take her away.

There is one more part to the story. Blue wanted me in at two the next afternoon. I took a long time getting ready. I would be like the lady in my mom's show who was so tough that no one would be mean to her. I would tell Blue to pay me back. No one would yell at me that day. No one would blame anything on me.

When I saw Jim Bell was in the office, I didn't feel so tough anymore. He shook my hand and kissed me on the cheek. He asked me what was wrong. I touched my face and felt the hollow place where the doctors could not fix the tiny fractures in my cheekbone. The wetness on my skin.

You should be careful, I said.

He tilted his head. Blue came into the office then with Mr. Lewis and a boy in a black shirt and tan pants. My head felt sparkling. Something was strange. The boy seemed like someone I knew, but at the same time I did not know him.

This is Nathan, Blue said. He is our student body president.

Jim shook his hand but did not kiss him on the cheek.

We are on a year-round schedule, Mr. Lewis said to Jim Bell. Which means we are on break right now. But I wanted you to get a chance to talk to a student. Get a tour from a young person you are allowing to get a college preparatory education.

The way Mr. Lewis talked made me think of choking. He made me think of drinking sand.

Nathan led Jim Bell on a tour. Mr. Lewis walked alongside with his hands clasped behind his back like he was out for a stroll.

We were going to the rooms with desks.

This is where I take AP calculus, Nathan said.

With enough community support, we could serve every underprivileged student in the city, Mr. Lewis said.

Nathan was applying to MIT. He wanted to study chemical engineering.

Jim looked at his watch and said, I'm proud of you, son. He patted Nathan's shoulder. I was jealous of Nathan. What would make Jim say he was proud of me?

When Jim left, Mr. Lewis walked off and Nathan, Blue, and I were alone.

Hey, Georgia, Nathan said. He had a sideways smile I swear I knew before.

Hey, I said. Pretending like I knew what was going on. I knew how to pretend.

I could pretend all day.

It's Nate, Blue said. Don't you remember him?

Think of me short, he said. Think of me following you guys around and begging you to play with me.

He was Nate from the home. Ten years later. Warm honey flowed through my chest whenever I remembered things I wanted to remember. It was a sweet feeling. A coming-home feeling.

You go here now? I asked.

Blue and he laughed. I'm here now, he said.

Blue wanted to show us something. We went outside to one of the older buildings, one that was round and full of windows. There was a giant stage and red-velvet seats and a balcony. I tried to picture the whole room filled with students and that just made the empty space feel lonely. Behind the curtains Blue flipped a switch for the lights.

We climbed stairs to a room of dusty couches and a window overlooking the stage. There were tools left behind. A screwdriver. A hammer.

Nate said, This place is haunted. I would not come here at night.

Would you for a thousand dollars? Blue asked. She sounded far away. She put her fingers on the window.

No way, said Nate.

Would you for a million? Blue tapped on the glass.

Nate pulled his shirt out of his waistband and said for a million he would. He cracked his knuckles. Blue took the hammer off the ground and smashed the glass. We watched the pieces fall to the stage below and catch the lights like stars.

In the office, Blue wanted my bank password and username.

I didn't say anything.

Then she said, So I can pay you back. You didn't think I was going to pay you back?

Blue taught me how to drive a stick shift. She taught me how to rig a locked window so I could escape at night and climb back in when I wanted. She taught me that the Yum Yum Donuts on Franklin Boulevard put out free donuts by their dumpsters at night. She taught me not to take pills at parties and to protect my drinks and she taught me that somebody cared about me.

Blue hugged me tight. After I got home, I looked into my bank account and there was still minus seventeen dollars and twenty-four cents.

When I went to work the next day, the door was locked.

I texted Blue and got a red *Not Delivered* message. Maybe we were having a day off and nobody told me. My heart was beating fast when I walked home. I had a bad feeling.

That night, Blue tapped on my window. She crawled through and landed on my bed. Her ponytail was black through the back of her ball cap.

She told me I needed to listen. You are beautiful, she said. You are the most beautiful one who ever lived. Please don't forget that. Please don't forget *me*.

I never could, I said. Don't you know that? You are my best friend.

I was going to just leave and not tell you, she said. I thought that might be better for you. But I couldn't help myself. I had to see you.

She would not tell me where she was going. She warned me to never go back to the charter high school. She told me never to try to find her. She told me never to talk to Jim. If I saw him in the street or whatever, I needed to pretend I didn't see him. I needed to pretend I didn't know him.

Dye your hair back to brown, she said.

She hugged me so close she hurt my ribs. My mom called through the wall.

I'm sorry you went to jail, Blue said. It was my fault what happened to you. She put her hand on my face. She patted my messed-up cheek with soft fingers.

I love you, Georgia, she said. Don't forget me, she said, and she was gone.

Mr. Lewis is superintendent someplace else now. The charter school has somebody else in charge. Sometimes I see kids around my neighborhood in black shirts and tan pants and I wonder if they are the kids I never saw in the school. I dreamed I saw Jim Bell. I'm proud of you, he said in my dream. He shook my hand and kissed me on the cheek. I know this will never happen. I don't go the same places Jim Bell goes.

A man came to our house because Jim Bell hired him to find me, which he did through the bank card Blue used to pay for dinner. The man knew about me. Knew about my mom and my brain injury and that I was hurt in County. He wasn't a mean man. He wasn't mad at me. He just had questions.

Do you know where the other woman is? Jim says she went by Bea Andersen. I'm not law enforcement. I just want to talk to her. Jim Bell wants to get some answers. He deserves that, I think. Don't you think he deserves that? The man won a Purple Heart. He thought he was giving money so kids could learn, and instead this woman embezzled the funds. That means she took the money for herself. You're not in trouble. You're as much a victim as he is—that's what Jim says, and I agree.

I said, Please tell Jim I am sorry. I literally don't know.

He left a card. *Sergio Castillo. Private Investigator*. I was glad my mom wasn't home. He never came over again.

One more thing happened.

A year later on a full moon, Cousin who got arrested same as me came to the gym where I work. I give out towels at the desk and keep things nice. My hands smell like cleaner a lot but I like the job. I go by my own name. Coach Carl who owns the gym is nice to me. No one ever yells at me.

Blue's cousin waited by my car after I closed up because he said he wanted to show me something. I went into his van and I saw there was a circle cut out of the floor. Our van from before had been confiscated by the police. This was another van.

I almost said, No thank you, but he told me not to worry. We drove down Highway 99 past Elk Grove and then took an exit past Lodi and went until we hit the river and took that snaky road for over an hour.

I asked if we were going to see Blue. I missed my friend. I wanted her to know that I wasn't mad about her using my bank card to pay for the fancy dinner. I made that five hundred dollars back and more. I worked a lot. My mom wanted me to save up for school but I didn't want to go.

Cousin didn't answer me. We went on a dirt road.

My shoulders got cold. Cousin was never really mean to me, but this wasn't right. I looked at my phone. No signal.

I thought about jumping out while we were moving, but what if I broke my legs? Then Cousin slowed down. Stopped. Looked at his phone. Backed up some. Killed the engine and the lights.

The moon was bright enough to see by. We parked at the edge of a field under a big oak with branches like knuckles. This is it, Cousin said. I ducked because I thought I was going to get hit. He ignored me and went to the back like in the old days. But instead of a bolt tool, he had a posthole digger. He put on a headlamp and pushed the digger into the soft ground, pulling up soil and grass. After a couple clods thrown out the back door, he clanged on metal. He got on his stomach and pulled a box out of the hole.

One thing about Blue, Cousin said. She always tries to make things right.

He put the muddy metal box on my lap. It was a safe with a combination lock.

She called me last night telling where to find it, he said. Half for you, half for me.

I wanted to know how much.

He would not answer but he said that Blue said that I was smart enough to be careful with this amount of money. I couldn't buy a Lamborghini. Nothing flashy that police would notice.

I said okay.

You can't deposit this amount in a regular bank account, he said. The IRS will want to know where the money came from. The police will want to know. Do you hear what I'm saying?

I said I did.

He turned on the radio. Hummed along. More relaxed now. Happy. She told me you're smart, he said. I guess we both are.

We hit the road that snaked along the river, taking the Delta way back to Sac. The moon played around on the surface of the water and I thought, This place is haunted.

I thought, This place is free.

A REFLECTION OF THE PUBLIC

BY WILLIAM T. VOLLMANN

Del Paso Heights

S unny was one of those people who from a petit bourgeois point of view cannot be helped because they
cannot or will not help themselves. (So was Matthew.) From her point of view, life was pleasant. For years she
worked at the coffee shop for not enough pay simply because
she lived next door, so that was easy. Whenever she could,
she stayed at home with the door locked, sleeping or watching television. She was afraid of people. If a windfall came
her way, instead of saving it or fixing her teeth, she'd rescue
another cat or dog, and go without food to pay the veterinary
bills. She almost never took the garbage out. Mold grew on
the dirty dishes in the sink, and the floor was rotten with cat
urine. If she found something on the street, she would take it
triumphantly home to add to her treasures. She was sure that
her battered old chairs were antiques which could bring in
money. Like TRAILBLAZER and Cheney, she lived the op-
timistic life. Her back had been hurting her for years, because
she never exercised and so had gained fifty pounds. A customer who loved her offered to buy her good shoes with in-
soles in them, but she couldn't be bothered to get to the store.
There was a free clinic, but she never got around to making
an appointment, so her back got worse and worse. Customers
gave her marijuana, which was harmless, and when that no
longer rescued her, they gave her miscellaneous pills, so she

medicated herself until she got addicted to this and that. She started coming to work late, and then the proprietress caught her stealing from the till—for her medications, of course. Upon being fired she could not make the rent. The landlady, who pitied her and used to like her, gave her a month to move out, upon which she locked the door and lay in bed. On the last day she departed empty-handed and in tears. It cost the landlady a thousand dollars to have the apartment fumigated and refloored, and another five hundred for the junkman to haul away Sunny's hoarded treasures. Now here she was, living with equanimity in her own filth.

She and Matthew were just friends, but loving friends. He considered her *really, really nice*. When her jailbait niece Tanosha had to run away from a forty-two-year-old boyfriend in Vallejo, Sunny happened to be at the hospital getting her stomach pumped, so it was Matthew who took the call on Sunny's cell phone and met Tanosha at the bus stop down the street. He showed her where Sunny's tent was and introduced her to West and his other friends. —I feel dirty just being here, she said in disgust. I mean, why doesn't anyone pick up the garbage? —Yeah, I, I'm really sorry, he said, and it speaks well of his modesty that he never mentioned his effort to do just that. Once in a while, you see, E.S. used to advise him that he was in need of an *attitude adjustment*. Of course that was so; we could all do with one, especially the enemy. Proudly denying E.S. the opportunity to adjust him, Matthew remained, as you might have noticed, quite prepared to submit himself to various other adjusters, which in this case included the rotting food and excrement left in plastic bags which formed hillocks here and there, playgrounds for rats, roaches, and disease. And here it might as well be noted that although America's homeless, or at least the ones who survived, were at least as ingenious as they needed to be, the wastes from which they foraged were of such luxurious comparative quantity and quality—almost-new shoes, tarps, blankets, and watermelons for the taking!—that while a curious *citizen* might sometimes discover hidden behind grapevines on some riverbank a carefully constructed shanty, maybe even showing off glass or plastic windows, when it came to anything more portable than that, here in America the taking was far more practical than the making, unlike in, for instance, Bagram Air Base, where numbers of our cunning Afghan detainees fashioned shoes out of orange prison scrubs; and come 2021, when the Taliban finally retook the country, ever so many orange shoes could be found in the ruins of Bagram, whose cells were convenient to enter now, thanks to the holes which the Talibs had made in the walls while freeing their Al Qaeda colleagues; whereas in the open slum where Matthew lived, there were very few locally manufactured items to be seen, aside from a couple of handmade crack stems made by old-timey addicts, and maybe every now and then a sharpened screwdriver or other improvised weapon, most evidence of human habitation consisting of those stinking hillocks of plastic bags; sometimes they heaved like sea waves, thanks to hungry rats within. Even Matthew felt oppressed by the stench—what was he to do? Why, adjust his attitude, of course—remembering that he liked *dirty jobs*, he took up the topmost bag and threw it over his shoulder. It dribbled a feculent liquid down his back, but he kept himself in mind of Hui: *One bamboo dish of rice, one ladle full of drink, living in a wretched lane, others couldn't have stood it.* In other words, Matthew was still *going straight!* His arms and legs glowed with labor happiness. Six blocks later he found an unlocked garbage bin behind a supermarket, looked right and left, then discreetly left his offering. He took a bag a day there for a week, but after that the garbage bin started to be locked. Nor did any of the neighbors help him. —Look, said West, it goes against my principles to enable all these litterbugs. Besides, it's pointless. And one day a demented man not entirely un-like Michael but maybe more dangerous snarled at Matthew that he had better *keep your fucking hands off my fucking garbage, 'cause it's mine!* Moreover, K.J. was furious at the locking up of, or at least so he alleged, his *main food supply.* —Sorry, said Matthew, and I can save up to buy you some bolt cutters, or if you just want the money for . . . —Finally, said K.J., a man who takes responsibility! I want fifty dollars, and until you get it, I expect you to feed me. Sunny's friend Tannika was about to in her words *go off on him,* but Matthew had dealt with such challenges for years, so he respectfully murmured: K.J., if you walk a few steps with me, I might have something for you . . . And he solved their differences with another apology and a baggie of meth about which he most fortunately had not told his friends, at which K.J. hugged and forgave him as follows: I don't talk about this with many people, but my best buddy was shot in the head, and I carried his body for two klicks, back to Camp Lejeune. Wasn't anything he wouldn't have done for me. And you know what? I'm sixty-four years old, and you see how I put my eye out when I had a stroke and fell right onto the bedpost, but if they asked me to be a soldier again, I'd do it in a heartbeat. Freedom ain't free, bro; just ask a vet. I came into this world alone and I'll leave it alone, but you know what I have, Matt? *America's* with me. I love America so much, bro. In consequence of which, Matthew gave up on sanitation, and heaved his refuse right with the rest of them; the first time he did it three people even applauded, which was how he knew he was still *going straight.*

The best part was that he now realized that even though his other friends disliked the man, K.J. was *wonderful.* — Snort a little crystal, said this *really nice* individual. Here you go—no, buddy, it's on me. Have a seat right there on the picnic cooler while I kind of stretch out and . . . You never served, now, did you? I can always tell. You just don't carry no discipline in your bones. —Well, my father . . . replied Matthew, astonishing himself. —Air force? inquired K.J. — How did you know? —I always do, the tweaker replied. And since he served, well then, he knows: anyone that's been overseas, they go from *hero to zero* real quick. —I'm already a zero, confided Matthew. Most people got weirded out or they feel sorry for me, but I know I can tell *you.* —You can tell me anything, Matt. And someday maybe you'll even come around to working with the president. You know what I like the most about him? He always tells it like it is. —Yeah, said Matthew, thanking K.J. and wondering whether Tannika liked him. That morning while touching himself in his tent, he had pretended that his hands were hers. He was pretty happy here, aside from the stink. Whenever he began worrying that continuing on as he was might not be the best way to keep *going straight,* the Ute woman Josephine's assurance shone out comfortably from his notebook: *As long as we're not hurting others, the sun will shine bright.* So the year kept passing right through him, and in December a reporter and photographer who claimed to represent the *Sacramento Bee* wandered wide-eyed through the squalor. Matthew hid in his tent. Then the cold weather finally came—cold at least for California—thereby reducing not only the number of people in the camp but also the stench's carrying power, so that Matthew could sum up the matter of sanitation more or less after TRAILBLAZER's immortal wrap-up of the Iraq War:

MISSION ACCOMPLISHED. —Sorry about that, was all he said to Tanosha. When he was about to go home to his tent, the girl wept for loneliness, so he stayed and chatted with her. —And egrets, sure, he said. I've been around a lot of those . . . And smiled to recall circling around Lost Isle with Audrey, grateful for her hand on his thigh and the smoothly groaning ride through the water; there had been palm trees like watchtowers peering out; and an old dark car came rolling along the levee road, trailing them, flashing past tree-screened logs as Tanosha said: Is it true that they sound like what you would imagine a pterodactyl would be like? Matthew thought about that. Then he said: Well, I, honestly, I don't know about dinosaurs. Maybe I should, since I, I, when I was a kid I went to the science museum in Pittsburgh.

When Sunny got back she was much impressed, and praised Matthew to all the neighbors: And you know what? He didn't even try to jump that little bitch's bones. Now that's what I call a motherfucking gentleman.

Sunny had an occasional girlfriend named Lorabel, who told him: I think that this place is a reflection of the public. I believe the public doesn't wanna see the sores on the world or whatever. Everybody just needs to help everybody . . .

Then is it okay if I ask something?

Sure, honey.

What's your idea of what America should be?

America is the Land of the Free. So everything should be free—well, free to have the rights to have housing of some sort. If they have housing, why is this going on? This tent city started farther down on Stockton Boulevard and then they crushed us out of that place . . .

Still hoping that he could uncover more of the American idea than this, as he maybe could have, Matthew smiled in polite disappointment, and three more years went by. Ashamed to be homeless, he rarely visited his aunt.

He tried not to think about Karl anymore, except sometimes to wish that he had been a better son to that old man. But frequently he would think or dream about going through the tules to Suzy's and the dogs rushing and growling, until they would remember his smell and commence snarling and licking him at the same time; he found the white bitch especially pretty, and Suzy said: Oh, she *likes* Matt; she won't even let *me* touch her, but look at her now . . . ! And he had felt proudly special. Sadie and Valentine had loved him better than they loved Audrey, probably because she had been too *restless* to stay in America and work with them as much as he had. And, speaking of love, he was getting interested in Tannika, who encouraged him. She told him that she would *do anything*, and he promised her the same, so that it seemed like the perfect adventure for Mr. and Mrs. Hui to anticipate in their leaky hut on the wretched lane in the *Analects*. Meanwhile, Matthew wanted to talk with West about *The Grapes of Wrath* and that Weedpatch camp in Arvin, because at Weedpatch, at least according to Steinbeck, there had been something like cleanliness, safety, community, and democracy. So didn't they have that here, in which case was this the true good America of his seeking?

The thing about those Okies, said West, was that they were all fucking rednecks. You think they would have cut *me* a break? —I don't know, said Matthew. —Why don't you know? You don't think Tom Joad must've been a racist? —The reason I don't know is because I'm *stupid*. But I want to believe in, you know, something good. —Be my guest, brother. Just don't spoonfeed me that crap. So Matthew kept quiet again.

Instead of a new notebook, he now kept pieces of scrap paper in his pocket for when he would go to the library, which activity still made him feel as *au courant* as had the Stasi's mole Günter Guillaume when, as yet unexposed, he rhapsodized: *There were days when the information exchange with the world's political centers assumed such dimensions that I felt . . . intoxicated by the implications of the rising possibilities for my own information-gathering activities*; and one of these loose sheets Matthew pulled out the next time he dropped by to smoke meth in K.J.'s tent, thereby teleporting them both back to that July in 1788 when North Carolina was debating the proposed Constitution, when a certain Reverend Caldwell *thought some danger might arise* on account of the Founding Fathers's refusal to make Christianity our national religion. *In the first place, he said, there was an invitation for Jews, and Pagans of every kind, to come among us.* —He's not wrong, said K.J. That's why we need to make America great again. Goddamnit, Matt, when will you finally wake up and see your own interest?

Although he never felt as he had when he lived in his own America—namely, that he was living exactly how and where he should—occasionally he did now get to cuddle up with Tannika. She invited him in for a night, and then for the day after, but after that she had to make some money. Two mornings later she crawled into his tent and began frantically kissing him, with the pupils of her beautiful eyes so huge he called her *Star Child*. To him she was what bygone William Bartram (whom he still occasionally discussed with his notebook) would have called *charming*. Oh, she was! She admitted to having been a thief every now and then, but promised not to steal from him, and she never did. What kind of love was best for him? Thanks to his *solid talent*, maybe almost any

kind! So why not Tannika? —She's a fireball, chuckled West,
although K.J. advised him to *remember your white pride*. —
Baby, she said, I'm lonely, and so are you, so why not hook up?
He suspected that something significant had just been offered
to him, although he could refuse it without consequences,
except that maybe nothing worthwhile would ever come to
him again; but since he did not know this for a fact, he wrote
it off as a mere stoned and ominous musing. Meanwhile, they
were having fun. They both sought out that typical marijuana effect, the expansion of everything, so that fucking her
in between inhalations of extra-strong sativa introduced him
to the sudden immensity of her cunt, which could have been
a canyon of pink sandstone split deep and narrow at the horizon's edge for him to plumb with his ten-mile erection which
went slowly in and out, taking an hour or maybe a century for
each thrust into what he now thought of as her hundred-mile
red smell or her thousand-mile *underwater concerto*, every in
and out of which differed from anything in the universe before, because sometimes she drew up her left knee in order to
tighten her slit, or moaned in a brand-new way, or caressed
his back instead of his face; this was almost like being back
in the empire of hissing tules; how could he keep up with it
all? Nor even *should* he—for as Jung once explained about
the neuroses of his patients: *I have made it a rule myself to
consider every case an entirely new proposition about which I do
not even know the ABC*; and having now entered that into his
notebook, he tried to apply it to *everything*, not knowing that
E.S. had also liked it and even when he was young tried to
go by it at the office. Again she opened her legs for Matthew
to kiss her, and this time it seemed to him (for now he was
extremely stoned on an indica-sativa hybrid) almost as if he
were back at Aunt Denise's baking persimmon bread, and he

now pulled open the oven door, ready to conduct a fork test of the mahogany-colored loaf, whose perfume was of cinnamon, vanilla, nutmeg, dark-brown sugar, whole wheat flour, and pureéd fruit, all hot and moist against his face in the perfect ripeness of present time, which of course was actually as past as those days when he could still pass for a damaged but guidable boy, for what could he now hope for from this sweet old relative but pity, or at best resigned tolerance? Now the loaf was out of the oven, Aunt Denise had praised it, he had scrubbed the bowls and baking pan, dinner and its dishes were likewise history, Aunt Denise lay on her recliner snoring over a simulcast version of some Berg opera, with her glasses halfway down her nose, and Matthew had stretched out on the futon in the guest room, which was across the hall from Cousin Amy's bedroom; after thinking about Abu Ghraib, he lay gazing out the sixteen-pane window at the slate-blue and peach inflammations of the November dusk; then Jessica came into his mind, so he began touching himself until he realized that what he actually felt was Tannika's hard, sweaty, experienced hand as the door to her oven opened wider and wider and he plunged into her fresh-bakedness. Happily lost, he buzzed all over her like a cheerful bottlefly. After her third climax and his second, he tried to consider whether it had ever been like this with Audrey, which question precipitated him into sleep. In the morning he decided that it had, which was nothing against Tannika. Anyhow, when had she ever pretended that he was different from the others? And there had been legions of those, for she rented out her pussy from time to time, although right now she house-sat for a kind of living which she was not about to risk losing by smuggling Matthew into one of her establishments as Jessica used to do. In March he turned thirty-four and told no one. Then the lovemaking grew less frenzied, maybe because they were economizing on meth. In April he studied up on Guantánamo at the library, and in June it struck him that she wasn't so much of a bad fuck as a tired one. Sniffing at himself, he perceived that he might not be the most attractive bedmate, so he rode three buses to the river with Sunny, in order that they could take turns watching each other's shoes, money, and identification cards while one of them bathed, fully clothed, scrubbing inside and outside with dishwashing soap. After smoking too much hash, he got happily confused as he scrubbed, and began supposing that he was eating gingerbread pussy, and Sunny kept giggling: Honey, you're a kook but you sure are fun! Afterward he itched and itched but at least he was clean for Tannika, who was by nature so clean that even when she was dirty, he never minded. Then she did desire him more, so he was grateful and decided to adore her, at which point he perceived what a beautiful person she was. They smoked more shatter, and through the consequent slowing down, he could better perceive the texture, not merely of music but of what seemed to be everything he could sense. When he went down on her, his tongue went more slowly, registering the separate existences of the big lips and the little ones, the inside of the slit, the inverted-V-shaped plateau just above it, the shy clitoris; while his finger inside found four distinct rings of muscle. Once he commenced riding her, he could gather just as many complexities from moving his tongue inside her mouth, while her beautiful brown-eyed face was its own infinity. There came a night when she wept in his arms and repented allowing the doctor to tie her tubes after her third crack baby because she wanted to carry his child in her womb. Well, Jessica and Liz used to say the same thing, but it was still sweet, so he said: That's okay, because I'll be

your baby and you can be mine. When she fell asleep, he lay
with her head pillowed in his arm as he thought about Aunt
Denise's past (he almost never thought about Cousin Amy),
wondered whether Jessica had died or gotten sober, and remembered from what he now called his *best time* the freshness
of winds in his face all through a certain happy night, when he
lay beside Audrey in her little boat, just offshore of America.

All the boarded-up homes and everything, Lorabel was
saying, I see people come ask me for help with Code Enforcement. I met with the city attorney at the police department
at Del Paso Heights and I had papers to prove that so-and-so
has been my payee for years and years and years. Well, they
took my work away saying I been homeless. Well, how can
I be homeless when I been paying my mortgage? Well, they
moved me out to a hotel way out there in East Sac, so I
couldn't meet my insurance adjuster, and then Code Enforcement pulled my house down. I went to triage and I tried that,
and my dog and me, they took her to the animal control for
being vicious and they put her to sleep.

Let it go, girl, said Sunny. You always got your spot with me.

Lorabel could not get over the death of her dog. This
and the razing of her house reminded Matthew of what had
happened to Suzy. Jacob Rosen, who sought to *represent the
homeless as a class*, could with *high* probability have explained
how common this was and what it signified. Then Matthew's
approaching lesson about freedom and property grew imminent, but first he needed Tannika to keep calling him her *little
cherub*, because a morning had come in which she threw her
arms wide apart when she smiled at him, with such love in
her face that he felt warmly at home within her heart, safe,
rested, nourished, and ready for a long gentleness. The more
he saw that smile, the more beautiful it became to him. It

was giving, and her eyes were happy and aware. Maybe he had finally found where he was supposed to be. Although he so much needed to love and be loved again, it had begun to seem as if he had reached the end of all that, as he had now reached the end of America-hunting or even traveling at all; and then it had happened; once more a woman's grace illuminated him, with the same beautiful unlikeliness as that tiny kumquat which he had seen growing up a grapevine in the Underground Gardens of Fresno. He kissed her lovely sweaty neck. He inhaled the fragrance of her sweaty hair; and every time he stood guard while she squatted behind a bush or garbage bin, he felt so joyous that he could be a help to her as he had once been for Jessica (and in fact he had a sweet dream of being in a tent with Jessica and kissing her cold wet feet, after which he woke up realizing that this had been a mysterious inversion of the time when *his* feet had been wet and loving Jessica gave him her own warm dry socks). At the beginning of August, when Tannika felt as she put it *crusty and itchy and just plain nasty*, they asked Sunny and West to watch their belongings, borrowed a grimy half cake of soap from Lorabel, and set out to bathe on that honey-rich, hundred-degree summer evening, with dogs snortingly swimming in the rippling river between the bike bridge and the train bridge, and footprints in the sand now filling with shadow, people's shadows long and then longer, radios strangely muffled by the humidity, a few empty bottles at the river's edge, a can of tomato juice, rags. They stripped to his sneakers and underpants, her sandals, bra, and panties. They hid their money and drugs in their clothes, and he rolled a boulder on top. Then they waded out into the water. —Baby, this is motherfuckin' romantic! said his goddess as he held her against him, rubbing her down with soap and cool river water while he kept his gaze on their clothes. After soaping him, he slid her hand down his underpants, and he remembered what he and Audrey used to do to each other when they were swimming in the slough by Karl's island. —You look kind of far away, said Tannika. They took turns ducking their heads underwater and washing their hair, while a fire engine sounded across the river. Then he retrieved their clothes and laundered them. She sat on a rock with their valuables, smiling and waving to him.

Feeling as his Grandpa Dale used to say *like a million bucks* (could *he* still be alive?), they headed for the bushes, with his arm around her sweet hips.

They were still together in time for the early Thanksgiving party at that place called the Island, where Tannika used to live with two of her boyfriends, so she knew all about it and led him there along with Lorabel, K.J., and Sunny (West refused to go on account of his unstated *principles*). Their host was a middle-aged Latino in jeans and worn polyester fleece; his name was Pat. He said that sometimes he didn't want to do this anymore, but every time he tried to bow out, God dragged him back. This year the Department of Parks and Recreation had threatened him with a fine for Health and Human Services violations related to serving food to hungry human beings. (*Why?* asked Matthew. —No idea, said Pat.) He got a permit for six hundred dollars and then Health and Human Services said he didn't need it. Parks and Recreation said his name would be on the attorney general's desk for prosecution, and he said go ahead. He never heard back from the attorney general. These were the stories that Pat told.

Matthew asked for something to do, maybe even a *dirty job*, so Pat told him to pack the juices and coffees in the two big coolers and layer them with ice. He and Sunny started working happily, facing each other over the coolers, while

Tannika laid out paper plates, danced and hugged everybody, the most intimate embraces being applied to two just-arrived ball-capped young men, one Black and one Latino; the Black man wore his army pack and uniform, as if he'd just come straight back from our good war in Eye-Rack. West talked about that war all the time. And Tannika went on dancing with the man in uniform. Matthew felt more sad than jealous. Maybe she was leaving him right now. Then Jacob Rosen arrived; he was rinsing out a big juice pot while Pat and Tannika were passing back and forth big bags of food. The sign said, *NO DRUGS AND NO ALCOHOL*; what was the world coming to? Then Tannika whirled over to say: *Baby, you're the one!* and kissed him until the two ball-capped young men applauded. They all had turkey on paper plates, and for dessert Tannika and Matthew went hand in hand behind the restrooms to smoke marijuana in defiance of the *NO DRUGS* sign so they could better apprehend the mellow sun on the fallen leaves and the pretty long shadows on the grass. Pat turned on the microphone to say: *I pray to the Lord to help everybody remember this is a community and you all need each other.*

A TEXTBOOK EXAMPLE

BY LUIS AVALOS

Broderick

Three crumpled stickers had already made their way into my pockets as I scratched the name *Danny* onto another one. Students behind me were engaged in chitchat, picking at snacks, and drinking from small soda cans. All of them were a variation of Latino—some looked sporty, others were framed by timid glasses, and most were full of anxious energy—but none of them were focused on my desperate scribblings. Instead, they'd found their own ways to pass the time: checking their phones, fidgeting, scanning the size of the meeting room, or looking straight down toward their restless heels as they tapped against sterile linoleum.

"I know they caught him," said one, "but what if this is just a setup?"

"Yeah," said another, "we'd all look pretty dumb when they took our mug shots."

The group laughed. They struggled to push time forward in this way, to move the needle of progress along, and yet I saw myself at the edge of this little world known as a support group. Time spun much more quickly for me as the threat of graduation loomed above, just waiting to throw me into the uncertainty of the job market in a few months. I felt bad for them. Some of them had only just begun their college careers, and there I was, about to complete a PhD in psychology. I sat there, mouth agape, until finally, one of my other, younger reflections nudged me back into existence. Out of embarrassment, I lost the urge to talk, but someone in the circle reminded me that this would likely be the only time we could share this space, in this way, together.

"So where did you start?" asked my therapist, May.

Where I work: the social sciences and humanities building. In that terrible maze commonly known as the Death Star. I was in my office, knee-deep in research, studying the effects of framing and negative bias. A few weeks away from finalizing my findings, I was to present to my chair in support of the idea that our minds are hardwired toward negativity. I was feeling the crunch, however, the vastness of variables, the puddles of flat water that dripped from open cans of Liquid Death, and an impossible number of questions left unanswered. I tried to focus, though all I could see was a chamber of endless Excel sheets, a wormhole of spiraling columns and rows with empty figures.

It would be so easy, I thought, *to just lie down on the couch*. I could feel that corner of the room tempting me. That's when my colleague in suffering, Vic(kie), stormed into the office, all in a huff. Her dark skin was like twilight, with a cold blush and an undertone similar to sapphires. The scent of strawberry vape escaped from the folds of her multicolored checkered scarf. Her curly braids seemed to sway with the motion of her whims. The palms of her hands were reddened by the weight of a Dunkin' Donuts box and two Electric Berry Rebel drinks. I could see her desperation in those trembling hands as she placed our snacks on the table.

"Danny," she said, "there's been a stabbing,"

I prepared myself for another distraction. I assumed this was the latest in celebrity gossip or perhaps an event that had made the national news. It had been like this since the moment I stepped back into Davis. First, it was the billowing stacks of smoke and ash from nearby fires; the following year it was COVID; this year, we began with the university strikes; and last quarter, we returned to a storm that brought down trees, pummeled houses and cars alike, and the school decided it was just one more thing to overcome. Despite all the debris, I often found myself beside Vic, flipping the light switches, desperately straining ourselves to find the optimal study environment in this dingy little office. Perhaps, in another time, one would think that this was a city on the verge of madness, but for us it was just another Thursday. We told ourselves the undergrads had it worse. Neither of us had to wait outside of an apartment complex with tents and blankets just to secure a lease. Nor did we ride our bikes through splintered branches, or suddenly sink beneath an underpass, or walk through ash-filled clouds with lungs wide open.

"What do you want me to do about it?" I asked.

"I want you to walk me to my car," she said.

"Wait, you're serious."

"They found him upright on a bench," she said as her keys rattled.

"When?"

"I don't know," she said. "It just says some lady saw a suspicious man sitting still on a bench in the middle of Central Park. So she called in a welfare check."

We packed our bags, turned off the lights, and called it a night. I carried the ice-cold drinks; she held a box of donuts. As we walked, our voices echoed against the dampened streets as if trying to scare off wild animals.

"Why was he suspicious?" I asked.

"I don't know, maybe he was houseless. Have you seen

how people talk about them on Nextdoor? It's kind of why I don't trust Californians."

"Fair enough," I chuckled. "Still, this is a small town—that sort of thing isn't common here."

"It just feels too calculated," she said in a hushed voice.

She was leaping to conclusions, but I couldn't blame her. Davis was mostly made up of upper-middle-class white people and Vic was always made to feel as if she stood out. I remember our first conference together, the squirming tanned bodies, the darting eyes that hid behind bushy gray brows, the shift of shoulders that pulled away as soon as she approached. It didn't help that she was an out-of-state student, unaccustomed to curt greetings, awkward silences, and stilted subtext. It was natural to be skeptical of a city that seemed to be fueled by false niceties and words left unspoken.

"Well, the person they found is a guy," I said. "So if the killer pops up, he'll likely see me first, with my hair todo peludo, and you can get a head start."

Vic let out a small huff of laughter, but she couldn't release her tense smile.

Vintage dahlia street posts led the way with a line of warm round orbs that splashed across wet concrete. We were only a few blocks away from the incident. We kept a steady pace, half expecting someone to jump out of the shrubbery. The bubbles of light gave some comfort; they felt like a visible range we could use to anticipate movement. I couldn't help but stare at the elongated shadows ahead of us as we made our way to our cars.

"You sure you don't want to take some food with you?" Vic asked.

"No thanks," I said. "That's all sugar."

"America runs on Dunkin'."

"That was during the depression," I said.

"What's the difference? Aren't we all, just a little?"

She got in her car and waited for my headlights to flick on before she started her engine. I knew she did this to be considerate, and yet I couldn't help but think she recognized how much I wanted to snoop around, or worse, stay on campus and continue the work we'd put aside. I waved as I watched her leave the parking lot and I made my way toward Sacramento. The glimmering lights of the city felt like a false promise of civilization.

I slept in the next day, brushing away my phone as it accumulated messages. It was my day off, after all. Didn't want to do a damn thing but stare at the ceiling. It reminded me of my time as a dropout, when all I could muster was to be a shut-in. I often hid in my sheets and watched the shadows beneath the door as my housemates crossed in and out of the hallway. The shadows grew heavier as my belly begged for sustenance, but I couldn't get myself to open that door out of shame.

Living alone, in my bare matchstick studio, I was free from embarrassment. I could get up when I pleased, leave my belongings spread across the floor, and eat a week-old chicken sando from Hotboys without a single person ready to question me when I decided to get up. I crawled through my dirty clothes, overwatered my dying plants, kept the blinds closed from the rest of the world, and embraced the silhouettes of silvery light that seeped into my room. It was a perfect little spot in Broderick, not too far from the university, yet close enough to the low side of the levee that I could afford my own space.

It wasn't until the late afternoon that I stepped out of the house to meet my friend Luci. The clouds were tight and compact, which gave a sharp contrast to a city layered with sheet metal, pavement, worn-down brick, imported trees, and neon graffiti. And in that sky, I began to see the empty spaces of an Excel sheet. Tower Bridge became a series of plot points on a graph that led me toward Downtown. Yet no matter where the empty space led me, I could still distinguish which side of the tracks I stood on. If anything, the city divisions had been made clearer. It was hard to stand still as I waited for Luci to appear. Perhaps it was the grit between the cracks, or the hollers of passersby that kept the city running. I could almost hear Vic's warm voice as she described the World's Worst Expo or Sol Blume in May. There was an intimacy among the people, some acknowledgment to be found from the eye contact of a friendly stranger.

Finally, Luci appeared, walking briskly toward me. He wore slick brown boots, a faded denim jacket, and corduroys. A hipster at heart, I expected to talk about some obscure movie, our vinyl discoveries, or some new game. We hugged one another like brothers who had survived a war. And once we finished greeting, he grabbed me by the shoulder.

"You check the UC Davis Reddit?" he asked.

"Who's got time for all that gossip?" I said.

"No, bro, the person who was killed," he said. "It was Compassion Guy."

"Not *him*," I said.

It took me a moment to catch my breath. We sat down softly on a concrete bench to reminisce. I imagined Compassion Guy as he'd been that summer, in a white tee, loose shorts, and orthotic sandals. The gray streaks of his hair flopping about as he jotted down another thought about compassion in his spiral notebook. I thought of all the people who would pass by, ignore him, hold their breath as they crossed 3rd and C.

"He was there, ever since you and I first started at Davis," Luci said.

"How many times did we wave at him?" I asked.

"Probably not enough. We barely knew him, and yet he was always ready to brighten anyone's day."

"You know, the moment my classmate mentioned it, I had a feeling," I said. "But I didn't want to believe it, I just hoped it was some other guy on a bench. Just awful."

"It's heartbreaking, is what it is. No one deserves that."

"I know. When did he start sleeping on those benches?"

"Hey," he said, "cut it out. Do you know what it'll look like if you start roaming around, looking for clues like you're Scooby-fucking-Doo?"

"More like Latinx Shaggy," I said as I tousled my hair.

"Be serious."

"Look, man, I don't have class for the next few days and we're about to hit the weekend anyway. By the time I get back, they'll have probably caught whoever it is."

"Fine."

"Come on, buddy, you know me," I said. "All my hours are spent in the Death Star anyway. I can barely find my way out of that damn office."

"Just be careful out there," Luci said.

When I got home, I began scouring the websites. It was sad that there was so little to be found on the news. All of them gave the same trinkets of information that leaned one way or the other. None of them quite captured him, yet I couldn't either. In a way I felt like his counterpart—the cynicism I held toward humanity could easily be found in any comment section. The forums were a clear indication of an agitated city. The parks were now "danger zones," and the campus was nearly "vacant," and everyone had something to say. Each comment spooled out like a rattlesnake from a creosote bush. I gave my sacrifice to the doom-scrolling gods, and felt the technocrats slowly taking over the city as I lost track of time. I tried to take my mind off it, rearranging the room in every which way but satisfied.

When it was time to return to Davis, an email came in at six in the morning informing everyone on campus that a second homicide had occurred the previous night. This time, the victim was a student named Karim; his hair was much like my own, but his beard was scruffy, and he seemed vibrant, filled with all the enthusiasm of a student nearing graduation. We were told to be cautious, to trust our instincts, to walk in groups, to avoid people and situations that made us nervous. The description read, *Suspect(s): Hispanic male adult, light-skinned, 5'7" to 5'8", 19-23 years of age, with long curly black loose hair. White shirt, Adidas pants.* How many times have people played the guessing game with my age? Or complimented my curly black hair? I'd always thought my skin was a bit on the darker side, but isn't that relative? If a cop saw me walking down the street, would he say, *Close enough?*

The drive to campus was long and construction made it worse. My car leaned toward the Jersey barrier in response to my unsteady hands. The yellow tickers flashed by as I pressed forward, trying not to scrape against a wall. With every turn, I felt more constricted, the lanes narrower. The drivers reeked of desperation, whizzing past at seventy, eighty, ninety, only to find themselves breaking a mere hundred feet ahead. Clenched fists beat the tops of their headliners and palms slammed against their steering wheels. It's no wonder this city is home to some of the worst drivers in the country. As I took the exit to Davis, I contemplated passing C Street. But it was too late; Luci's warning resonated as I imagined myself roaming through the streets. So instead, I went around the perimeter of Downtown, took to the residential roads, and avoided even the faintest glimmer of Central Park.

Alertness had ground me down to a nervous mess before I could even reach the parking structure. The grainy concrete and sharp angles left me isolated, in the dark, looking over my shoulder to gauge the mood of passersby. I stalled for time and looked at my phone. *Maybe you should stay home today,* said one text message. *Stay safe buddy,* said another. *Maybe it's time you rock a manbun,* said the last. I peered at myself in the rearview mirror as I parted my locks. *If I change my hair now, won't people be more suspicious of me?*

As usual, I made my way toward Memorial Union, the beating heart of campus. Students poured in and out of the building, bought their breakfasts, sat in the communal study areas, or waited in line for free groceries next to the Pantry. I couldn't help but notice the clusters of people, that no one seemed alone. Some moved in packs, others kept their laptops face-to-face, even a few pencils shook in synchronicity. And the closer I stepped toward any area, the more likely I was to create a wave of bobbing heads that would size me up. Every glance became a lingering thought, every phone was a possible call. How could I trust my instincts when every whisper carried an air of suspicion? At the market, I looked through the snacks I rarely bought. I stumbled through every gesture as I struggled to recollect what *normal* meant for me. I bought myself another can of Liquid Death and could not help but remark, "It's all just in poor taste." The cashier gave me an odd look, and I left without an explanation.

Outside, the gray sky became blinding, all-encompassing.

The roads were busy with the usual swarm of bikers, but the sidewalks were sparse. The students who normally waited outside for classes were gone, and everyone else seemed to have a direction in mind. I thought this would make it easier to avoid people. But the architect who'd built the Death Star never had an easy passage in mind. Visitors are often forced to ask for directions, since many of the sections lead outside and there are no obvious indicators to designate how or where the room numbers continue sequentially. And for those more experienced, the door locks rotate every so often, so you don't grow accustomed to any single route. Even the colloquially named "panic buttons" are meant to push you toward socialization.

I knew all of this, and yet I couldn't help but feel accosted by all the faces, even the familiar ones. It was as if my absence had been a pressure cooker of interest, especially among my peers. *I knew it wasn't you, that you'd never, that you're too kind*, they smiled. *But that new description, I couldn't help but think of you.* Every which way I turned, I heard another iteration of this comment—in the lobby, in slanted hallways, next to locked doors, in front of staircases that led nowhere, in the glassed-in catwalk, and before class began. I tried to understand the urge from my classmates, their inability to resist bringing up our similarity before they could move on. But I couldn't blame them either. I had my own list of students who resembled the profile, my own dossier of random people who happened to wear Adidas pants that morning, and my own list of people I wanted to comfort. How many rooms would it take to bring in all the "light-skinned Hispanics" with curly black hair for a therapy session? It sounds like the beginning of a convoluted joke, doesn't it?

When lectures began, I sat at the back of the class.

"How's everyone holding up?" asked the professor. For a

moment, I swore I caught a glance, but I brushed it off as my imagination. "I would be remiss to not bring this up with everything that has occurred, but if there's anything you'd like to talk about, please feel free to reach out to me."

I felt bad for the professors—they weren't being paid for the emotional labor. I wondered how many times a teacher started class this way, how many students responded, how many slipped away when no one was looking. Luci had certainly seen me duck out during my undergraduate career when advisors, faculty, and professors talked at me. I recalled my first day in class at Davis as a biology major. When the lights went out and the seminar began, the professor had spoken as if making a promise: *Look to your right, look to your left—before the end of the year, only two of you may remain. At the end of year three, it will likely only be one.* This, too, was by design; call it a dismissal, a weeding-out, a culling. And I was the ghost who looked at the shadows of students; how their heads bowed toward their notebooks, how they stretched against their tip-up seats, and how the restless rows and rows and rows of students shifted in discomfort.

By evening I was shaky with pent-up energy. I needed to tire myself out. So I went to the pickup games by Toomey Field. I stretched, ran around the track, and waited for others to show. I drank another can of Liquid Death and took in the air of freshly cut grass. When some familiar faces finally arrived, they smiled, waved, and beckoned me in.

"Haven't seen you in a while," said Josue. "Where have you been?"

My hair prickled. "Out stabbing people."

"I was just about to tell you," he laughed, "you're on my team today. I don't want any problems."

"And what about you," I mocked, "is that a new cut or are you getting a little thin up top?"

"It's my new regimen," he said. "I just think *thinner* and voilà, with age comes wisdom. You should consider it. And try not to worry, the latest description has the guy at 160—you're well above that."

I chuckled, and for the first time I felt some of my tension release. Everyone else seemed to have the same idea. We ran our bodies to the ground. We forgot everything but the green grass, the mud, and the fluorescent white ball we chased after. I pushed myself as hard as I could, hoping that later the soreness would keep my mind occupied.

At the end of the night, I found myself lying on the grass, staring at a silhouette of the Death Star. Its sharp angles bled into the sky, making it hard to distinguish where nature began. My stomach growled and churned. For a moment, I looked toward C Street, and just as quickly turned away. My muscles strained to push forward, but I couldn't muster the energy to drive home as the others had. Instead, I gathered some clothes from my car and decided to bunk down in my office. I did this a lot in my first year as a researcher. After my undergrad career, jobs had been limited. I blamed it on a poor GPA, but my return to Davis was filled with gratitude, especially since my bank account was well below zero. I counted my blessings despite Broketober, a portmanteau passed down by graduate students to emphasize they wouldn't get paid until their second month of teaching. I was just happy to have an office where I could store a couch, a car where I could keep a rotation of clothes, a storage unit for the rest of my belongings, the campus gym to take a quick shower (except over summer since I couldn't get a fee waiver), and a cluster of nearby friends who would let me crash in their living rooms.

I was grateful because no one but Vic suspected the state of my living conditions. And as far as I knew, no one else in my cohort knew the cold touch of the late hour in this office, or the sound of locks resetting in the middle of the night, or the sirens that wailed in the distance as frat row came to life.

By the third stabbing, I was exhausted. But how could I complain when the latest victim was a sixty-four-year-old houseless woman named Kimberlee? Her only protection had been a tent and her houseless neighbor who was able to fend off the assailant before calling it in. What must she have gone through to have been left so vulnerable? Meanwhile, I had been surrounded by brutalist architecture and polished glass as I tried to block the day out with headphones. My paranoia was reaching a fever pitch. And I was nearly out of Liquid Death. So I'd resorted to drinking the plain filtered water down one of the halls. As I turned the corner toward the water fountain one afternoon, I almost ran into two students, a young brunette woman and a big awkward guy with a unibrow. They froze like deer in front of a curly haired semi truck. I froze a bit too. They were jittery, glancing over their shoulders at each of the rooms as if looking for an escape. My fingers struggled between the locks of hair that tangled around my headphones. Fear coated their stutters.

"Did you need help?" I finally managed.

"Oh no," said the woman with a tense smile. "We figured it out."

She grabbed her friend by the arm and hustled in the opposite direction. The guy kept one eye over his shoulder the entire way out. I wanted to explain it away, to say it was the shock of a near collision, but deep down I knew their true fear, and it could not be overcome by force. Is this how it had been for Compassion Man? Did he deal with this every time a person got a whiff of him? I thought back to my days in under-grad, when life was a little less busy, on the days I happened to pass that corner for a meal, to roam around, to get some air.

"How are ya?" I'd ask.

"Peaceful," he'd say.

I spent the rest of the week locked up in my office. Lights dimmed. I turned my back to the latticed wall and stared at the foot of the door. My headphones played lightly on my desk. It took them long enough, but they'd finally caught him. The Internet was riddled with questions about the kid who had tormented a campus for a little under a week. His name was Carlos and when I saw his picture, he seemed pale, his hair slick, the way mine was after a few days of not showering. *Did you see he was Salvadoran?* someone wrote. He was also Puerto Rican and loved to play football. He was a high school honor student who came to the US as an unaccompanied minor. *His roommates should have noticed,* said a Redditor. A week prior, the university had sent him an email to inform him he'd been kicked out, just like me, for academic reasons. I wondered if anyone had talked to him, if he had been told that he could possibly return if he just raised some funds and his grades through a community college or even a retroactive withdrawal. I hadn't been told, at least not by the school. I'd been lucky—I'd found people who'd been through it before and helped me with every dreadful appeal as I begged for my worth. *Must have been out of retaliation,* said a commenter be-low one of the articles. The boys in blue took all the glory as if he hadn't been found in an encampment by a group of con-cerned citizens. He'd been wearing the exact same clothes as he had when this all began. It was as if he'd wanted to be found, aimlessly roaming the park with a knife in his bag. *Fuck this monster, I hope he rots*, someone else wrote. I wanted to cry, because the depth of his pain felt familiar, and yet I could not grasp what would make him go so far.

And that was the thing: it was easy to see him as some outlier, a monster. It was harder to stomach the idea that he was just another person lost in the maze. I listened to the steps of my peers, the students, and faculty, and my heart paced with each new shadow. It became a meditation. Easy come, easy go.

As the sun began to set one evening, my eyes grew heavy. Until a knock on the door startled me back into consciousness.

"Wake up, Danny boy!" It was Vic. "I heard your snoring from the ground floor, ya know."

"Just let me rest," I said. "Don't you have your own work to get done?"

"I wish you'd get off my dick," she said.

"You never had a problem with it before," I said.

"It's the modern age. We're allowed to be versatile."

"Right, right," I muttered, letting her into the room.

She looked at the cans scattered around my desk. "How many times do I have to tell you that Liquid Death is just water? Get a real drink. Maybe a tropical Red Bull."

"Thanks for checking in on me," I said. "Years ago, when I dropped out, if you'd told me I'd be here with people as talented as you, I would have laughed at you."

"Kindness? That's new," she said. "What's wrong?"

"You once told me you wanted to know more about me. So there you go. I can't stay, though—therapy."

"Are you okay?"

"We should all get our heads examined from time to time," I said.

"You know what I mean."

"I'm good." I felt the pressure in my dimples as I forced a smile. "Let's get lunch soon."

I took a long walk, bought some flowers, and found myself standing in front of a bench, chanting for a man I didn't know well enough. I was crowded by flowers and people with candles who sang a hymn, a dirge, or lamentations, I didn't know. I was too busy thinking of the days we'd sat beside one another. Sometimes he'd ask me a question, or I'd ask one back. Other times we'd sit in silence, and that was all I needed. Someone to be there. Present. Even when the whole world felt like it was falling apart on a Thursday.

"Well, that's quite the tidy bow," said May, as she penned her thoughts onto a yellow notepad.

I sank back into my therapist's couch and gripped the soft blanket in my hand. Next to me was a box of tissues sitting atop an end table. In front of me, a small trash can filled with more crumpled, tear-soaked tissues. The yellow glow of the lamp above obscured my view just enough to prevent me from recognizing all the careful details May put into making her patients feel comfortable.

"What do you mean?" I asked.

"Everything you've said up to this point has made sense," she said. "But it's as if you're keeping me at arm's length. The same way you did at that support group, or with Vic and Luci. I think there's something more."

"I don't know what to tell you," I responded. "I guess everything I've said does sound like intimacy, but I've always been able to talk about difficult things. I can go through the motions pretty easily."

"Why is that?"

"Because I'm just a bystander," I said. "When I see the people directly impacted, I can't help but feel as if where I am is pretty comfortable in comparison."

"And yet you've been crying since the moment you started talking. Were you feeling this emotional at the meeting?"

"No," I said. "I can't explain it. I don't know why this happens every time I talk to you."

"Well, what is it you're feeling right now?"

"I don't know," I said. "I'm just tired and upset. My eyes are like burning embers and they sting from all the rubbing, but I just can't get it to stop. I want it to, but I just can't."

PAINTED LADIES

BY NORA RODRIGUEZ CAMAGNA

Freeport

2006

buelita Arsenia began talking the minute the brown and orange butterfly landed on her flowered batita. "Mira, Pacito, it's a painted lady." Life filled her glassy eyes as her mind leaped back in time to find my seven-year-old cousin, Pacito.

My mother kept watering her birds of paradise and breathed in the smell of wet earth, hoping to enjoy a few more minutes of the cool morning air. An early, brutal summer gripped Sacramento. A pile-up of hundred-degree days limited the time my mother could bring Abuelita outside. Dawn and dusk were all that the heat allowed. For the last five years, Abuelita had lived with my parents; too many smoking frying pans and bruising falls had forced us to see that she was no longer firmly planted in this world. We would tend to her now, like she had tended to us most of her life.

"Pacito, the painted ladies are strong fliers," Abuelita was saying. She stared straight ahead and smiled. Then her smile deepened at the butterflies gathered around her patio chair. "For three days, they chased our camión from Reynosa until we arrived here to begin picking peaches. Ay, mijito, you loved to collect butterflies. Remember the day you finally caught the blue one? I never got to tell you its name."

I moved my chair closer. I would go back in time with her

today to visit Pacito. Mom touched my shoulder and went inside. The path Abuelita often ventured down was too painful for my mother to bear alone, so my sisters, my cousins, and I had been taking turns helping. The path always led to the same place: the small town Freeport, in Pacito's small backyard, thirty years ago, and the canal that flowed behind it.

1976

My mother had warned Pacito's father, Tío Picho, about the canal.

"Too few steps to death," she said.

"The backyard fence is tall," he responded, laughing away her worry.

Tío Picho had shed his family's cautious way of thinking when he had met my Tía Lola. Her family had been in the United States for two generations, long enough to adapt to the live-free mentality that had saturated the country in the 1970s. The women in Tía Lola's family consumed alcohol alongside the men, had tattoos, and didn't believe in stockings. The men wore their hair long, had earrings, and didn't believe that a man had to be head of the family. But, worse than all of that, Tía Lola's family had forgotten most of their Spanish. Any Spanish they retained was littered with English. My parents tried not to socialize with them. They didn't want their children exposed to that kind of American life. But there we were in their shadeless backyard, the scorching sun high in the sky, because Tía Lola had caught my mom off guard at the grocery store with an invitation to come celebrate their new home—a ranch-style house on a tomato farmer's land, where Tío Picho was the foreman. She couldn't say no.

"Manita, you can't worry about dying all the time," Tío

Picho said. He placed his Budweiser can on a rusty fold-up chair that bore the faded name of Pacito's elementary school. He grabbed my mother's shoulders, steadying himself. "You gotta live life while you can. Relax, enjoy the party. Be free, that's what the Americanos do, and look how well they're living." Tío picked up his beer can and stumbled over to the ice chest to get another one. Pacito was sitting atop it to stay cool, his skinny white legs propped up on Flaco, his shaggy black dog with friendly eyes. Pacito laughed as his father flipped him over his shoulder, pulled another beer out of the ice chest, and settled him back on top. Tío tried to readjust Pacito's black rectangular glasses, but the boy pushed away his clumsy hand and did it himself.

"Look at them," Mom whispered to Abuelita. "They're all drunk. The girls are never coming here without me, not with that canal back there and that monstro snatching the children."

Abuelita fanned away the beads of sweat that had gathered on her brown, unlined face. Periodically, she would wave her dime-store paper fan at me, my sisters, and our cousins, Rosie and Elvia. We were so small then that we didn't sweat much. "Ay, Emma," was all she could reply before Tío Picho approached with the new can of beer in his hand.

Pretending we hadn't heard, we girls sat on the dying lawn eating Tiá Lola's hot dogs and Abuelita's homemade rice and beans, ready to go back to Rosie and Elvia's bedroom and our Barbies.

Tío Picho held out the beer to my mother. "Everyone's drinking, manita," he grinned, "even the women—look at mi Lola, bien Americana." Tía Lola didn't work in the fields or the tomato cannery like my parents and my father's family. She ran a hair salon out of her home and called herself a Chicana. Tía Lola was the only proof my father needed to decide that we would go back to Mexico permanently this year—case closed.

"I don't want it," Mom replied, ignoring the beer can that Tío Picho tried to hold steady, and looked over to Tiá Lola.

Tía Lola stood in a circle with her six-foot-seven, fierce-looking brother El Indio, her heavily made-up divorced mother La Araña, and a few other people we didn't know, laughing hard at some joke. Her straight black hair fanned out behind her when she tilted back from the force of her laugh. She wore a suede headband, with black and turquoise beads stitched in an X pattern all around it. The black and red spider, tattooed on her arm, reached up for her unblemished face as she took an easy swig of her beer. I'd heard Mom call her "una mujer de la calle." A woman of the street. This was the worst insult my mother inflicted on other women.

"See how happy she is? You can be happy too." Tío Picho kept holding the beer out to Mom.

"Estás loco, Picho," Mom snapped, "I'm pregnant. It harms the baby." She let her gaze drift over to Pacito. Everyone knew there was something wrong with the boy. He was weaker than most of the other kids at school, running gave him coughing fits, he talked like he had two gumballs stuck in his mouth, and he needed his super-thick glasses to see two steps ahead of him.

Tío's red face fell.

"Ya, mijo, you know your sister doesn't drink," Abuelita said, getting up and laying a comforting hand on Tío Picho. "Come, let's get you some food."

After Tío finished two hot dogs and three more beers, he started talking about politics: "Cesar Chavez nominated Jerry Brown for president last week! Things good for you here, manito! Things good for Mexican people!" He looked at my father with a goofy grin and clasped him on the shoulder. Tío

Picho and Tía Lola were always trying to convince my father to stay in America; to them, Mexico was like a straitjacket, crippling one's free spirit.

My father felt like it was his duty to keep up with his brother-in-law's drinking. He finished his beer, put the empty can next to four others, popped open the one Tío Picho handed to him, and finally responded: "Even when a few of us get ahead, people will see Mexicans in the fields and believe that's all we're good for. We will never overcome the image of a lowly peasant. And when brown faces start outnumbering white faces, they will look for ways to send us back . . . or worse."

I waited to see what Tío Picho, or anyone else would say to that. I wanted my father's dreary assessment to be struck down. I wanted to believe what my teachers were telling me back then—that I could be anything I wanted to be. I wanted to be so many things: a baseball player, a tortilla maker, a cake maker, a teacher, the president.

"Ay, Rogelio, don't pout," Tía Lola said to my father. She walked over to Tío Picho and stood behind my father. Tía's large breasts rose and fell in her low-cut, black tank top. She placed her hands on my father's shoulders and said, "You bought a home here, and you have a year-round job at the cannery. What more can you want?"

"Girls, tell your father I don't feel well," my mother called to us, her typical excuse when she was unhappy.

We were helping Rosie, Elvia, and Pacito with the ice cream machine. Even though we didn't want to leave before dessert, we knew better than to challenge our mother publicly. She gave us nalgadas as needed, regardless of where we were. Anyway, we had faith that our father would nurse a few more beers before he was ready to leave.

Pacito cranked the ice cream maker a few times before

we all started complaining that he was going too slowly. But Pacito refused to budge. He was only timid at school; at home he could encapricharse like the rest of us. Tía Lola came over and carried him away. She stood him on the ice chest, quietly instructing him about fairness, gently rubbing his tightly crossed arms, until he calmed down and started running his skinny fingers through her smooth dark hair. When she was done talking, she pulled him into a long, full-bodied embrace. It was the kind of hug every kid craves. El Indio came over and let Pacito hang on to his enormous bicep while lifting him up and down. Pacito and Tía laughed and laughed. For the moment, everyone forgot about the ice cream.

Our car ride home was hot and miserable. Dad snuck through the back-country Delta levee roads. The orange glow of the setting sun blanketed the labyrinth of rivers, streams, sloughs, and canals with an iridescent beauty. A heady aroma filled our car from the patchwork of tomato fields, strawberry fields, rice fields, and the peach orchards my parents had worked in and fallen in love in as teenagers. We crossed the narrow Freeport Bridge and headed to our house in South Sacramento. Normally, my sisters and I would marvel at the vast, swift-flowing Sacramento River, but not that day. Everyone was pissed off—me because I had missed out on the ice cream, and I had cranked the ice cream maker the hardest, my father because he'd consumed fewer beers than he'd brought, and Mom because of the knife. "A knife!" she fumed. "What kind of people are they? I'm telling you, the girls are never going over there again." When El Indio had thrown Pacito up in the air, his fringed black-leather vest had flown open to expose a knife. Mom had looked ill; she'd taken off to the bathroom and stayed in there long enough to worry everyone.

Dad was also angry because he had gotten into a heated talk with Tía Lola about why he wouldn't join Cesar Chavez's union. "We aren't staying here!" he'd said to us when we got in our car, meaning both Tía Lola's house and the United States. Dad kept a *For Sale* sign in our garage and every time he became infuriated or disillusioned with our behavior or anyone else's, he would pound the sign into our lawn right next to the *Stop* sign.

True to her word, Mom stopped letting us go over to Pacito's house. Instead, our cousins visited our house; Mom wasn't thrilled about them coming over because she thought Rosie and Elvia were bad influences. Pacito she loved like an injured bird. We lived fifteen minutes away from where Dad worked as a machine maintenance technician at the Del Monte cannery and twenty-five minutes away from Pacito's house. Our two-bedroom, one-bath house was shaded by a fifty-foot sycamore and had a white picket fence. Sandra, Marisol, and I used to walk five minutes to our elementary school, until another kid had gone missing. Now, Mom or Abuelita walked us to school. Abuelita was the default babysitter while the adults worked picking peaches, nectarines, or apricots in Freeport until the cannery season started.

Dad would come home after his shift smelling of stewed tomatoes and mechanic oil. His smile would fade under his thick black mustache when he saw Rosie and Elvia. Their dirty-blond hair was disheveled, their clothes wrinkled and stained, and they'd be sprawled on the floor looking bored while we watched *The Brady Bunch*.

Elvia was ten, only a year older than me, and Rosie was three years younger, but both were much worldlier than I was. Whenever my sisters and I played Barbie with them, we would learn something new about love; like if Barbie kissed Ken while she was topless, he would like her better. Tío and Tía took them to the drive-in almost every Friday, and instead of sleeping when the adult movies were on, Rosie and Elvia would stay up learning stuff they would pass along to us and other kids at school. I envied them for their grown-up knowledge. Knowledge they acquired daily when Tía came into town to run errands and dropped them off on Franklin Boulevard. Rosie and Elvia would roam around, counting their change to see what they could buy, running down the sidewalk laughing, their long untamed hair waving teasingly behind them, or they'd sit on the corner in front of the beauty salon licking double-decker ice cream cones like they were practicing French kissing. Sometimes Pacito trailed behind them nervously. Usually, he begged to be dropped off with Abuelita.

One day, when we were coming out of La Esperanza grocery store, we found Pacito leaning against a brick wall, breathing hard. He started crying when he saw us. "Tía, Rosie and Elvia are in a fight."

"¡Ay, Dios mío! ¿Dónde, mijo?" Mom asked.

Pacito wiped his nose, hitched up his shorts, and started running. "Come on!"

We charged behind him for two blocks, past the donut shop where Mom practiced her limited English, past the hardware store where all the farmers hung out, and past the library that taught me what my parents could not. Pacito turned the corner into a trash-filled alley and stopped. Rosie and Elvia stood there, hands on their cutoff shorts, slinging some serious swear words at the Márquez brothers, who happily slung them back. The Márquez brothers took off when they saw my pregnant mother.

The Márquez brothers were our latest nemeses back then. Once, Rosie, Elvia, and I had run like hell across the school playground to stop them from breaking Pacito's glasses. We found Pacito on the ground, and they were standing over him laughing—but not for long. We crashed into them from behind, kicking and punching until the glasses were ours. They couldn't hit us back, we were girls. The men in their family would have given them unos chingasos if they had. Blood trickled from Pacito's bony knee as he had slowly stood up. Of course, he was crying. *Never cry.* I don't know how many times we had told him that. Pacito was the only boy we knew who cried.

Mom let the dry-eyed Rosie and Elvia have it, and they were smart enough to take it silently. We ended up leaving them in front of La Esperanza to wait for Tía Lola. The usual spot she picked them up, they told Mom, whose indignant eyebrows stretched so high I thought they would snap. Pacito came with us, and I hung back to walk with him.

"Were the Márquez brothers picking on you?" I asked.

"Yes, Rosie and Elvia chased them down. I couldn't keep up."

"Don't worry, Pacito, we'll always protect you, but you have to stop crying. Act tough, pretend El Indio is behind you."

"Papí says I should smile more. That a smile will protect me, make people like me." Pacito's sweet face looked up to me for confirmation.

I couldn't help but smile back, even though I knew that wouldn't save him either.

Tío Picho was all smiles and jokes. My mother told my father that the joke was on Tío Picho. He worked like a pinche dog while Tiá Lola drove around searching for who knows what? Rosie and Elvia were developing bad reputations, and

Pacito barely survived the mean kids at school. Dad never responded to her judgments.

"Valeria, could El Indio have saved her?" Pacito asked me, and pointed to the *Missing Child* poster tacked up to a telephone pole. A school picture of Shelby Porter sat underneath the Sacramento Police Department logo. Her description was listed below the picture: fifty-five pounds, four foot nine, born on April 16, 1970, and what she was last seen wearing—a white blouse with blue polka dots and a pair of red pants. A phone number to call was printed at the bottom. Shelby smiled shyly from the poster, like she didn't want to be a bother. A flood of images of her crying, whimpering, screaming filled my head and made me want to tear down the poster. Shelby Porter was the latest kid who had gone missing, making it three in the last two years. Their faces stared out from the posters tacked up all over town, haunting everyone. The evening news featured them nearly every day, but from our parents and other Mexican families we heard about even more missing kids whose families were undocumented, so they never got reported to the police, pobresitos.

"She wasn't connected to El Indio like we are," I said to Pacito, leading him away from the poster. I don't know why I told them that. I think I was trying to convince myself that even though we weren't related to El Indio by blood, he would still protect us.

At nighttime, Marisol, Sandra, and I would swelter in our twin beds. Our pink camisoles and underwear would stick to our little bodies. Outside our window, through the long, curved branches of the sycamore tree, the full moon looked like it was speckled with bruises. The Sacramento night air cooled to ninety degrees, but we were forbidden to open our window, so our room remained a furnace.

We wished we lived with Rosie, Elvia, and Pacito. El Indio slept outside Rosie and Elvia's bedroom in a screened-in porch so they could leave their window open, they had told had us smugly when we complained about the hot nights. El Indio had lost his job in construction after he punched his boss for disrespecting him and now worked on the tomato farm with Tío Picho. "You have *me* to protect you," our father had snapped at us when he heard us talking about El Indio. We had nodded, but there was something otherworldly about El Indio, not just his massive size, but his turquoise and bead jewelry, his Aztec tattoo of Quetzalcoatl, the god of light and wisdom, lord of the day and wind, and his knife.

Marisol, Sandra, and I would talk about what we thought the kidnapper looked like, a shriveled old railway worker who scooped up children with his long, yellow, grimy nails and put them in train car full of rats, human bones, and chunks of bloody hair. When he was hungry, he would poke their eyes out, slit their throats, and drink their blood.

"Let's start," I would say after we had scared ourselves sufficiently.

"Shelby, Tommy, Julie, María, Pilar, Blanca, José . . ." We would chant the names of the missing and rub each bead of our first-communion rosaries until we reached the silver crucifix. Back then, in our young minds, we figured if the rosary beads worked to connect prayers to the Virgin Mary, maybe they could also be conduits to the missing children.

One night Sandra said, "What if the missing children are dead and we are drawing them to us?" I closed my eyes tightly and clutched Marisol's sweaty hand, then Sandra left her twin bed and squeezed into the bed with us. The sound of the train roaring to a stop at the Fruitvale station, a few blocks from our house, made us jump.

"We need more protection," I whispered.

We asked Rosie and Elvia to bring us a feather from one of El Indio's dream catchers so we could be connected to him through his dreams. As payment, they demanded two of our best Barbie outfits and that we become blood sisters with them. Once we had secured the long brown and white feather, we placed it next to the glass of water we always had by our bedside. Abuelita had told us that if you gave spirits water at night, they would leave you alone. We felt better with our double protection.

When Tía came to pick up Pacito that night, Mom met her at our front door with my youngest sister, Esperanza, latched to her hip, and clinging to her cherry-patterned apron. Mom had applied her best red lipstick, Ruby Rose, darkened the beauty mole next to her right eye, and had taken her shoulder-length brown hair out of her pink rollers.

"Thanks for bringing Pacito home. The girls said he got tired again." Tía held her cigarette low at her hip. The smoke floated behind her like a tail.

"Pos mira, Lola, the girls were fighting with those maldito Márquez brothers. Language was used that girls shouldn't hear."

In the dusty blue Chevy station wagon, parked halfway on the sidewalk in front of our house, Rosie and Elvia stared straight ahead. The Chevy's windows were down, so I knew they were listening. Abuelita and Pacito stood behind Mom. My sisters and I peered out the family room window, wanting to see Tía's reaction.

"Ay, those Márquez boys, ever since their father left, they've been wild. Good thing Rosie and Elvia can take care of themselves," Tía said with a shake of her head, followed by a proud smile that ground into Mom and puzzled me.

I wondered if Mom would bring up the new missing child; I had heard her and Abuelita talking about it, mad that Tía wasn't worried like they were.

Mom was smart to keep quiet about Tía's careless child-rearing, because a few days later she was on the phone pleading to Tía for a ride to the grocery store. "The ice is almost gone, Lola, the food will spoil." Our refrigerator had stopped working the day before and we had to keep our food in an ice chest until Dad's next payday so we could buy a new one. If it had been spring or winter, Mom would have walked to the store rather than beg Tía Lola for a ride, but it was already a hundred degrees at ten a.m. Our street was shaded by tall sycamores and California blue oaks, but once you hit Franklin Boulevard, where the grocery store was, there wasn't a tree in sight. Mom was seven months pregnant so the walk would be impossible for her. "We are all out of peanut butter. Yes, the bread too." Mom's face pinched with anger and shame. "Ay, gracias, Lola, sí, we will pay for the gas."

Half an hour later, Tía showed up and gave Mom an unsparing look. When Mom came home from the grocery store an hour later, she vowed she would never again ask Tía Lola for a ride.

But a few days later, Mom had to ask Tía Lola to pick us up from school because Dad had to take her to the doctor. Tía pulled up in her Chevy station wagon and honked her horn several times and waved us in. "Who's up for some ice cream?" she said cheerfully, with a big toothy smile.

When we arrived at the Frosty Hut, Tía gave us some money and told us she would be back in a little while to pick us up. Esperanza started to cry.

It took Tía a few moments to register the fear on our faces. "Oh, I forgot, your mom doesn't let you do anything. You poor girls." Her sad look made me wonder why she wasn't worried about the missing children like everyone else. After buying us the promised ice cream and reassuring a hiccupping Esperanza that she wouldn't leave us, she silently drove us to her house.

During the ride, I couldn't stop staring at the black and red spider tattooed on her arm. I wondered if that was the reason Tía Lola was so different from our mother. I caught my sisters staring at it too. There was something bad about the tattoo, something that had happened before she married Tío Picho, but the adults guarded the story from us. Even my mother kept quiet about it.

Tía Lola and her spider waved goodbye to us as we scrambled out of the station wagon and raced inside. We found Abuelita and Pacito out in the backyard. Pacito had missed the last few days of school because he was having problems with his breathing. Abuelita said it was the peach pollen; Mom later said it was Tía Lola's poor housekeeping.

Abuelita sat on a worn rocker hemming some garage-sale pants for Pacito. He sat cross-legged in a miserly bit of shade the house was casting. In the presence of Abuelita, I quickly forgot about the spider and our near abandonment at the Frosty Hut. Abuelita wore one of her flowered summer dresses that made her look like a spontaneous bouquet. She had a slight hunch from a lifetime of fieldwork, and dark-blue veins bulged through the dark, papery skin on her shins. Two black bobby pins kept her graying brown curls away from her face.

"No butterflies yet, Abuelita," Pacito said, disappointed. Abuelita looked down at his sweaty face, light-brown hair, blue magnified eyes, and crooked smile; except for the glasses, he could have been his father's twin.

"Keep watching, mijito, they'll come, they always do."

A few minutes later, Pacito jumped up laughing. Waves

of butterflies cascaded into the backyard. We weren't obsessed with butterflies like he was, but we left our Barbies and ran over too. The butterflies formed fluttering umbrellas over the rosebushes before landing. We pinched them from the red petals and held them for a few seconds before their pulsing frantic bodies forced us to release them.

Trancelike, Pacito circled around the butterflies. He caught two at a time, and then held them high over his head before letting them go. He had started collecting butterflies ever since Abuelita had first told us their story: *The brown and orange painted ladies begin their lives in northern Mexico where your parents began their lives. When your abuelito decided to migrate to California, the painted ladies followed us. They chased our camión, riding the winds to el norte. When your abuelito and I return to Mexico, they follow us back. They will always return, mijito, because they are always eager to see you.* She had taken Pacito's hand in both of hers, and they'd exchanged smiles. None of us minded that Abuelita had directed this to Pacito. We were so full of her love that we didn't mind the extra servings she gave to him.

"Look, Pacito, a blue one," Elvia said now.

We froze. Pacito had been talking about the blue one for weeks. He tiptoed over and expertly pinched it off the rose. Abuelita was somehow ready with his glass jar. She cupped it over the straining butterfly, Pacito released it, and Abuelita quickly capped it in.

I had never seen Pacito happier. He held up the jar, and we formed a circle around him. The blue butterfly flew about, angrily bumping into the glass, while we passed the jar around, admiring its brilliant blue-silvery wings.

"Abuelita, here." Pacito handed her the jar. "Is it telling you its name?"

Abuelita whispered something to the butterfly, tilted her head over the air holes sprinkled across the gold lid, and listened. Then she chuckled. "She says she won't tell me until we release her."

"Tell her I'll let her go in a few days. I want to paint her picture first."

Pacito never kept the butterflies. He didn't want them to miss their families, so he painted their pictures instead. Tía had them tacked up all over the house; our mother tossed our art into the trash the minute we left it unguarded. I remember that after all the missing posters went up, the butterfly paintings made me feel uneasy. One day I wrote, *Missing Butterfly*, in black crayon across the top of one of the drawings—no one thought it was funny.

"What a wonderful day," Abuelita said. "Pacito has his blue butterfly, and your cousins are visiting when I need them most. I've been craving some buñuelos, but it's too hard to make them alone."

And just like that, happiness came. We spent the rest of the afternoon rolling out paper-thin dough into crooked circles, laughing when Abuelita jumped back from the frying pan to avoid the sizzling oil that shot out when she put the dough in. All of us admonishing Esperanza and Pacito for eating the sugar and cinnamon, instead of sprinkling it on the buñuelos. And finally, eating the sugary crisps until we felt sick.

The next day we were at Pacito's house again. The doctor had ordered our mother to rest for a few more days since she was bleeding and the baby needed another two months to finish growing. Mom told us it was because she'd already had four kids and her body was getting worn out. We prayed for a boy so Mom could stop making babies.

Abuelita was kneading a huge mound of tortilla dough when we walked into the house. She saw it as her duty to supply everyone in the family with fresh tortillas daily. Tía was out buying beauty supplies for her business. Tío Picho and El Indio were working in the back fields, harvesting tomatoes with a work crew of mostly undocumented workers.

I followed Elvia outside to see her and Rosie's latest secret, something Pacito's restless dog Flaco had done at night. He'd worked a plank loose in their fence. Elvia smiled smugly at me as her pink nail–polished fingers pushed aside the splintering plank. It lifted, revealing the canal that lay about twenty yards away.

The canal, I later learned, was part of the Central Valley Project, created in 1933 after droughts had destroyed California agriculture and the Dust Bowl devastation loomed large in everyone's minds. The project included a system of dams, reservoirs, water pumps, and five hundred miles of canals that provided municipal and irrigation water to most of the Central Valley by diverting and controlling water from the Sacramento and San Joaquin rivers. About five million acre-feet of water was provided for farms, enough to irrigate three million acres, approximately one-third of the agricultural land in California. At school, we kids were taught to be proud of California's ingenuity and natural resources. El Indio, however, said that the water was stolen from the indigenous people to make a bunch of farmers rich and that the canals cuts through the earth like they cut through the native tribes.

A few houses down, we saw some kids sitting on the edge of the canal, their chanclas littered around them as their dirty legs cooled in the olive-colored water. Some of the kids poked sticks into the waterfalls that cascaded over the flow-controlling metal gates, squealing as they got sprayed. A dingy white sign said, *NO SWIMMING ALLOWED*.

A few of them waved over at Elvia and shouted for her to join them. Jealousy swept over me as I pictured her, later, dangling her long legs into the water, collecting those kids around her like a movie star.

"Have you gone out there?" I asked.

"Not yet, we're waiting for the right time," Elvia whispered. She glanced over to Pacito. He was sitting with his legs spread in front of him on the brown grass, his back to us, playing with a few marbles. Flaco flopped down beside him.

Pacito heard us whispering and looked back at us, his eyes questioning us through the thick lenses. Flaco looked up and barked.

"Pacito, come be Ken!" Rosie shouted from the sliding-glass door. My sisters were sitting around a pile of semi-nude Barbies, sifting for the best outfits.

"No, that's boring."

"Come on, Pacito, it's better when a boy is Ken."

"No."

"We'll give you some of our candy."

"I have my own. Anyway, you know what Flaco will do."

The dog's head jerked up to peer at Rosie and the treasured Barbies.

"Just leave him out there."

"He'll be lonely."

Tía Lola had brought Flaco home from the Dairy Queen a year ago. She liked to say that when she first saw Flaco, with his stringy matted fur clinging to his pathetic ribs, trying to sneak some of her fries while she sat outside, she knew she had to bring him home, because any dog who preferred fries to a hamburger when they were starving to death was her kind of dog. Flaco was Pacito's best friend. Not only did he eat all of Pacito's unfinished food so everyone wouldn't worry that he was too skinny, he also saved the boy from having to play Barbie with us. Flaco was crazy for the Barbies. The minute the tarted-up Barbies made an appearance, Flaco sprang into action. Circling nonchalantly, he distracted us with a few well-placed licks before lunging and clamping onto a Barbie. The first few times he had made off with them, ravaging them before we had managed to wrestle them out of his slobbering mouth. When our collection of chewed-up zombie Barbies outnumbered the living, we decided to release Pacito from Ken duty so he could keep Flaco away.

"We'll have to take turns being Ken," Elvia sighed, heading inside.

"What about Pacito?" I asked. Mom would've gone crazy if she'd known we were out back without Abuelita for even a few minutes. The loose plank. I can't even imagine her rage.

Elvia gave me an exasperated look, and then called out, "Abuelita, Pacito won't come inside!"

"Ay, mija, let me finish the tortillas. You know how much your papí loves them."

"I'll stay with him," I said to Elvia. "You go in and help set up. Make sure I get a good Barbie . . . Pacito, want to practice catching?" I hated that he couldn't catch. Our father had taught us to catch almost as soon as we could walk.

"Okay," he said, to make me happy. We dug a semi-chewed glove and baseball out of a crate full of junk and positioned ourselves in as much house shade as possible.

"Are all your fingers in?"

"Yes, go ahead." He stuck his glove way out in front of him, already cringing at the thought of impact.

I threw the ball underhand as lightly as I could. It landed on the tip of his closed glove.

"Come on, Pacito, your eyes have to be open," I said, exasperated that we always started like this.

"Okay, this time I'll look. I promise." He spread out his arms and gave me a placating smile.

Again, I threw an underhand lob. Again, it hit the tip of his glove and plunked to his feet, but at least he had kept his eyes open. We did this for about five minutes. He never caught the ball.

"Let's practice hitting now," I said. "I'll go first so you can see how I stand."

He nodded and tossed the ball underhand to me. I swung and the ball sailed over the fence.

"You're too strong," Pacito said, laughing.

I agreed, but I needed to get the ball. It was the only one we had. "Don't follow me," I said, and pushed through the loose plank. The ball had landed in the opposite direction of where the kids were sitting by the canal. A few had seen the ball and were racing toward it. I got to it first and was heading back to the house when I heard Pacito shout for Flaco. Flaco had escaped through the loose plank and the boy was chasing after him.

"Pacito, wait!" I shouted, and ran after him.

"I have to get Flaco!" Pacito responded, and raced farther down the wide dirt path toward the canal. Flaco was running toward the canal kids, wagging his tail, excited to be free. Pacito pleaded with Flaco, trying to get him to come back, but the dog ignored him.

"Pacito, come back here!" I yelled. "If Abuelita sees us out here . . ."

He shook his head no and sped up. Pebbles tumbled into

the murky water as he and Flaco dashed through the kids. Some of them pushed to move out of the way or to help catch Flaco. Then somebody bumped into Pacito.

I watched Pacito's body stiffen; he scrunched his eyes shut, like he didn't want to see what was happening, and then he stretched out his arms for help before he fell into the dark water. I screamed out his name. Several of the older kids hurried to the edge of the canal and plunged their arms into the cold water, hoping to grab him before he sank underneath the gushing waterfalls.

Flaco barked crazily at their side.

I froze in terror. My thoughts went wild. I needed to save him, but I wasn't a good swimmer—I spent my time at the community pool clinging to the edge at the deep end. I ran back to the house.

"¿Dónde está Pacito?" Abuelita shouted when she saw my crying. She grabbed my shoulders.

"He r-ran after Flaco, through the fence," I stammered.

Abuelita ran outside and squeezed through the loose plank. Her flowered batita snagged on the rough wood and a nail caught her sleeve, ripping it and her skin. She kept racing toward the canal's edge, where Flaco was still barking frantically.

Elvia, Rosie, and my sisters had followed Abuelita out and were sobbing at the edge of the canal. By now, the men working out in the tomato fields had heard the commotion. El Indio was sprinting toward us, then he jumped into the canal and we watched him disappear under the gray water.

He surfaced thirty seconds later with Pacito. The boy's favorite orange and brown–striped shirt glistened in the sun. His face was blue.

Flaco started to howl.

* * *

The day of the funeral, Abuelita didn't sit with us. She sat alone in the front, talking to no one. Since Pacito's death, she hardly spoke. His death had changed the way everyone looked at her; it changed the way she looked at us. Mom kept us at the back of the church. She was furious in her grief. She could barely talk to Tía, Tío, or Abuelita. For days she'd badgered me about what had happened. "How could Pacito have gotten out?" Her eyes dug into me. "He wasn't strong enough to climb that fence." I told her about the loose plank, but not that I had gone through it to get the baseball. Relief and vindication filled her eyes. Their careless ways had hurt us all, she ranted to my father.

I looked up at the stained-glass saints, hoping to find the usual comfort in their beauty, but they didn't seem so beautiful to me that day. Why hadn't they protected Pacito? Why hadn't they let Abuelita know about the loose plank? Why hadn't they made me faster or braver? Why hadn't they heard our prayers? Why hadn't El Indio come sooner?

I looked over at Tía Lola and Tío Picho that day as we filed out of church, the sky shining a radiant blue over the tops of the oak trees, heating up the day without mercy. They smiled sadly at people's condolences and remembrances of Pacito. Tía turned and saw me watching, but Mom pushed me toward our car. The smell of incense had made her dizzy, she claimed.

I broke away from her grasp, and walked over to Tía Lola. She bent and pulled me into the kind of hug she used to give Pacito. I ran my fingers through her thick hair and cried. I was protecting her, I said to myself, by not telling her that I had seen the look on Pacito's face before he fell into the water. It would have haunted her, like the missing kids' faces on the posters.

ABOUT THE CONTRIBUTORS

Jessica Lam

LUIS AVALOS is a fiction writer and essayist of Salvadoran-American descent who is currently earning his MFA in creative writing at UC Davis. His writing interlaces social, political, and theoretical lenses to move beyond one-dimensional narratives of marginalized people. On his off time, he enjoys playing soccer, snowboarding, and drinking rose aloe tea.

Anita Scharf

SHELLEY BLANTON-STROUD writes historical mysteries, including the Jane Benjamin novels—*Copy Boy*, *Tomboy*, and *Poster Girl*. She works and lives in Sacramento in the former home of a family whose mother-in-law was reportedly crushed by the Hippodrome marquee.

Beth Baugher

NORA RODRIGUEZ CAMAGNA grew up in California migrant labor camps, Texas, and Mexico, and graduated from UC Berkeley. Her work has been featured in the *Common*'s Farmworker Portfolio, the Bay Area Book Festival, and Stories on Stage Sacramento. She works at 916 Ink, a Sacramento nonprofit literacy organization, teaching creative writing to underserved students.

Ruby Aragi

JOHN FREEMAN is the author and editor of a dozen books, including *Wind, Trees*, a collection of poems; *There's a Revolution Outside, My Love*, coedited with Tracy K. Smith; and *Dictionary of the Undoing*. A Sacramento native, he lives in New York City, where he is an executive editor at Alfred A. Knopf. Once a month, he hosts the California Book Club for *Alta Journal*. His work has been translated into twenty-two languages.

Ara Arbabzadeh

REYNA GRANDE is the author of three novels and two memoirs, which are required reading in schools across the country. She is the recipient of an American Book Award, a Premio Aztlán Literary Prize, and a Writers for Writers Award, among others. She lives in Woodland, California, with her husband and two children.

Jalil Kochai

JAMIL JAN KOCHAI is the author of *The Haunting of Hajji Hotak and Other Stories*, a winner of the 2023 Aspen Words Literary Prize and a finalist for the 2022 National Book Award. His debut novel, *99 Nights in Logar,* was a finalist for the PEN/Hemingway Award for Debut Novel. His short stories have appeared in the *New Yorker, The O. Henry Prize Stories,* and *The Best American Short Stories.*

Alejandra Pérez

MACEO MONTOYA is an author and visual artist who has published books in a variety of genres, including four works of fiction: *The Scoundrel and the Optimist, The Deportation of Wopper Barraza, You Must Fight Them,* and *Preparatory Notes for Future Masterpieces.* Montoya is a professor of Chicana/o Studies and English at UC Davis, and editor of the literary magazine *Huizache.*

Jason Sinn

MAUREEN O'LEARY lives in Sacramento and her writing has appeared in *Bourbon Penn, The Esopus Reader, Nightmare Magazine,* and the *Tahoma Literary Review,* among other places. She is the author of *physics of weight: collected poems,* and is a Pushcart Prize nominee and a graduate of the Ashland University MFA program.

Mike Rivera

JANET RODRIGUEZ is a writer, teacher, and editor living in Northern California. She is the author of the memoir *Making an American Family: A Recipe in Five Generations.* Most recently published in *Hobart, Pangyrus, Eclectica Magazine,* the *Rumpus,* and *Cloud Women's Quarterly Journal,* Rodriguez engages themes of duality in faith communities and mixed races in a culturally binary world. She earned an MFA from Antioch University in Los Angeles and is currently the interviews editor at the *Rumpus.*

Haley James

JEN SOONG, a daughter of Chinese immigrants, grew up in New Jersey and now lives in Northern California. An alum of Tin House and VONA, her writing has appeared in the *Washington Post,* the *Audacity, Black Warrior Review, Witness,* and *Waxwing.* She received her MFA in creative writing from UC Davis, and her memoir-in-progress is a reckoning of myth and migration.

Bobby Gordon

JOSÉ VADI is the author of *Chipped: Writing from a Skateboarder's Lens* and *Inter State: Essays from California.* His work has been featured in the *Paris Review*, the *Atlantic*, *PBS News-Hour*, the *San Francisco Chronicle*, *Free Skate Magazine*, *Quartersnacks*, *Alta Journal*, and the *Yale Review*.

William T. Vollmann

WILLIAM T. VOLLMANN is the celebrated author of over twenty-five books, including the National Book Award–winning novel *Europe Central*; the seven-volume *Rising Up and Rising Down*, based on his career as a war correspondent; and the two-volume climate-change investigation *Carbon Ideologies.* He has won the Whiting Foundation Award and the Shiva Naipaul Memorial Award for his fiction.

Joella Aragon

NAOMI J. WILLIAMS is the author of the novel *Landfalls*, as well as numerous short stories and essays. A biracial Japanese American, she was born and partly raised in Japan. She has a master's degree in creative writing from UC Davis and has made the Sacramento area her home for over two decades.

Also available from the Akashic Noir Series

LOS ANGELES NOIR
edited by Denise Hamilton
318 pages, trade paperback original, $16.95

BRAND-NEW STORIES BY: Michael Connelly, Janet Fitch, Susan Straight, Héctor Tobar, Patt Morrison, Emory Holmes II, Robert Ferrigno, Gary Phillips, Christopher Rice, Naomi Hirahara, Jim Pascoe, Neal Pollack, Scott Phillips, Diana Wagman, Lienna Silver, Brian Ascalon Roley, and Denise Hamilton.

A *Los Angeles Times* bestseller, SCIBA bestseller, and SCIBA Award winner; includes Edgar Award–winning story "The Golden Gopher" by Susan Straight

"Noir lives, and will go on living, as this fine . . . anthology proves."
—*Los Angeles Times*

SAN FRANCISCO NOIR
edited by Peter Maravelis
272 pages, trade paperback original, $18.95

BRAND-NEW STORIES BY: Barry Gifford, Robert Mailer Anderson, Michelle Tea, Peter Plate, Kate Braverman, Domenic Stansberry, David Corbett, Eddie Muller, Alejandro Murguía, Sin Soracco, Alvin Lu, Jon Longhi, Will Christopher Baer, Jim Nisbet, and David Henry Sterry.

"An entertaining anthology of overheated short stories by local writers . . . Here the city becomes the central character, the strongest on the page."
—*San Francisco Chronicle*

BERKELEY NOIR
edited by Jerry Thompson and Owen Hill
256 pages, trade paperback original, $15.95

BRAND-NEW STORIES BY: Barry Gifford, Jim Nisbet, Lexi Pandell, Lucy Jane Bledsoe, Mara Faye Lethem, Thomas Burchfield, Shanthi Sekaran, Nick Mamatas, Kimn Neilson, Jason S. Ridler, Susan Dunlap, J.M. Curet, Summer Brenner, Michael David Lukas, Aya de León, and Owen Hill.

"[E]ach story evokes the dark side of a Berkeley neighborhood and pays tribute both to the city's history as a haven for outcasts and as a literary metropolis. If you race through it, consider picking up *San Francisco Noir* and *Oakland Noir*."
—*Diablo Magazine*, a Top Ticket choice

"At first consideration one might wonder if Berkeley has enough of a seedy underbelly to produce credible settings and stories for such an anthology? The writing proves it does."
—*Berkeley Daily Planet*

OAKLAND NOIR
edited by Eddie Muller and Jerry Thompson
272 pages, trade paperback original, $19.95

BRAND-NEW STORIES BY: Nick Petrulakis, Kim Addonizio, Keenan Norris, Keri Miki-Lani Schroeder, Katie Gilmartin, Dorothy Lazard, Harry Louis Williams II, Carolyn Alexander, Phil Canalin, Judy Juanita, Jamie DeWolf, Nayomi Munaweera, Mahmud Rahman, Tom McElravey, Joe Loya, and Eddie Muller.

"Wonderfully, in Akashic's *Oakland Noir*, the stereotypes about the city suffer the fate of your average noir character—they die brutally. Kudos to the editors, Jerry Thompson and Eddie Muller, for getting Oakland right." —*San Francisco Chronicle*

SEATTLE NOIR
edited by Curt Colbert
276 pages, trade paperback original, $19.95

BRAND-NEW STORIES BY: G.M. Ford, Skye Moody, R. Barri Flowers, Thomas P. Hopp, Patricia Harrington, Bharti Kirchner, Kathleen Alcalá, Simon Wood, Brian Thornton, Lou Kemp, Curt Colbert, Robert Lopresti, Paul S. Piper, and Stephan Magcosta.

"The protagonists of *Seattle Noir* are all running scared in Seattle. But beyond that, there are as many layers of class and race as there are stories in the collection." —*Seattle Times*

PORTLAND NOIR
edited by Kevin Sampsell
280 pages, trade paperback original, $15.95

BRAND-NEW STORIES BY: Gigi Little, Justin Hocking, Chris A. Bolton, Jess Walter, Monica Drake, Jamie S. Rich & Joëlle Jones, Dan DeWeese, Zoe Trope, Luciana Lopez, Karen Karbo, Bill Cameron, Ariel Gore, Floyd Skloot, Megan Kruse, Kimberly Warner-Cohen, and Jonathan Selwood.

"The home of Chuck Palahniuk, Powell's City of Books—and the place with more strip clubs per capita than any other city in America—gets its due in this splendid entry in Akashic's noir series . . . The sixteen stories in this anthology demonstrate that a little rain is never a deterrent to murder." —*Publishers Weekly*